DREAM CAPTIVE

by

REESE GABRIEL

I0517543

Published by **CHIMERA**
ISBN 9781780806150

Chapter 1

Tesra slipped gracefully through the pale blue waters, her slender body arcing its way towards the surface of the rock encrusted pool. Eyes closed, she invoked Persistrata, goddess of inner dawn, mother of all who see what is yet to be. What the golden-haired nymph could not see, however, was the presence of another form, large and powerful beneath her, closing fast to intercept.

They met at the waterline. Intending to scream, Tesra opened her mouth, but a hand quickly clamped over it.

'Do not resist,' said the deep-voiced creature, holding her from behind in a grip of iron. 'There is no escape. If you understand me, nod.'

Tesra bobbed her head, eyes wide in fear and shock.

'You must draw a deep breath,' said her captor. 'Enough to carry you to the bottom and beyond. If you obey me we shall both live, if not, we shall both die. Nod if this, too, you understand.'

Again Tesra acknowledged, though in truth she understood nothing. What sort of being was this - strong like a beast and yet able to speak as a human? Could this be a member of the other half of her own species, the ones she had never before seen but whom she knew from her teachers were called men? If so, it had no place on the Isle of Dreams - none at all. And what was his intention, this mad beast-man, in dragging her down to the bottom of the sharp-edged Pool of Reflection - and beyond? It was suicide!

Treading water to keep them afloat, the talking beast wrapped her midsection tightly with a cord, the other end of which was attached to his own. 'This is our lifeline,' he told her. 'As you see it is relatively thin. If you have deities to whom you pray, I suggest you do so now. We dive at the count of three.'

'Wise Persistrata,' she called in voice unspoken. 'Spare me. Descend from your high clouds and give me rescue.'

'One,' pronounced the insane man-creature with utter calm. 'Two. And three.'

Tesra was pulled like a toy doll, her lithe body sucked down as if by a stone. Her first instinct was to resist, but she saw quickly what he meant about their fates being tied, for if she were to pull upward against him they would drown somewhere between the top and bottom.

But where could he be taking her, except to certain death?

The man was a fast swimmer and Tesra added the motions of her own arms and legs, conveying them knife-like at a steep angle of descent towards the far edge, where the rock floor met the wall. The reds and blues and greens of the jagged crystal surface loomed ever closer and Tesra was certain they would be cut to ribbons. At the last possible second, however, nearly in the teeth of the deadly shards, the man held out his fist, upon which was a single ruby ring. The light from this ring reflected onto a long crystal of equally brilliant red. There was at once a shaking of the entire pool and a loud rumbling sound. Impossibly, the rocks along the wall began to slide aside, as though they were not a fixed barrier but some doorway.

The opening was just large enough to allow them through. There was water in the tunnel and Tesra was terrified because she did not know how she could hold her breath much longer. The man pulled her as she lagged, dragging her onward, just in time as the rocks crashed closed once more behind them. The tunnel was rounded and very narrow. The rock was a dark color, decorated with various tiny jewel-like stones of many different colors. There was also writing, the ancient hieroglyphics of the First People, who came in the Time Before Time.

Tesra had never dreamed of the existence of such a tunnel beneath her island. Had her teachers kept the knowledge from her and the other initiates into the sisterhood? Or was it possible even they did not know? Doubling her effort, desperate to convey them forward, Tesra wriggled her body in the cold water, like a dolphin or one of the other sea creatures she loved. Time was running out. She saw no end ahead and she was already feeling the build up of dead, poisonous air in her lungs. By the goddess she must make it - she must!

The world was going black. So, tired. Let me rest, she thought. Let me sleep, if only for a moment.

Then, in the midst of the agonizing silence came a rushing roar, like an underwater wind pulling them upward into the light. Tesra opened her starved lungs and tasted precious oxygen. Waters were circling about them, as if to greet the weary travelers. They had surfaced! Again the man took her by the waist, pulling her forward, this time onto the sandy shore of what looked to be an underground river.

Tesra clawed at the gritty surface, gasping on hands and knees.

'There is no time to rest,' he informed her, already on his feet, seemingly unaffected by the ordeal. 'We must make haste to my ships.'

Tesra beheld him, climbing behind an outcropping, seeking to pull something large from behind the jagged, red and blue stones. The man was at least six foot tall, with powerful arms and shoulders and an iron chest, far larger and harder looking than her own. His biceps were massive; the heavy muscles marked with inked designs, creatures whose names she did not know. His legs were equally imposing, like those of a horse or verr-beast. Most curious of all was the animal skin covering his midsection, very short and concealing his groin area. There appeared to be something beneath it, protruding. From the little that she knew there were certain physical differences in the male and female of the species, but that they were of no import to higher developed beings such as the sisterhood.

She herself had a depression between her own legs, through which she eliminated liquid waste. Among lower creatures this was an entry point for seminal fluid, to pollinate the feminine womb. Such fluid came from the projecting organs of the male through an action of thrusting, or rutting. It was said to be pleasurable, though Tesra had no interest, having been born parthenogenically, like all the seers, through the power of the goddess.

'Your ships?' Tesra rose to her feet, the impact of his words sinking in. 'You intend to take me from here?'

'You are my captive,' he confirmed, pausing to shake out his mane of hair, long and dark and wet. 'What else would you expect?'

Tesra took a step backward, bare heels pressing into the sand. Could she make a run for it?

'No person may take another captive,' she informed him. 'That is the law.'

The man's back was turned now, the awesome muscles fully engaged in the overwhelming task of pulling a concealed wooden boat down to the water. 'Women's law,' he grunted in response. 'Not men's law.'

'There is only one law.' Tesra took another step backward. Was she fast enough to outrun him? 'Pray to the goddess if you are in doubt.'

'I have no goddess,' he said. 'And if I were you, I would stand still from this point forward.'

Tesra raised her head haughtily. 'I will not be commanded by anyone, let alone a man-creature.'

She watched him push the boat to the very edge of the gurgling, foamy white water. 'Get in,' he told her.

'No,' she defied. 'I will not.'

The man-beast drew from his waist a leather binding strip. 'Get in the boat,' he repeated.

'What do you intend to do with that?' she wanted to know.

His answer came in graphic form. Quick as lightning he seized her wrist and forced her down. Positioning himself on one knee he drew her across his knotted thigh.

'What are you doing?' she cried, squirming fiercely against him. 'How dare you?'

'I am Marcellus, King of Pirates,' the man-beast introduced himself, the belt doubled in his fist, his arm poised high overhead. 'As my captive you are compelled to obey me under threat of punishment.'

Tesra screamed as hot leather seared the unblemished cheeks of her soft pink bottom.

'Remove your hands,' ordered Marcellus as she tried to cover her exposed skin. 'Or it shall go worse for you.'

She lowered her arms and he struck her again, even more viciously than before.

'Please,' she begged. 'You are hurting me.' Tesra had never known pain, not like this. Once she had cut her leg on the rocks and another time she burned herself, but this was persistent and deliberate.

'That is the point,' Marcellus replied, letting loose the strap yet again. Fire radiated through the young woman's body. She wept and wailed, but he did not seem to care, either for her suffering or the noise she was making. This fact caused her to fear even more, that perhaps they were in a place so remote that already she was too far from her people to be helped by them.

'No more,' she cried. 'I will obey you.'

Thrice more for good measure he struck her. 'Get in the boat,' he said simply, releasing her.

Tesra, sniffling, choked back fresh tears as she scurried across the sand, and it was only as she stood in the boat that she saw a new problem. 'I cannot sit; it will hurt too badly.'

'That is not my problem,' said Marcellus, King of Pirates, thrusting the boat completely into the river. 'I am not the one who disobeyed.'

4

Tesra shrieked as the momentum upended her, landing her flat on her inflamed buttocks on one of the two weathered boards that served as seats. 'You are a monster,' she protested as he jumped in after her, taking the other seat, his body facing hers.

'No more or less than any man.' He seized the oars, one in each hand, propelling the small craft forward down the snakelike waterway.

Tesra studied his powerful muscles, smoothly expanding and contracting with each stroke. He was like some force of nature, some instrument of the divine.

'They will come after me,' she promised. 'I will be rescued.'

Marcellus' breathing was steady and deep. 'Very soon you will not wish to be rescued,' he predicted.

Tesra contemplated the meaning of these words. Could it be he himself was a seer of some kind? If only she could read his mind; if only she had been taught to use her powers in the dark and dreaded world of men.

All at once the sunlight streamed in from behind her back. Turning she saw the mouth of the cave, a great maw, spilling out into the ocean; that vast blue carpet which, until this very day, she'd thought a perfect and invincible protection against all forms of invasion.

Who was this barbarian to break through the defenses of the Isle of Dreams, to escape the notice of the Mother Seers?

'Nephisos,' murmured her captor, with a tone and solemnity clearly not directed to her, 'convey me safely. Grant your blessing for this journey.'

A god of the sea. So this is what he worshipped. Did Persistrata know of this deity?

'Have you a name?' he asked her, as it if were some mere afterthought.

Tesra squared her chin with all the confidence of her heritage. 'I am called Tesra Bel-ahn Tes-ya Shin-dara Meala-sirea,' she informed the uncouth barbarian, scarcely human. 'Daughter of Neyria, granddaughter of Tera-Nyeria, direct descendent of the goddess Persistrata herself.'

His laughter, ripe and bawdy, caught her off guard. 'So long a name for such a slip of a wench.'

Tesra's pride burned deeply as her inflamed buttocks. 'I will see you defeated and destroyed,' she vowed. 'If it takes the last breath from my body.'

Marcellus inclined his head, directing her to turn. 'I would advise you to learn the extent of my power before declaring yourself my enemy,' he advised. 'Oh, nymph of many names.'

Tesra's breath was taken away. There were a dozen of the massive vessels; tall, elegant masts, billowing white sails, curved bows, fiercely painted with dragon's teeth and decorated shields upon the sides. For the first time the unthinkable occurred - that her people and even the goddess might not be able to free her from her newfound captivity.

'I am Marcellus,' he completed his introduction of before, when he had beaten her over his knee. 'Pirate king of all the sea, from this to the next horizon. Scourge of the deep, thorn in the side of mighty Talassia, lord of men and master of women.'

It was this last epithet that set her heart racing. 'Do you intend to kill me?' she enquired.

'No,' he reassured her. 'Only to use you. Mercilessly.'

The pirate king conveyed them to the side of the tallest vessel. Pulling a blanket from beneath the seat he commanded her to wrap herself.

'Why would I so cover my body?' she wished to know.

'In my world a naked woman can be only one thing. And you are not that thing.'

Tesra studied the expression on his face. There was something he was not telling her, something important and profound, but which she did not yet understand. And yet understand it she must, along with everything else about this man and his self-professed kingdom, for like it or not her fate, her very life now lay in his hands.

A rope ladder was lowered from the deck. Marcellus helped her up, his body pressed close behind hers, warm and strong. The proximity of the man was creating a strange tingling in her own body, at the tips of her breasts and also in the open place between her legs. It was his arrogant power that seemed to intoxicate her as well as her own sense of vulnerability; to his belt, his hand, and maybe even to the sex between his legs.

'Ahoy, captain!' bellowed a short, yellow-bearded man, his dirty crow's nest head appearing over the edge. 'What booty do you bring? Is there more where that came from?'

The captain thrust Tesra into his waiting arms, bidding him deposit her on the deck. The smell of the little man made her want to retch, so too the spaces between his teeth.

'No,' said Marcellus, planting his leathered bare feet upon the worn and sun-blistered deck. 'There is nothing more to be had on the island. Neither in treasure nor women. Prepare to weigh anchor. We set sail at once.'

The craggy-faced man, his yellowed hair dry as broom straw, eyed the captain, uncertain. Two other men, in red bandannas, bare chests and ragged knee-length pants flanked him, looking equally dismayed. Tesra did not like the look of them, particularly the sharp metal blades hooked at their waists. If they were able to see through the captain's lie, there was no telling what might happen next.

'What's this, captain? You say we take no booty?'

The company turned towards the rugged, bald-headed man, both ears pierced with gold bands, his mouth and chin ringed with a layer of shaggy black hair. He was an inch or so shorter than the captain and slighter of build, but his dark eyes were fierce and he had about him the look of a seasoned predator.

Marcellus stood his ground. 'Am I required to repeat myself, Rodrigo?'

The one called Rodrigo approached the captain so the two were eye to eye. Tesra sensed the tension between the two, the hawk-eyed Rodrigo ready to square off against the stalwart, blue-eyed Marcellus.

'I do not ask you to repeat, majesty, only to explain. You have taken but one woman - surely she has sisters, aunts, cousins, someone besides herself out there? And where has she lived all these years? In a tree? Is there not at least one small, measly palace to ransack? Or do you stand here now and tell us that this one scrawny female is all we have to show for this journey of six months?'

6

Marcellus neither flinched nor blinked. 'Actually, Rodrigo, "we" have nothing; the wench is mine alone.' Grumbles passed through the growing assembly of fierce men, most of them bearded and bare-chested. Clearly Rodrigo was not the only one left unsatisfied. 'If you wish to take issue,' Marcellus went on, 'we may finish with steel what cannot be resolved in words.'

Rodrigo's gaze narrowed, his hand at the hilt of the long blade at his waist, the name for which came to Tesra's mind now as a sword.

'Go on, Rodrigo,' he taunted, making no move to reach for a weapon of his own, 'come at me. See if you are ready for the kingship.'

The eyes of the bald, goateed man flashed. For long moments he considered, then at the last moment he faltered.

'You are king,' Rodrigo conceded, lowering his eyes.

Marcellus, gracious in victory, clapped him on the shoulder. 'Come, my brother, let us not quibble over a mere female. Let us sit and drink and talk of the things of men. Give me ear, my noble lieutenant and I will tell you what plans lay ahead for our stalwart company. Montrego,' he called to the yellow-bearded man, 'lock this wench below with the slaves and fetch us rum. The good stock we liberated from that Talassian governor's shipment last spring. The rest of you - prepare to sail. I wish to be back in Talassian shipping channels in time to fish gold for tomorrow's supper.'

The men scattered to do Marcellus' will. Whatever challenge had just been mounted, it was passed, thanks to the cool confidence of the pirate king.

'Where are they taking me?' asked Tesra, who had no desire to be separated from the one and only man she knew in this or any other part of the outside world.

'To a place of education,' he smiled wryly. 'Where perhaps you will learn that your position as captive is not so terrible as you think.'

Tesra cared not for the tone of the man's voice, and still less the dark-edged laughter that followed from the assembled pirates. 'Marcellus, wait!' she cried.

The one called Montrego, though he was barely her own height and looked ancient as a sea turtle, clapped her wrist and tugged her forward with a strength that nearly pulled her off her feet.

'Where are we going?' she asked, attempting to continue her conversation with this minion of the king.

'To the hole,' said Montrego, kicking open the hatchway with his blackened foot. 'Where sluts like you belong.'

It was pitch-black below deck. Tesra was forced to follow him, keeping her balance as best she could on the slimy steps. Twice she fell forward, colliding into the knotted back of her new jailer.

'Clumsy bitch,' he snarled finally, tossing her straight down into the seemingly bottomless abyss.

Tesra cried out, thinking she would fall to her death, but almost at once she was met with a soft though stinking layer of hay.

'Ow!' cried a female close at hand. 'Watch where you're falling, you stupid cunt!'

'Who said that?' demanded Montrego, reaching down into the hay.

The woman cried out again. 'Mercy, master. Forgive me, master; I thought it was

7

only some new slave thrown in our midst.'

'Well she's not,' he pulled savagely at her hair. 'Vorra,' he bellowed, looking for another. 'Where in the Dragon's Inferno are you?'

Tesra felt a rustling in the hay, a body crawling, a head lowering itself to the filthy pirate's feet.

'I am here, master. Forgive me for the outburst of the slave Drusia. I will see to it she is punished.'

The pirate shook her off. 'Don't give me that.' He pressed his foot down on Vorra's back, the surface of which Tesra could now make out dimly in the shadowed light. 'You're a lazy slut. You don't deserve to be slave warder.'

'I will try harder, please master, give me another chance.'

'You!' He pulled up on the girl whose hair he was still holding. 'Drusia, you are warder now. Fetch fire from above, light me the lamps.'

'Yes, master!' exclaimed the very relieved Drusia. 'Right away, master.'

Tiny feet scampered up the moldy steps. Tesra waited in blind terror for her to return, the only sound that of the labored breathing of the former warder, the now humbled Vorra, her back under the grinding foot of Montrego.

Drusia came bearing a clay pot in which sat a large burning candle. The pot hung from the end of a long stick which allowed her, one by one, to light lamps along the wall of the ship's hold. With each new lamp Tesra was able to see a little more, till at last her surroundings were made crystal clear. Sitting up she tucked her legs beneath her, wrapping herself as best she could in the captain's blanket.

To her horror she saw that she was in a damp, rounded chamber, like the belly of some great whale, the entire bottom matted with straw and occupied with the reclining bodies of naked females, their limbs variously attached with chains of steel.

'Listen up, you stupid sluts,' announced Montrego, showing what to Tesra seemed to be a complete lack of respect and dignity due an assemblage of his fellow human beings. 'This new one here is private property. Special stock belonging to the captain himself. Untouchable. Is that clear?'

'Yes, master,' chimed the voices, almost in chorus.

'You, Drusia!'

The candle-bearer ran to him, kneeling at his feet. In the light, Tesra could see the girl was short and brown-haired, with flaring hips and a pair of full breasts. She was olive-skinned and seemed to have been in some accident, owing to the network of scars, long thin lines crisscrossed over her buttocks. Was it some farm machine, perhaps, or an accident in the mountains? And what was that tiny circle on her left buttock - like a birthmark, only more regular?

'Listen closely, Drusia,' he lifted her chin cruelly, forcing her to look him in the eye. 'Anything happens to this slut and you answer for it, personally. Is that clear?'

'Yes,' replied Drusia, her eyes wide and eager to please. 'Master.'

He snatched the clay pot from her. 'Consider this insurance,' the pirate tilted the earthenware bowl over her gently peaked breasts, the nipples softly pink and prominent. 'Hands behind your back,' he ordered.

Drusia obeyed, arching her back and offering no resistance as the man poured the accumulation of hot liquid wax over her chest. Confining herself to whimpers, the well-disciplined slave did not move a muscle.

'You may thank me,' Montrego extended his bony hand. 'For your promotion.'

The freshly tortured woman lowered her lips, covering his knuckles with eager, reverent kisses.

'Farewell, ladies,' the pirate chuckled, when he had sufficiently enjoyed her humiliation.

Tesra did not dare speak till the man had climbed back up the stairs and slammed shut the door to their freedom. 'Why?' she asked Drusia in all innocence. 'Why did he wish to hurt you like that?'

Drusia, who wore a band of steel round her throat like the others, looked at her in utter disbelief.

'Are you some sort of idiot?' hissed tall, dark-haired Vorra, who had been warder until Tesra's untimely arrival. 'You must be to ask such a question.'

Vorra was standing above her, legs akimbo, hands on hips, her well-toned arms suggesting that it was not only men who were capable of exercising force.

'I am not an idiot,' said Tesra, more than a little frightened of the girl. 'I come from the Isle of Dreams.'

'Isle of what?' scoffed the ruby-lipped slave.

'The Isle of Dreams,' completed Drusia, knowingly. 'I once heard the captain mention it in his sleep. Vorra,' she stood authoritatively, 'sit your arse down before we tan it for you.'

'Try it, you fat cow!'

'I am warder,' said Drusia, reminding her of the new order. 'Or have you forgotten?'

Vorra's eyes narrowed fiercely. Like Rodrigo she seemed ready to fight, but before she could make a move Drusia struck her hard in the stomach with a fist. The big girl went down with a yelp to her knees.

'Montrego hurts me,' answered Drusia, dealing at last with Tesra's question, 'because he can. Because I am below and he is above, with the others. They are the masters and we are the slaves.'

Tesra looked at the girl's red breasts, the nipples and swollen globes encased in a coating of hard white wax.

'I do not know these words,' she said, though she had heard them just before, from the lips of Marcellus on the boat. How long ago that little trip seemed now. How innocent had seemed her existence before learning of the world of men.

Drusia sat down beside her. 'A slave is one who is the property of another - a master,' she explained. 'The slave is at the master's mercy and must endure whatever abuse the master wishes to heap upon her.'

Tesra reached for the ring of steel around Drusia's neck, strangely fascinated. 'How terribly you must suffer.'

Drusia arched her neck, allowing the blonde to touch. 'Masters give pleasure as well,' she said softly. 'I would not seek to trade my collar.'

Tesra shuddered at the feel of the metal on the other woman. A master, a male, had put this on her; a seamless circle of iron, with an eye-ring through which could be run a length of chain to secure her like an animal.

'You'd like one too, wouldn't you?' teased Vorra. 'Nice and tight around that neck of yours.' Vorra was crouching behind Tesra now, nibbling her neck. It was making her feel uncomfortable, crowded, like she was choking - only the tension in her body wasn't painful, just a tingling warmth, like a spreading itch needing to be scratched.

'Back off, Vorra,' warned the new warder. 'You heard what Master Montrego said.'

Vorra slipped her hands under the blanket, snaking her way to Tesra's breasts, cupping them. 'I don't see Montrego here or any other masters either, and since I don't have a cock, I hardly see how I can spoil the slut's orifices for his highness' gold-plated organ.'

'Vorra,' appealed another of the girls, a thin redhead with perky breasts who was chained by the neck to the wall of the ship. 'You will bring punishment on us all.'

'Who asked you, Kasandra? Why don't you lap up your water like a good little doggie and stop bothering the rest of us? Or better yet, why don't you bark for Bothar to come and prong you again like the little bitch you are?'

Tesra fell back against Vorra, no longer able to resist, no longer wanting to even if she could. Why had her teachers never told her of these feelings? Why had she never known her body capable of feeling them? It was driving her mad, this need to touch. To be touched.

'You are no better than her,' said Drusia to Vorra. 'We have all seen you lick at water pans in heavy punishment chains, not to mention the puckered arse-hole of Rodrigo. And I guarantee, if red-haired Bothar wants you barking, you'll howl just as loud as Kasandra.'

'I am a slave,' declared Vorra, the hay strands matted heavily in her uncombed hair. 'I do not hide the fact. Unlike this little bitch who acts like some kind of queen.'

Tesra sucked in her stomach as Vorra's fingers moved across her belly. Why were the woman's hands on her body so disconcerting? Why were they provoking her so? And why did her senses feel so fully assaulted at every turn, from the odor of the hay and the smell of the confined females to the taste of the salt on her own perspiring lips?

'What's so special about her? Why is she allowed to cover herself, and why can't she be touched?' persisted Vorra. 'That is what I want to know.'

'If you do not let her go, Vorra, you will be beaten. First by us, then by the men when I call for them.'

'Beat me, then,' she challenged. '*Warder*.'

Drusia and Vorra were quickly locked into a tumbling, twisting, hair-pulling battle for supremacy. Tesra could only watch, trembling inside her blanket and strangely overheated in spite of the cool dampness of the place.

The two seemed little more than animals, nude and dirty, their necks collared, their bodies covered in the strange marks, which increasingly Tesra was thinking, were due to the men. There was no pride in their fighting, only a petty, churlishness resulting in a kind of impotent, powerless romp. In the end it was the newly

10

elevated Drusia who prevailed, seating herself, chest heaving and slick with sweat on top of the facedown body of the vanquished Vorra.

'Mercy,' cried Vorra, her arm twisted high on her back, her legs thrashing. 'Please, Mistress Drusia.'

Drusia extended her leg, curling her toes round Vorra's face for her to kiss. 'You may suck them,' she declared imperiously, 'slave.'

Vorra paid wet and sloppy attention to the warder for several minutes before being allowed off her belly. Unless Tesra missed her guess, the arrogant girl had given plenty of this treatment herself to the others before falling so suddenly out of favor.

'Good girl,' said Drusia as the raven-haired beauty presented herself on all fours for inspection. 'Now you may stand and tell our guest what it is like to be a slave. Mistress,' Drusia addressed Tesra, 'may we ask your name?'

'I am called Tesra,' she whispered, dispensing with the lengthy surnames of her ancestors. 'Of the sisterhood of seers.'

'Mistress Tesra,' Drusia knelt gracefully before her, legs apart, palms on her thighs. 'We humbly present ourselves for your questions. May we suggest you use the body of Vorra as a beginning point for your enquiries?'

Tesra surveyed the magnificent naked body, the seeds of her first query already taking root. 'The marks, Vorra, on your buttocks, your back and breasts - they are very odd.'

'From the whip,' she said harshly. 'I have been whipped by my masters on many occasions.'

Tesra flushed as she remembered the belt, and Marcellus telling her that her punishment had been the result of her disobedience. 'You are beaten when you do not obey?'

'Sometimes. Other times they do it just for their own pleasure.'

Tesra felt faint. Up to this moment it had not dawned on her that these men-creatures might take their pleasure in the pain of females.

'Mistress Tesra, you are not well?' It was Drusia, scooting very close, concern in her eyes, and also a heat; a strange light she had never before seen in a woman. 'Does our slavery so discomfit you?'

'I just need to lie down a moment, I'm so tired,' she murmured.

Tesra lay down in the damp straw, which for these women was both mattress and covering. Above her the dark underside of the deck-head swirled, the shadowed patterns of the dancing lanterns casting an eerie glow to the wood-slatted roof of their prison, or more appropriately, an animal pen. Tesra had never been so confined before. On the island there were always the stars to see, and though she was still but a few miles from it now it felt a million miles away.

'Let us help you,' Drusia was saying, brown hair dangling down over her face, their lips inches apart. 'You are not well.'

Tesra lacked the power to fight. She did not understand why Drusia was opening the blanket and baring her naked flesh, especially since she had so admonished Vorra not to touch her just minutes ago.

'Drusia!' exclaimed the defeated Vorra. 'What do you think you're doing? Have you lost your mind? It is one thing for me to have enjoyed a harmless grope, but this, this is too much!'

'Be silent, Vorra,' said the warder, parting the legs of the captive. 'Or I will have you gagged.'

'I shall call for the guards.'

'No, you will not. Girls, deal with this slut. Now.'

Tesra turned her head to the side so as not to miss what was transpiring between Vorra and the other slaves. Six of them, those not chained in place like Kasandra were attacking, pinning the former warder down on her stomach. One by one they took turns smacking her buttocks, reddening them considerably under a hail of slaps, the crack of each sending chills down Tesra's spine.

Meanwhile Drusia was astride her exposed middle, in readiness to stake her command over this guest of their dingy slave hole. 'Mistress Tesra,' she said with a stiff pinch of her nipples, causing Tesra to cry out, 'if I may have your attention. Hands above your head.' Drusia doubled the pressure, her voice and manner and even appearance wholly transformed into something dark and sinister. 'Do not move them again.'

Tesra placed her arms as ordered, rendering herself helpless in the process. Drusia licked her lips, and then bent her head to bite. 'You enjoy pain, I see,' she observed clamping and releasing one of Tesra's coral-pink nipples.

'No, no,' Tesra thrashed her head, the conflicting emotions raging in her head. 'Please, let me go.'

'But who will let me go?' she asked, moving her savage lips to Tesra's for a kiss. 'I am chattel. Flesh for my masters to enjoy and abuse. All of us are exactly that, Mistress Tesra. All of us are property, born to crawl, to writhe at the feet of strong men, to please them with the appearance, touch and taste of our bodies. Somewhere between the value of a good hunting dog and a carving knife, that is the worth of a female.'

'That cannot be,' she protested. 'My sisters and I are the pride of the great blue sea, a shining gem. We touch the hands of the gods and goddesses, we see what they see, know what they know. You too are females, you too have a tribe, a goddess of your own, you must.'

Drusia hooked a finger in the open place between Tesra's legs.

'What are you... no please, stop.'

At first it did not feel good, but suddenly there was distinct pleasure and also a sensation of moistness, like when she swam only the liquid was not from outside.

'Confess it,' Drusia persisted. 'All of this excites you. You long to be where we are; to face the paradox of womanhood, to yearn for subjugation, to gush between the legs knowing you belong to men strong enough to take from you everything - stripping you, whipping you, forcing you to live like a domestic animal, to the point of being branded.'

'B-branded?' The word poured out unbidden, like the liquid essence of her onto Drusia's torturous fingers.

'Oh, yes,' Drusia used her free hand to guide Tesra's down her back to the swell of her bottom. 'Can't you feel it?'

Yes. There it was. The raise of skin, like a scar, only far more substantial and round. The circle, inside of which was a capital 'T' in cursive. The circle she thought she'd seen earlier.

'It's permanent.' Drusia read the seer's eyes, wild and hot. 'It was placed there by a red-hot branding iron. I was marked as one would a horse or verr-beast. The Talassians did it to me. Theirs is the most horrible slavery on earth. I served onboard a galley of the Talassian navy till the pirates took me. Now I am theirs. Just as Vorra and Tesla and all these others, and even you. How does that make you feel - knowing men have that much power over our bodies? Does that spark your fire? It does mine.'

Drusia slid down, placing her mouth on Tesra's nexus. 'Such a sweet thing. I'm going to get you off right now, just like you had a cock in you.'

Tesra cried out, first from the sensation of Drusia's mouth and then from the sudden, unexpected sight of Montrego looming over them, his face filled with rage.

'Get off her you ravenous little cunt!'

Drusia recoiled as the whip struck her hack. 'Forgive me!' she wailed. 'Master, please, forgive me!'

The man continued to strike at her. 'It's too late for that, cunt! Far too late. Bothar!' he called up top to another man. 'Put this one in heavy irons, and the yellow hair, too! I'll deal with them both after I've finished my supper. Yes, yes, little captain's slut,' he purred to the cowering Drusia, her body balled at his feet, 'I will enjoy punishing you, tonight - while your new friend watches.'

Bothar was a red-bearded man with a flattened nose and scars across his cheek and neck. His chest was covered in fiery locks and he had round his neck circlets of heavy, clanking irons. Drusia was limp and utterly passive as he shackled her, hands behind her back, both ankles drawn tight to the wrists. He left her on her belly, her body bowed, a bit in her mouth attached to light chains drawing her neck back painfully towards her feet. For good measure he tied back her auburn hair, taut at the roots. Tesra was dealt with far more leniently, being required to offer but a single wrist, the shackle being attached by a length of chain to an eyebolt in the deck nearby.

Minor though this might seem by slave standards, it was for Tesra an unbearable confinement, terrifying and humiliating.

'There must be some mistake,' she pleaded to Bothar, who had paused to scratch the wild red head of his obediently yapping Kasandra.

He made no response and long after he had left she continued to pull at the chain irrationally, finally giving in to a flood of tears that soaked the metal, threatening to rust it. Drusia, meanwhile, her body scourged, her limbs contorted, looked stoically away, her eyes focusing on some distant point.

Vorra alone seemed pleased, for while she had not yet gotten her old job back, it was a virtual certainty she would, given Drusia's transgression. 'Just you wait,' she taunted the helpless warder, carefully wiping the sweat off the woman's brow to drip into the wounds on her back. 'I will make you pay for every bit of treachery.'

And what did Vorra know of treachery? Tesra thought bitterly. Had she endured

13

kidnapping and cruel abandonment all in one day? Had she been taken from all she knew by a strange man, only to be forgotten by him, left to linger in despair? How could she possibly understand, or Marcellus either? Indeed, the next time she saw the man she would give him a piece of her mind. She would make him comprehend who she was and how it was she must be treated. She, Tesra, would speak and he would have to listen.

Then again, what if he didn't? What if he told her things were as they were and she could not change them back? What if he took out his belt to enforce his decrees? Or took down a whip like Montrego had used? The idea angered her, but it also made her wet and squirmy, the way Drusia's fingers and tongue had. Quietly retreating to an isolated spot, Tesra tucked herself tight into a ball in an effort to make the feelings pass.

It did not help that Drusia was close by, being forced into whimpers by Vorra's girlish tortures. Oh, Persistrata, she prayed, you who are most powerful among female beings, descend now and defeat these males and Vorra, too. Give me courage and dignity.

Closing her eyes, she awaited a response that was destined not to come.

Chapter 2

'Behold, Rodrigo,' announced the pirate king, placing the ancient medallion into the hands of his much-mellowed second-in-command. 'My greatest treasure.'

Rodrigo, his temperament much improved by the Talassian governor's rum, grasped the hammered medal in slow motion, fighting as he did to focus his deep brown eyes, which turned black as a sea storm in times of rage. 'Not gold,' he muttered from across the heavy oaken table in Marcellus' chambers. 'Bronze, is it then?'

Marcellus nodded his head. 'Yes. It is not the metal itself that is of value, though, but the source of it, and the inscription. See here, at the bottom?'

He pointed to the beveled edge, just below the stylized ship and sun emblem, superimposed over a vaguely rounded shape meant to represent an island. 'This is where we were today, and this ship belonged to my grandfather.'

Rodrigo raised his teetering head. 'The same island?'

'Yes, Rodrigo, it is.' Marcellus only hoped he hadn't gotten the man too drunk, or else he'd wind up explaining the whole thing again tomorrow. 'My grandfather came to this place nearly a century ago. He told an incredible tale, which in turn he passed to my father, who left it to me. This medallion alone bespeaks its truth, and yet the men of my family have had no rest on account of its eating away at their brains like a phantom. It drove my grandfather and father mad, the seeking of it, and now I, Marcellus, have found it.'

'You never said anything,' Rodrigo slurred, holding out his dented iron goblet for yet another refill, 'about a magic island.'

'It is not the sort of thing to advertise,' he tipped the rum bottle, upending the dregs. Indeed, Marcellus had intended to tell nothing of this to his crew. The severity of Rodrigo's and the other men's reaction upon his return from the island, however, had caught him entirely off guard. Apparently his authority was not as ironclad as he would have liked to think. A pirate king should not have to explain himself nor ask permission for anything. Those who follow obey, at the price of blood, the rewards being measured in the booty he brings to one and all in his campaigns.

Of late there'd been little in the way of treasure, thanks to the ever-increasing efficiency of the Talassian navy. It was no secret that the new dragar had vowed to end the menace of piracy on the high seas forever. What his Imperial Majesty Teranos the Fifth did not know, though, was that Marcellus, latest and greatest of the pirate kings now had a secret weapon, one he'd been searching for surreptitiously his entire life.

'Rodrigo,' he leaned forward, capturing the man's shoulder in his grasp, 'what if I were to tell you the female has a power greater than that of all Talassia, greater than the dragar... greater even than the gods?'

Rodrigo pursed his lips, and after a thoughtful moment began to laugh. 'I would say you were mad,' he shook off the hand of his captain. 'I would say the slut is some witch who has cast a spell on you. Give me half an hour with her, captain, and I will fix her right enough.'

Marcellus had no doubt he would. The slave girls lived in terror of the man, especially those of his own ship and for good reason. It was not only their bodies he took, but their minds and hearts as well, playing upon their worst fears, breaking their wills and reducing them to levels scarcely recognizable as human.

'No, this one cannot be treated as a slave. She must be cultivated till her powers are gauged.'

'Powers,' he spat, landing a thick ball of sputum on the slanting wooden floor, gently swaying with the rest of the ship. 'What power does a female have but the ability to take a cock? They are animals; they should not even open their mouths except to cry out or suck.'

'This one is different, Rodrigo. This one can see the future.'

Rodrigo looked ready to laugh again. This was the tricky part, the part Marcellus had wished so much to avoid. It would almost be worse if the man believed him than if he thought him mad. Were it not for the high probability of mutiny, Marcellus would keep his mouth shut. Earlier today, on deck, he had deliberately provoked his vice king to test the depth of the resistance. Looking about, reading the men's eyes, sensing the tensions in the air, Marcellus had read his own fate. Montrego, Baltar and Thosar were nearly ready to switch sides, and there were others who would have followed suit. And these were men of his own crew. How matters might stand on the other ships he was only now learning from his spies. Prudence had been the watchword upon his return. Had it come to steel today, he - the pirate king - might have prevailed in the melee. Or not.

Marcellus did not like to play odds. He preferred to be master of his own fate. Better to retain Rodrigo's alliance, at least for now until their coffers were filled, after which time he could make whatever moves he needed. Since the story was so fanciful Rodrigo would never convince anyone else anyhow, so in that sense the secret was still protected no matter what.

And if worse came to worse, which it sometimes did, he still had the ring, safely hidden once more, which would allow him to go back for another slut, or even to hide out himself till the trouble blew over.

'She is a seer,' Marcellus continued. 'Uncultivated, but definitely the genuine article. They live in seclusion, as part of a holy order, under the care of nuns belonging to a sort of sisterhood. They are raised as virgins, with no knowledge whatsoever of males. They live in perfect harmony, contemplating the beauty of the heavens their entire lives.'

Rodrigo slammed his fist, shaking the wood. 'Now you are pulling my leg, my friend. I am sure of it.'

Marcellus' face bore no expression as he rose to his feet, military fashion. 'The proof shall come, all too soon. Keep the crew in line, maintain discipline, and see if we are not snatching fat-bellied Talassian galleons out from under the nose of the dragar within the week.'

Rodrigo was not too drunk to understand that he was being dismissed. 'I obey you, captain,' said the dumbfounded man, as dazed and awed as Marcellus had hoped he would be.

'You are my arm,' he saluted in formal pirate code.

'And you, my heart,' Rodrigo replied. 'For now and always.'

Marcellus hoped there was some sincerity still left in the stock salutation. Rodrigo had been with him on many missions, but it was a known fact among pirates that a friendship was only as strong as the rum that poured, only as brilliant as the gold that shines fresh off a newly taken vessel.

The seer was brought to him shortly after Rodrigo's departure. She had been cleaned up after her time in the slave hold, though its effects seemed very much writ on her lovely face.

He greeted her standing, hair braided down his back, his body covered by a short loincloth and nothing more. 'I see you have found something more suitable to wear,' he observed, noting the linen lace-up shirt hanging nearly to her knees.

'It was given to me,' she informed him, much accusation in the sky-blue eyes. 'After I was dunked in the ocean upside down, a rope tied to my ankle.'

Marcellus suppressed his amusement. 'That is a slave's bath,' he confirmed. 'For which the girls are generally most grateful after lying so long in their own filth.'

'The gods shall punish you,' said the still haughty nymph, far too beautiful for her own good. 'They shall hunt you down and dispatch the whole of your evil crew and all of your ships besides to the pit of eternal flames.'

Marcellus thought it interesting that in her account so far she had not brought up her being confined in steel, a fact brought to his attention just before her arrival. Nor did she seem anxious to discuss the incident with the naughty and ever horny Drusia, in which she had experienced a tiny awakening of her dormant sexuality.

'I cannot help noticing,' observed the pirate king, arms folded across his bare chest, 'that your nipples are fully erect.'

Tesra crossed her own arms. 'That is a reaction to the cold of the ocean and nothing more.'

'Return your arms to your sides, captive.'

She did so, furious. 'As you say, *captor*.'

'I had an interesting discussion with Rodrigo,' he said, enjoying immensely this game of cat and mouse, 'in which he told me what he thinks should be done with you.'

'Oh?' she tossed her wet yellow curls, born to be clenched in the hands of a possessing master. 'And what is that?'

'That which is done with the others,' he shrugged, going to the cabinet for a fresh bottle. On a whim he chose a different spirit entirely. 'Do you know what wine is, Tesra?'

'It is a drink made of fermented grapes,' she said dismissively, returning to the other matter, as he knew she would. 'What things in particular did he mean - among those done to those poor prisoners below deck?'

'Slave girls,' he corrected. 'Come here and kneel.' He snapped his fingers, pointing to the edge of the table. 'As for what things Rodrigo meant, I suspect you know better than I, having spent some considerable time with the girls.'

'Why may I not sit down?' she enquired, noting the presence of two seats.

'Because,' he sat himself in the one, 'females do not sit in my chambers.'

'Then I shall stand.'

'Not an option,' he shook his head. 'In my chambers females remain on their backs, bellies or knees. Take your pick.'

'Go to hell.'

'There is the whip,' he inclined his head. 'Fetch it for me.'

Tesra turned to face the wall on which hung the leather device, some foot-and-a-half long, made of braided leather.

'I will obey,' she lowered herself hastily, her face a shade whiter. 'Please do not beat me again.'

He held out the cup for her, allowing a distinct look of amusement to creep across his face. 'Drink.'

Tesra understood she was to lean forward with her lips. Deliberately he fed her too much, sending blood-red rivulets down her neck and chest.

'Leave it,' he commanded when she tried to clean herself. He liked her this way. The borrowed white shirt soaked in the red wine, her peaked breasts outlined in the material, rendering her neither fully clothed nor gracefully nude, but somewhere between, in the category of whore or slut.

'Rodrigo would enjoy this view,' he mused, taking a sip for himself of the tart, dry liquid, liberated from the island stores of sun-baked Rotura on the eastern gulf of Pheraria Minor.

Tesra held her tongue, the recent reminder of her status as a captive subject to the whip having curbed her temper somewhat.

'You seem very curious,' he said, 'about what Rodrigo might do to you. What exactly was it you saw in the hold? You will tell me, in every detail.' She frowned very slightly - an expression he found quite fetching.

'I saw women, slaves, abused,' she began, attempting to make her account seem voluntary though in fact she had been commanded. 'Chained and confined in a vile hole.'

'Were they clothed?' he enquired as if he had no idea.

'No, they were naked.'

'Your knees are closed together,' he observed. 'This is another thing I do not permit in my chambers.' Tesra spread them, uncertain. 'Wider.' He waited as she opened herself further, the shirt riding up nearly to her waist. Were he to check he was fairly certain he would find her already moist.

'Drink,' he commanded, and this time he gave her no chance at all, pouring the entire contents of the goblet down her throat and over the front of her sopping wet top.

'S-stop,' she sputtered, the liquid splashing pleasantly between her dependent orbs. 'Are you trying to drown me?'

The captive earned a cuff to the side of her face, strong enough to knock her to the floor. 'You will no longer speak,' Marcellus informed her, 'unless spoken to. Resume your position.'

Tesra returned swiftly to her knees, newfound fear and respect in her eyes. She was learning that there were limits and that while he might give her play from time to time, she must never forget on whose leash her lovely throat resided.

'As I recall,' Marcellus refilled both their goblets, 'you were telling me the things that are done to slave girls, as was revealed to you by the ship's sluts below deck.'

'They are kept naked,' she reiterated, fighting the tremor in her voice. 'Some wear chains, collars even.'

'Men are wont to secure their property,' he nodded. 'Are you hungry?'

Tesra's mouth watered visibly at the sight of the piece of dried beef in his hand. How long had it been since she'd eaten?

'Yes,' acknowledged the wine-soaked blonde. 'Very.'

'Tell me then, captive. How do slave girls take their meals in the hole?'

'I think they must eat on all fours. Scraps are thrown down for them or else they are given bowls.'

'For a slave to take food from a master's hand, then,' he prompted, 'would be a privilege.'

'Yes,' whispered the girl, her eyes daring to look up into his, their emerald centers hot and helpless for many things besides mere meat.

Marcellus tore the strip in half, placing one part in his palm. 'You may feed, captive.'

The feel of her teeth and lips, soft and needy was pleasing on his skin. It occurred to him that he might take her here and now, on the floor if he wished, or else in his storm-tossed bed. He must walk a fine line, however, if he were to get the control he needed over her subconscious. 'In addition to feeding like animals, what else do these sluts endure?'

'They may be whipped,' said Tesra throatily. 'I saw the evidence. Scars from beatings, recent and not so recent. Whippings and floggings and canings administered to their recalcitrant flesh. One girl was even punished in my presence.'

'So much disobedience,' he mused.

18

'No,' she shook her head with a most intoxicating eagerness, 'it is not only that. Slaves may be marked simply for a man's pleasure.'

'And they have no say whatsoever?'

'None.' She arched her back instinctively, revealing her charms. 'None whatsoever.'

The kiss was neither gentle nor brief. Marcellus, having bent to receive her, drank his full, absorbing the wine from her lips and also the taste of blood where he had struck her.

Never had he felt lips to match his own so fully, never had he sensed a female so ready to yield to him, to the very depths of her heart and soul. And never had he been more ready, more explosively hard and surging.

But this was not how it could go. Pulling himself back at the last possible second, barely avoiding the point of no return, he rejected her.

'Not yet.' He met the confusion and pain in her eyes. 'Not now.' Not ever, he meant to say, though he hadn't the heart. This poor creature had no idea what he must do to her, nor, in a doubly cruel twist, did she know what she must forego in order for him to have a pure and mental union with her, untainted by physical love. If he'd sought to break her down physically so far, and clearly he had, it was only for this greater purpose; one that did not allow him the luxury of taking pleasure from her willing and needful body.

'You will go and find Montrego,' the captain rose to his feet. 'Tell him that he is to bind you to the main mast and give you a half-dozen lashes of the cat o' nine tails. After this you are to be thrown back in the hole. Naked. Though if any touch you, male or female, they shall answer to me. Is that understood?'

Tesra looked up at him, more a child than a woman. 'I don't understand.'

He clenched his fists. How could she understand - how could he begin to explain to such an innocent creature that he must resist seducing her body so as to take later on her mind?

'What is to understand?' he said curtly. 'You will leave now and do as you're told, or face the consequences.'

'Yes.' His prisoner rose shakily, the heat of her more than a little apparent to his nostrils. 'Sir.'

'Captive,' he called just as she was about to close the door.

'Yes?' she asked expectantly.

'Tell Montrego to send Drusia to me. I am in need of a slut.'

The girl was unable to hide her fallen feelings. 'Yes, sir,' she whispered, her face a crumbled mask.

Tesra ran humiliated from the captain's chamber, hot tears stinging her face like the man's belt. How she hated him! He was worse than a monster; he was a sadistic, cruel madman, a deranged being who delighted in the senseless torture of living beings. How could he work her up like this and then abandon her? How could he awaken needs, show her things about her body not even the mother seers had known and then chase her away, spurning her cruelly?

More than anything she wanted to crawl into some dark corner and weep herself to death. Better to have jumped from the man's rowboat and drowned in the sea than to have lived to see such a day! Better she should drown now, in fact, than live a moment longer. Climbing to the top of the railing she prepared to throw herself over the prow, but at the last moment, in the shifting pattern of the waves, she saw the face of the goddess, restraining her, warning her against the evils of suicide.

If she were to end her life now, this way, she would not see the Golden Hall of her mothers and grandmothers. Rather she would plunge to the pit - the dark inferno where Marcellus himself was destined, along with his minions.

'I have no sin in this,' she told the goddess, her reassuring face staring back. 'Whatever is done to me is on their hands. Let the men-beasts be damned, and their hideous god, Nephisis.'

The sudden rush of wind knocked her back overboard on her bottom. She took the timing to be coincidental, in no way evidentiary of the efficacy or even the existence of the barbaric sea god. 'I do your will,' she cried, looking skyward. 'Persistrata, my divine queen.'

Tesra drew stares, hungry and lean, along with outright leers as she made her search for Montrego. Twice she asked for help only to have sailors shrug indifferently, as though she were a mere fly pestering them.

It will soon be dark, she thought, carrying her search to the rear deck, where the sun could be seen as a great red orb slipping down beneath the waves, obliterating all in its wake including the memories of her island home. I will have to be onboard this ship at night. With no light at all. Why this should be any worse than the day she did not know.

'You, woman, what do you want here?' A dark-skinned man with an even darker beard was glaring at her, looking as if he wished to devour her in her wine-stained shirt, barely adequate to shield her from his lust.

'Montrego,' she managed to say, conveying as best she could her mission.

'In the galley,' he grumbled, pointing to a set of stairs.

Tesra descended reluctantly, the slave hold fresh in her mind. There was no darkness here, however, and no smell. Reaching bottom, she felt her feet impact pleasantly on dry sanded wood. So far so good.

The sound was coming from behind a stack of barrels, just to the right of some sacks of flour. It was a female sound, a kind of muffled whimper, half pain, half pleasure. Tesra felt an instinctive tingling between her legs. Once again there was moisture. Heart pounding in her chest, feet falling step by step toward an unknown fate, she rounded the corner to see what, or rather who was behind the barrels.

Tesra had to steady herself against the nearest one.

It was Vorra, on her belly, over a grain sack, her arse under assault from the stiffly engorged sex organ of Montrego. He was showing her no mercy, slamming the full length of himself inside the tightly puckered opening. Tesra felt her own buttocks clench instinctively. She had no idea such a thing was possible for a male, much less that a female could submit to it. But Vorra was a slave, which meant the say was not hers. If Montrego enjoyed this act she had no choice but to endure it.

Tesra wanted to retreat, to turn away, but she was too engrossed. Montrego was so big - did all men swell like this between their legs, Marcellus included? Was this what the captain had wanted to do to her - sticking his thing inside her, pushing her to the floor like Vorra, forcing her sweat-covered body to bear the weight of him, the smell, the press of his hand on her back, the feel of his saliva dripping disgustedly from the corner of his mouth? Was that what Marcellus had in mind? And what about Vorra? Was she enjoying this? Did Montrego care?

'Worthless sluts,' he snarled, talking to no one in particular. 'The whole bunch of you. And you can take this godforsaken crew as well. And the captain; what possessed him to bring back that little slut and rub her in our faces, eh?'

Vorra's head was bowed, the man's craggy hand pulling back on her hair, threatening to tear the roots. 'I - I don't know master.'

'Of course you don't.' He slid his dick from her arsehole, withdrawing it completely. 'You don't know anything; you're a piece of flesh, nothing more.'

'Oh, master,' she moaned as he took her other hole. 'Yes, master.'

'The captain ain't right in the head,' the man continued, fucking her in punctuation to his cadence. 'I'll tell you that right off. First he drags us halfway across the sea for one little cunt, and he won't even fuck her proper. Then he throws her in the hole, so all hell breaks loose and I have to clean up his mess. And do I even get to finish the job? No, because on top of every other blistering thing, now he has to have Drusia to bed for the night. When what she really needs is a few hours of being dragged in the ship's wake, or maybe in the dunking cage.'

'Master,' Vorra dug her fingernails into the grain sack, 'please, may I?'

May I what? Why did she not finish the sentence? Tesra wondered, her fingers slithering almost invisibly to her own wet opening. Yes, this felt good. Just as it had when Drusia touched her there, and when the captain looked at her where she knelt at his feet in his chambers, his deep voice giving her commands as he toyed with her, making her open her legs, spilling the wine and, above all, kissing her.

By the goddess it was happening again. That strange nether earthquake she had narrowly evaded in the hole with Drusia. Only this time it was far greater, stronger and more completely irresistible. 'Oh, save me, Persistrata,' she moaned, both hands at her pussy, leaning ever backward in the process and finally collapsing.

The barrels! Oh no, the barrels!

'What in blazes?' roared Montrego. A moment later he was towering over her, his interrupted cock dripping with the intimate juices of Vorra. 'Are you demon possessed or just simpleminded?' he wanted to know. 'Do you know the penalty for eavesdropping?'

'I - I didn't mean to spy on you,' she cried, scrambling to her feet and doing her best to cover herself. 'I was sent by the captain to find you.'

'Find me?' he snorted. 'And exactly how long were you standing there "finding me" as you put it, eh girl?'

'I only just got here,' she lied.

'That's not true, master,' declared Vorra, kneeling at his side now like some kind of pet. 'I heard her all along. Breathing. Masturbating. She wants to be a slave, in the worst way.'

21

'Liar!' cried Tesra, hating herself at once for becoming involved in such a demeaning and petty debate.

'It's true, master,' wheedled the obsequious Vorra, kissing her way round Montrego's hip to his hairy arse. 'The yellow hair wants to be a slave, but she is nothing more than a frigid captain's bitch. Like Drusia. She cannot please you like I can.'

'I seek to please no one,' Tesra declared, wishing for somewhere to wipe her wet fingers.

'Silence, both of you,' Montrego barked. 'Or I'll feed you to the sharks myself. You,' he grabbed for Vorra, 'finish me off.'

Vorra gave Tesra an evil smile before planting her lips around the man's penis, and Tesra's eyes widened in shock as inch by inch the girl took him, till the whole of his cock was buried in her cheeks. Eagerly, making little gurgling sounds, Vorra sucked him, intending to bring him to what Tesra understood would be his climax, the shooting of the sperm which biologically belonged in the girl's womb.

'What was the captain's message?' Montrego wanted to know, his interest shifted for the moment from the naked, utterly abased girl at his crotch.

Tesra flushed crimson, as much for what she had to say as for what she was seeing. 'The captain has ordered me whipped,' she said, her voice barely audible. 'Half a dozen lashes at the main mast. Then I am to go back in the hole. Naked. But no one is to touch me. And also,' she swallowed, feeling the need to clamp her legs together, 'he orders Drusia to be sent to him... though it seems you already know this.'

'Aye, he sent me another messenger, he did. Seems you were a little slow.'

Tesra feared Montrego would be angry with her, but he had already shifted back to Vorra, his eyes rolled back in his head as he pressed his hands to the side of the girl's skull. The look on his face both frightened and aroused her; his teeth so fiercely bared, the sinews on his neck so thickly exposed as he manipulated her into place for maximum penetration. What was going on in Vorra's mouth? What was she feeling and tasting?

For several moments he held her like this, the spasms continuing as he released himself with the deepest satisfaction.

'May as well take it off now,' Montrego told Tesra, indicating that she should begin her sentence of nudity.

Her fingers moved to the hem of the damp shirt, numb, her senses oblivious to everything but Vorra who - having taken his seed - was now licking him clean, paying homage to this organ which had been not only in her mouth but in her sex and arse as well. For some reason Tesra was not revolted, but rather jealous. Vorra seemed to know this too; from the way she was licking her lips and narrowing her eyes catlike, staring directly at the free woman who she somehow had deemed her rival.

'Was I good, master?' she looked up at the pirate, for Tesra's benefit.

'To the hold with you,' growled the cantankerous yellow beard, kicking her away.

'And you, to the main mast,' Montrego turned Tesra about, moving her forward with a cupped hand hard against her bare buttocks.

To Tesra's shame she lingered, deliberately, so that by the time she reached the mast he'd had to spank her twice more, each blow a little hotter and more exciting than the last.

'I've never been whipped before,' she told Montrego as he commanded her to lift her hands over her head while pressing her tummy, breasts and sex against the rough wood.

'I'll be sure and hold your hand,' he mocked.

Montrego - who was scarcely taller than her and a full three inches shorter than Vorra - yanked Tesra's wrists high so as to affix the well-worn manacles dangling down in front of her. The steel bit cruelly into her wrists, forcing the girl to her tiptoes. Tesra did not like what was being done by the wood to her nipples, or to the tender slit between her legs. Sensitized as she was, she feared the effect of any additional rubbing she might experience.

The cat o' nine tails was long, with a series of braided leather strands. From the man's mind she garnered that he was looking to teach her a lesson with it. It was happening with more frequency that Tesra could read the thoughts of these male beasts. Unlike the females with whom she had grown up, they seemed to have no guard over their minds, no discipline in their consciousnesses. The only exception to this was Captain Marcellus, whose inner sanctum was as well guarded as any fortification of stone.

Was he with the girl now; the small and eager slut Drusia who had tried to take from Tesra the pleasure that belonged only to her captor? She hoped the slave would be richly punished for her crime. On the other hand, she did not wish the girl to in any way arouse Marcellus, provoking him to her use. No doubt Drusia would sweat and squeal for him, as well or better than Vorra. The thought made her sick. The curvy brown-haired girl had no place with the handsome captain, no right to his kisses, to his commands, to the back of his hand at the side of her face, correcting her when she'd done wrong.

'One,' called Montrego, wielding the device with devastating accuracy.

Tesra's back exploded with red-hot pain. Compared to this Marcellus' belt was nothing but a delicate tap, his hand imprinting her face the merest tickle. It was different too, in that here she was exposed, gawked at and lusted after by one and all, attacked with impunity by an uncaring stranger, while with Marcellus there was an intimacy, a connection born of their relationship as captor and captive.

But what was she saying? Marcellus was no less a stranger than any of these others. In fact, whereas these men were merely following orders the pirate king was the one who had invaded the sacred pool in the first place, dragging her from her home, humiliating and beating her till she agreed to go with him to his ship. And then he'd systematically teased and brutalized her, reducing her to a mass of quivering need, a bundle of confused, surrendered flesh with no will, no backbone.

'Two,' called her abuser, letting loose the terrible rain of leather for a second go. This time he struck low, across her bottom cheeks. Tesra moaned, having no option but to retreat against the unforgiving mast. Predictably her sex was split, the delicate lips puckering open against the un-sanded wood. She was wet, the juice of her female self flowing freely, enhanced it seemed by her brutalization at the hands of the man-beast.

The third blow found her panting, her cheek scraping against the mighty cylinder. Shamelessly she was humping it now, her body in tune to her beating.

'Four,' he called, striping the back of her thighs.

How thorough he was. How well qualified to mark and humble a woman. For all his ugliness Tesra was beginning to see why tall and beautiful Vorra so willingly abased herself, allowing him to use her orifices at will, to treat her little better than one might a household animal.

She shuddered at the fifth blow. Was this what Vorra was seeking? Some kind of resolution or release to this building tension, to this spiral of need and satisfaction, of pleasure spiked with pain?

'Six,' growled Montrego, his voice coming to her as if in slow motion. It was in the time between his call and the fall of the last blow on her defenseless, beaten back that Tesra experienced her orgasm. How she knew the name she was not sure, but there was no doubting what it was, and the power it had over her body. It was like all the good feelings of life, all the itched scratches, pleasant tickles, cool spring rains and hot cups of milk combined, in one sudden burst of energy.

Enough energy to lift her high, but also to send her crashing back down. For in as much as this experience must be empowering for Montrego and the other male beasts, she knew instinctively that for her gender it was a sign of intimate submission, a profound confession that the deepest controls to her own body belonged to them - to whichever man was clever enough or strong enough to take and exploit her.

'What a waste,' muttered Montrego, running a ripe thumb down the crack of her backside, lightly teasing the entrance to her still spasming hole. 'A hot little piece like you would serve half the Talassian navy and beg for more, wouldn't you?'

The man was directly behind her, his hands on her arse, his mouth an inch from her ear, pronouncing the words, hot and wet.

'Oh yes,' she moaned, on the verge of another explosion, far, far bigger. 'Oh yes, master.'

Montrego let her go, cackling in triumph. She'd called him master, though she was purportedly a free woman, beholden to no one at all, except the man who claimed her as captive.

'I didn't mean that,' she made a point of telling him as he released her from the manacles. 'I was under stress... I misspoke.'

'To the hold with you, milady,' he grabbed her by the hair, his voice crusty with sarcasm. 'Time for your beauty rest.'

The last rays of the sun, angry red, were already below the horizon as Montrego forced her down into the dank black hole for the night. She contemplated begging him to keep her in the open air, just a little longer, but she knew in her mind it was no use. Wasted breath to a man - to men like these.

The air felt damper to her than before, the moisture already clinging to her naked body, and as the hatch was slammed shut above, Tesra got that closed in, panicked feeling she'd had in here the last time.

'Hello?' she called out, hearing no one about in the unlit hold. 'Is anybody here?'

'Silence, slut,' sizzled the voice of Vorra. 'You have nothing to say down here.' Vorra's fingers came from nowhere, clamping her nipples. 'Isn't that right, you little whore? The men may drool over your perky tits and yellow hair up there, but down here you're my bitch. Is that clear?'

Tesra winced at the rough treatment. 'Yes, Vorra.'

'Such a pretty one,' she whispered. 'It will be a joy to make you cry. Have they told you I am warder again?'

'No, Vorra, but you mustn't touch me. No one is supposed to, not even a man.'

Vorra was licking her lips, like a cat at a bowl of cream. 'I've news for you, my trusting little free woman. The men do not know what transpires down here unless someone tells them. And unlike Drusia, I run a tight little ship within a ship.'

'What will you do?' said Tesra, looking at the woman with new respect.

'Whatever I wish,' Vorra replied, pushing down on her shoulders till she was kneeling. 'Now kiss my feet... slave.'

Tesra lowered herself all the way down, practically burrowing under the straw to reach Vorra's toes. Touching them with her lips she imagined Marcellus once more, a surge of heat shooting through her belly.

'Suck them,' Vorra demanded, and that is precisely what Tesra did, one by one till all ten were cleaned to the satisfaction of the haughty and vindictive slave.

Chapter 3

'You have been a naughty girl, my little Drusia.'

'Forgive me, master,' begged the naked, collared wench, lying stretched at the captain's feet, having crawled across the floor of his chambers on her belly.

Marcellus pressed the toe of his calfskin boot to the lips of the vivacious slave, his personal favorite among the herd, though he would never let on. 'Perhaps the sharks could teach you some manners, little girl.'

'Please no, master,' rasped the very grown up Drusia through her naturally pouty lips, even as she began to lick the surface of the dusty boots, her tongue moving with sweet desperation, 'your little girl begs you for another chance.'

Marcellus allowed her to abase herself a while longer, demonstrating in the process his complete and total power over her, to the point of life and death. It was this aspect of the ownership of a female that most satisfied him; even more, in fact, than the ability to use her sexually in any way shape or form. Marcellus, like most strong men, craved power in every area of his life, sexual relations included. To accept a female as equal would be as absurd as allowing democracy for his crew, or piloting his rowboat to the nearest station of the Talassian navy to throw himself on their mercy.

'Another chance?' he exclaimed. 'And how many would that make in total?'

'Your slave girl does not know, master,' she answered coquettishly, no mean feat in her present position of total subjugation. 'Little Drusia cannot do math, nor can she read or write the words of men.'

'You, Drusia? You read better than I! By the salty beard of Nephisis, girl, that tongue of yours will be the death of one of us yet.'

'Drusia's tongue exists to please her master.'

'Indeed,' he noted dryly, 'when it is not otherwise engaged in pleasuring the pussies of my new acquisitions. And who was it, exactly, my dear slave, who gave you license to diddle in the hole of the nymph?'

'I sought to warm her up for you, master.'

He reared back, enjoying his first good laugh in days. 'You make as fine a liar as you do a cocksucker. What do you suppose that says about my cock? Is it as easily covered over and manipulated by your lips, do you suppose, as the truth?

'Master, allow your girl to please you.'

'My naughty girl,' he corrected.

'Punish me then, master. Beat me and use me like a naughty little slave.'

'Fetch the cane, and lie across my sea chest.'

Drusia enjoyed this game as much as he, though it was her flesh that ended up bruised and welted, her body invariably teased and tormented to breaking point. Breathing hard, her nipples tight, her crotch already thickly oiled, she presented the dastardly rattan. 'Position, master?' she whispered.

'On your back,' said the captain; sentencing her by his words to a far longer torment than if he'd ordered her immediately to offer up her arse.

The slave girl shivered visibly at her sentence, but made no delay in obeying. Prettily, with pure feminine grace, she sat upon the curved, metal-banded chest, as old as his grandfather's grandfather, and immediately reclined, her head lying at one end, her knees over the other. Raising one foot she hooked it on the edge, so that the captain had full access to her crotch. Drawing a sharp breath to outline her ribs and push out her breasts, she let fall her hands down to the floor, giving him access to her torso as well.

How beautiful she was, stretched out for love yet destined for pain.

'Perhaps I should marry you,' he ran the tip of the cane over the hollow of her belly.

Drusia closed her eyes, already priming herself to move as the slut she was. 'Your slave would make a poor wife, milord; forever crawling to you, begging to be leashed and fucked.'

'True. Still, I am tempted, which is why it is fortunate that I came across you already branded.' He smacked her on the inner thigh, inviting her to spread herself more widely.

'And yet that thought makes you jealous - that it was another who burned my flesh, who gave me my first whipping, making me beg for it on the deck of a ship belonging to your enemies.'

Marcellus struck her on the cunt. 'You push me, slave, time and again, why?'

Drusia writhed. 'So that master will be stronger with me.'

'Good answer,' he nodded, using the end to masturbate her. 'Indeed, one day I hope to be strong enough to feed you to the sharks, which as we both know is the only way we will either of us find any peace with regard to our relationship.'

'I would die for you, my captain.'

26

Marcellus retracted the cane, depriving her. 'Bridge.' Drusia assumed the required shape, responding like the trained animal she was. Marcellus enjoyed her this way, watching her acrobatics, her utter vulnerability as she placed herself, cunt in the air, hands grasping ankles from underneath her arse. 'Beg,' he told her, placing the cane suggestively over her bowed belly.

'I am at your mercy, master,' she evaded.

He ran his hand under her quivering buttocks, feeling for visceral responses. Simply holding this position for any length of time could be quite painful, even without any form of corporal punishment attached. 'Which will be stronger today,' Marcellus speculated, his left hand sneaking up to her pussy, his right brandishing the punishment stick. 'Pleasure or pain?'

His timing, as always, was impeccable, for at the very moment the thin, resilient piece of wood crashed down on her naked belly, he was tickling the underside of her clit in that way she loved best. 'Beg,' he repeated, determined to outstrip her martyr's will, just this once.

'No, master, please, I can take more.'

He hit her again. 'I can do this all night,' he warned, 'the whole time keeping you on the edge, a hair's breadth from orgasm.

'I am yours,' she breathed, her voice and form slipping on over to that other place, to that realm where torture is received as a sacred rite and where the feminine is elevated to the most devastating of levels of anguish.

'That means nothing to me,' he growled, moving north to strike at her helpless tits, wanting to see them as red and bruised as her belly, wanting to see every inch of her marked and abused so that no matter how he chose to fuck her tonight it would be agony. 'Your coy words are wasted. You are an animal - beg as one, that is all I require of you.'

Though in truth it was Drusia who brought out the animal in him. More than any of the other girls, in his hands, she was slave and he master.

The sensation had seemed unique, up to tonight, when he'd had his first encounter - or more properly his first training session - with the blonde seer. Instead of remaining impassive, full of professional pride and satisfaction, he'd been overcome with the desire to possess her completely, as his personal object of conquest.

Perhaps this was a result of his having bonded with her in capture, or else an overeager lust for her as the proverbial golden goose to fill his coffers with shiny eggs. In either case it fell to Drusia, unwittingly, to make him forget, to drain off his raging manhood enough to let him think straight around the arrogant and quirky little yellow hair.

'You're nothing but a cunt to me, Drusia. A mouth, an arse, or tits if I have need of them.'

'I am your cunt, master. I am your mouth, to be filled. I am the arse you may beat or screw as it suits you.'

'Turn over, girl. Arse up high.'

Drusia lifted herself painfully from the chest. To lie now on her stomach was excruciating, but this is what Marcellus required from her, the ultimate sacrifice.

'How many times, girl, have you been promoted to warder?' he wanted to know, the cane poised to strike.

'Seven,' said Drusia, no longer claiming ignorance with regard to her counting skills.

'And each time you were demoted, within hours. Why?'

'I do not know, master,'

He sliced at her soft cheeks, landing a blow directly across her brand. 'Liar,' he accused, though probably she was telling the truth.

'Yes, master.'

It was satisfying to unleash his wrath, moving the weapon with cold efficiency, again and again and again till Drusia's bottom was a network of welts, a crisscrossed, throbbing horror.

'Spread your cheeks,' he told the sobbing girl, this being the only forewarning she would receive of imminent penetration.

Drusia had nothing more to say, no witticisms to share as he buried himself with dark satisfaction into her anus. Hands on her hips he showed no mercy, taking his fill of slave arse, his fill of slave suffering.

'Touch yourself,' he demanded, though in all probability she did not want any pleasure right now. 'Show me what a greedy little cunt you are.'

Drusia buried a tired hand into her tired pussy, working it as required till, after just a few minutes she was groaning with need.

'Tomorrow you will beg the forgiveness of Tesra,' he declared. 'The free woman whom you have wronged.'

'Yes, master,' groaned the arse-fucked slave, having no choice but to answer.

'She is not like you,' he felt obligated to tell her, though he knew not why. 'She has a mind of her own and will not be bent to the opinion of anyone. What are you in comparison to her? You, who lies naked in the hold, dreaming and praying of moments like this, when your master will take you up into the fresh air for a nice beating and a fresh vanquishing.'

'Oh yes, master,' she hissed, prodding him. 'Vanquish me. Take me and make me yield to you.'

Marcellus pushed her hand from her cunt in blind rage, forgetting for the moment she was doing this only by his orders. 'Whore,' he roared, taking her pussy. 'Slut of a slave. Chattel bitch, I'll teach you to taunt your betters.'

She began to convulse at the third thrust, her body a tangle of conflicting sensations. Like a dagger he kept at her, hands clamped to her hips, forcing her to feel more, to take more. He surged with seed, flooding the womb of her, overfilling the channel so that as he withdrew it began to pour back out of her well-caned cunt.

'On your knees,' he told her, the sight of her conquered body rousing him to life again already. 'Your work is not yet done.'

'Yes, master,' whispered Drusia, eager to apply her lips where in truth they had belonged all along. 'Thank you, master.'

'You are welcome,' he slid comfortably home, grasping her hair like a well-worn handle. 'My very naughty, very horny little girl.'

She looked up at him lovingly, in a way that gave him much grief. 'The sharks,' he reminded her, forcing her to refocus on the matter at hand. 'Never forget the sharks.'

The girl sucked him as if her life depended on it, which of course, it did.

Vorra did not dare to openly molest the yellow-haired newcomer, but there were plenty of other things she could do, much to Tesra's great dismay. Not to mention her sexual frustration. After the toe sucking Vorra sat upon the back of the smaller woman, bending her arm till she begged for mercy.

'We know your kind,' Vorra snarled at her. 'Pretending to lord it over the slaves, all the while stealing the attentions of the males, begging them with your eyes, taunting them to have and possess you. Yours is the worst kind of woman, dishonest and hypocritical. All you yellow-hairs are like that. You think you are better than us.'

'No,' gasped Tesra, the pressure on her arm threatening to break it. 'I am not like that. All women are my sisters.'

'Sisters?' Tesra scoffed. 'Now there is something truly laughable.'

'It is true,' Tesra craned her neck, hoping to enlighten the downtrodden female. 'The man-beasts seek to keep you in these conditions, treating you like animals, but you are born free, destined to serve Persistrata, the great goddess of inner dawn.'

'Here,' said Vorra, pushing Tesra's face into the mulch. 'Here is your great destiny. Here is where it all ends and begins for females in this world. Unless you happen to be born a queen in some tower - or a madwoman on a nowhere island like you. Know where I was born, *Sister* Tesra? In a whorehouse in Braxia. My mother was a nineteen-year-old prostitute impregnated by a garrison soldier twice her age. They let her go to term because it turned out this particular officer and his friends had a thing for pregnant girls. They chained her by the ankle to the bed for the whole nine months, where she continued to serve them till the day I was born.'

'Please,' cried Tesra, starved of air and wanting to retch, 'I can't breathe.'

'What's the matter?' Vorra yanked her up by her ruined curls. 'Is it too lowly and un-goddess-like for you down there?'

Tesra sucked down mouthfuls of relatively clean air. 'Oh, thank you!' she exclaimed, seeking to placate the woman. 'That is much better.' But her docility seemed to have the opposite effect.

'Call me Mistress Vorra,' the warder decided. 'As a matter of fact, yellow hair, I think I should like to tell you the rest of my story while you give me pleasure, the way we are forced to pleasure men from morning till night. I assume your virgin tongue can manage? Certainly the men won't be able to check *that* for purity, will they?'

Vorra used the back of a fellow slave for a seat, having called a pretty black-skinned girl over on all fours. In this position Vorra could open her legs wide, giving access to the kneeling Tesra.

'Eat my pussy right,' Vorra pulled cruelly at her ears, forcing her into place. 'Or I promise, we will find ways to make you suffer that will make you pray to your goddess you'd never been born.'

Tesra had no clue how to pleasure a woman, though to a certain extent she assumed it must be instinctual. The lips of her were very soft, surprisingly so for the roughness of her slavery, and when the tip of Tesra's tongue parted the folds of velvet flesh she heard from Vorra a tiny girlish moan.

'Not bad,' she said approvingly. 'Now we can finish the story. Of my divine birth.' Several of the girls snickered at this, having gathered themselves round to view the entertainment. 'As I said, my mother was a special attraction, her ever swelling belly a source of great delight to the men who fucked her day and night. She was chained in place and deprived of all clothing, even the scraps usually allowed a slave whore such as herself. Towards the end they could only do her on all fours like a dog, though she was able to suck till the last possible second and immediately afterwards, which she did, as a matter of fact, to compensate the physician for his trouble in delivering me.'

'There was some debate as to who I belonged to, but in the end the soldier, who only wanted to sell me in the first place, gave me over to the brothel owner in exchange for free ale as long as he was stationed in the town. My mother was never allowed to see me and the very next day she was sold to the owner's cousin who used female slaves in his grist mill, forcing them to turn great stone wheels till they dropped, their bodies naked, scourged by whips and bound in heavy chains. Needless to say, I never laid eyes on her again.

'I grew up in the whorehouse, and the tavern downstairs. Almost from the time I could crawl I was put to work, scrubbing the beer-soaked floors, often under the very feet of the male customers. I was a favorite of theirs and I took pride in pleasing them with my smile and my singing voice. They told me I was pretty and ever since I can remember, all I have ever wanted to do is please men.

'As I grew older, closer to a woman than a girl, it was no longer appropriate to sit on the customers' laps and joke with them. I was retired to the stable behind, where I cared for the customers' horses. The whorehouse owner, quite elderly by now, took pity upon me and promised that when I came of age I would be given my freedom along with a small dowry, so long as I kept myself pure.

'I was bound and determined and as of my eighteenth birthday, I had not strayed, by great power of will. There was, however, a certain one of the stable boys, a handsome, curly-haired twenty-year-old, arrogant and cruel who had been trying to seduce me for the better part of a year. Finally, on the very night of my majority, he cornered me once and for all in the back of the barn.

'"You do not fool me," he said, "even if you fool the others. I know what you are. I know what you really want, deep in your heart."

'I was standing there in my shirt, breeches and work boots, back to the wall, terrified. The young man had this dark look on his face, like a smirk or leer and his own shirt was open to reveal his lean, lightly muscled chest. But it was the whip in his hand that frightened me most.'

Vorra's breathing had grown faster as she spoke and now she was clutching Tesra, pinning her by means of her strong thighs. The liquid of her trickled over Tesra's face, in her nose and even down the back of her throat, its flavor strong and heady, vaguely sweet and not entirely unpleasant.

'I told him I would scream and he said it did not matter, that in a few short moments no one would care what happened to me ever again.

'"You're a slut, Vorra," said the arrogant stable-hand to me. "And a slave. And I will prove it now."

'He ordered me to take my clothes off and when I hesitated, he lashed me with the whip, tearing open the front of my shirt and leaving an angry trail across my bosom. Tears in my eyes I did as I was told, removing my ruined shirt as well as my pants and boots.

'"You have a nice body, Vorra," he said to me as I presented myself for his inspection. "How about we teach you how to use it?"

'I reminded him of my upcoming legacy and the promise of my freedom, to which he merely laughed. "This is your legacy," he grabbed at his swollen crotch, "and it is high time you received it."

'He made me come to him on my knees, my breasts on fire from the lash of the whip, my cheeks stained with tears, my flesh nude and humiliated. As he lorded it over me, still fully dressed, I was compelled to open his trousers to receive his inflamed member. I was not naïve and I knew what was expected, though the act revolted me. He doubled my shame by stroking my hair, assuring me how good I looked this way down on my knees and how I was a natural sucker of cocks. At a certain point something deep inside me must have kicked in, because I began to feel something in the midst of my degradation, a distinct warmth in my body, a burning itch to have him push me down further and if possible, conquer me completely.

'"Would you like to swallow, my obedient little cocksucker?" he asked, having pushed himself by this time to the back of my throat. "Would you like to drink my come like the natural slut you are?"

'I did, but there were other things I needed as well. I did not know whether to be terrified or overjoyed when he shoved me away, telling me it would not end this way, no matter if I wanted it to or not.

'"On all fours," he commanded and I obeyed, though he was nothing to me, neither master nor husband.

'"You're a born slave whore," he said, walking about me, draping the whip over my body as he moved. "A sleek and pretty little beast." I could do nothing but shudder, my head down, my hair in my face, my flesh fully at his mercy.

'"Beg me to fuck you," he said, bending to stroke lightly my swollen, exposed pussy lips. The sensations overwhelmed me, and as I knelt for him on hands and knees in the straw I wanted nothing more than to be penetrated by his wicked hardness. Foolish cunt that I was, though, I held out.

'"I cannot," I gasped. "Please, don't make me."

'"Oh," he straightened himself, denying me my pleasure, "but I will."

'The whip on my arse and back was ten times what it had been on my tits. He gave no mercy as he tanned my arrogant hide. When at last he stopped there was no doubt what my response would be.

'"Beg," he said simply, and I immediately offered up the words, imploring and wailing for him to use me for his pleasure. Through my earlier disobedience, however, I had lost the right to his penis. It was the whip handle that would take my virginity from me, and in the end, brutal as he was I surrendered even to this, lifting my hips, straining against the invading leather device if only to obtain release.

'He used me thoroughly, leaving me collapsed on the hay, a naked wreck, sore, abused, marked and deeply broken in my spirit. I'd thought my ordeal over, but it had only begun.

'"Up here, girl," said he, commanding me back to my knees as if I were nothing more now than a tavern slave. I could barely keep myself righted. He had to put his hand on the top of my head, which left him the other to stroke his magnificent cock. After all I had been, I was denied the right even to receive his load in my mouth, taking it rather over my whipped breasts as well as on my face and in my hair.

'One final look at me, one final smirk and he was gone. "Happy birthday," he winked at me from the doorway, offering his parting shot as I knelt, whipped, violated, and covered in man-seed.

'I cleaned and dressed myself as best I could, using a blanket to hide my torn shirt. At first I was in shock, uncertain how to feel. Then I was angry, and a little fearful he would try to attack me again. When after three days of interacting with me he showed no sign of recognition of what we had been through, however, I turned my thoughts in a different direction. Feeling spurned, I now found I wanted him again.

'He made me humiliate myself, begging for his attentions. I had to practically throw myself at him and all so he would consider whipping and abusing me a second time. Not that it would or had been true abuse, since I wanted and needed it every step of the way. At last, one night after we had bedded down the horses, he condescended to shoot down my throat, though he would not touch or even look at my hot and willing body.

'The next day I threw myself at his feet, in tears, begging him to tell me why he had rejected me this way, tearing me apart and stomping on my heart. Did he not know that I loved him? Did he not see that in possessing and mastering me he had won my affection and obedience not merely for one night, but forever?

'He told me to get up, whereupon he explained that the real problem was my status. He could never love a free woman, only a slave. Having been completely deceived and manipulated by the man, I told him this was no problem as in my heart I was already his slave. He feigned hesitancy, indicating that he would need some real proof. It was thus that I was fooled into turning myself over for manumission. We left that very day for the court, after which, having signed the papers, we found a blacksmith to place upon me the brand. My new master wasted no time in enjoying his prize, taking possession of me on my back in a filthy alley behind the blacksmith's. Afterwards, a tether about my neck, my hands behind me in manacles, he led me down the main street of Braxia, my body black from the dirt and grease of the alley, my thighs oozing with the fluids of our mutual climax.

'I considered it my dream come true, to have the man I loved so proud of his domination over me, but my soaring happiness soon turned to crushing defeat as he revealed to me the true intent of our relationship. As it turned out, he had made a bet with some of his friends that he could corrupt me. For the price of a measly bronze coin I had been branded, whipped and used beyond imagination.

'"What will you do with her now?" had asked one of his drinking buddies.

'"I hadn't thought of it," he shrugged. "Sell her, I suppose."

'Which he did, though not after having the monumental gall to collect my dowry from the tavern owner, claiming that as my master he was entitled to all my possessions. Without so much as kissing me goodbye he deposited me for auction, whereupon I was purchased for the first time.

'So there you have it, noble sister - the story of my fine upstanding birth. And now, if you don't mind, I think I shall come on your face.'

Tesra received the woman's orgasm, a sensuous flood that made her feel hot and needy, dirty and deliciously subjugated. And yet at the same time she sensed real power down here, too: the power to arouse, to tempt, to invoke the wrath and desire of masters. It was an art she was determined to learn, if for no other reason than to help her escape and defeat the monstrous, arrogantly handsome captain.

The man she hated - and wanted.

Chapter 4

Tesra did not want the pirate anymore. She only hated him, and with a vengeance that would have done the goddess proud.

'To a certain extent our relationship will be that of a master and slave,' he was saying as he stood casually over her, the short, nasty whip in his hands. 'Though there will be certain fundamental differences.'

He paused, as if awaiting her response, but not having given her permission to speak he knew that none would be forthcoming. Biting her tongue, Tesra could only squirm uncomfortably. The sadistic Marcellus had added a new dimension to his game of torture this morning, having compelled the proud seer to kneel naked at his feet, her hands shackled behind her back.

It was a convenient posture for him, no doubt, allowing as it did ample opportunity to molest and abuse her helpless breasts. In fact, they already bore a pair of angry welts as punishment for two of her answers deemed unsatisfactory to his idiotic, demeaning questions. If he liked her remarks, by contrast, he would flick the tip of the outrageous leather instrument over the tips of her nipples in what was supposed to be a manner of praise.

'Among those differences will be your immunity from sexual penetration. Do you know what that is, my shy island sprite?'

Tesra thought of Montrego, having his way with naked, branded Vorra, her well-used body beneath him at the mercy of his hard cock, while she herself watched, fingers stuffed inside herself like a shameless slut. 'I have eyes,' she retorted. 'I've seen enough on this ship of yours.'

Marcellus slashed the side of her left breast. What a slow learner she was.

'Forgive me,' she hastened to correct herself, the pain shooting cruelly up and down her torso. 'I meant to say, respectfully, that I have observed the act of sexual penetration... sir.'

This was another new thing this morning; she now had to address him by a title rather than by his name. He, on the other hand, remained free to call her Tesra, Tes, girl, woman, nymph, slut or whatever else struck his fancy. She supposed she counted herself fortunate he did not refer to her as bitch, dog or cunt, as the other girls often were.

Just this morning, prior to being taken out for her humiliating ice water bath in the ocean, she'd witnessed the somber Bothar leash the slave Kasandra, forcing her to heal as he led her up the stairs, the girl's body flush and eager from having been called his 'good little pet'.

No doubt she'd been richly penetrated, in every orifice, to her master's content. Kasandra was said by Vorra to be a simpleminded slut, a natural slave who was only capable of finding her joy in strict, humiliating bondage. Vorra seemed to Tesra to be a similar sort of slave, though she dared not point this out, as she was already sore in her mouth from licking her and the others all night and had no wish to bring any further punishment on herself.

'You've observed it, have you?' He had that condescending look on his face, the one she so despised. 'Such a dispassionate expression. Did you feel nothing?'

Tesra hesitated. Another of the new rules was against lying. If he caught her out, the consequences would be severe. 'I did feel something,' she admitted, 'though it was complicated. I didn't understand it all, sir.'

He nodded approvingly, moving behind her to unchain her wrists. 'Well said. I shall help you work through it. Place your fingers between your legs and we shall talk of this further.'

The blood drained from her face. 'Sir?'

'Put your fingers inside your cunt,' he elaborated matter-of-factly. 'Bring yourself to arousal so we may get to the bottom of how you feel about sex.'

The nymph weighed out the pain of another whipping. The man did not know what he was asking, requiring her to bare something to him which was so deeply personal, so delicate and fragile that she had yet to fully grasp its full meaning and implications.

The seconds ticked, counting against her.

'Tesra, Tesra,' he sighed, sounding like a disappointed teacher. 'Whatever am I to do with you? I could threaten to throw you to the sharks, but I wager you're smart enough to realize I'm saving you for something special. I can, however, make you suffer in ways that might make death seem preferable.'

Tesra touched herself, and the sudden sensation made her jolt.

'Such a hot little thing,' he chuckled.

She looked down at his feet, unable to bear the sight of his tattooed chest and those red silk pantaloons, beneath which lay that snake-like rod of flesh she could not keep her mind off.

'Do you enjoy exciting men, Tesra?'

A question. By the goddess, he'd asked a direct question.

'I... I do not know, sir. I have known of them such a short time.'

He lifted her chin with the tip of the whip, the device to which she was subject, for beating or pleasuring. 'Come, come, my little sea-born wench, you're more intelligent than that. When you see a man, such as myself, how does it make you feel?'

'I want to run away, sir.'

'That's not all. Out with it, girl.' He ran the whip over her cheek towards her mouth, inducing her to open her lips. He could this and whatever else he wanted because Tesra was his captive, a prisoner of his ship as well as a temporary occupant, if not an outright resident of his slave hold.

'And I want to hide, as well,' she managed.

He smacked her hip, delivering an instructive sting. 'You try my patience, Tesra. Must I order you to your back so I can determine the matter for myself?'

Yes, called her secret self, a voice reckless and insane within her. Do that. Put me to my back; order me to lie for you, spreading my own virgin cunt lips with my fingers for your inspection. Then you will know my heat. My moistness as I crave your whip. Your cock.

'No sir,' said quickly. 'I will tell you. When I saw Montrego... when I saw him...' the word stuck in her throat. 'When I saw him inside Vorra, I got... wet.'

'Wet? Explain yourself.'

She flushed crimson. 'I... I am not sure, sir. It is like a juice that comes to me, and a powerful itching. I become slick and...'

'Yes?' He raised her suddenly lowered chin. 'The word you seek is ready. The liquid is a natural emission of the female as she prepares to submit to the male. It is how she readies herself to be used.'

Tesra shuddered.

'Tell me what you saw on deck that made you wet.'

'H-he was inside her.'

'Montrego was inside her how?' he prompted. 'Explain yourself.'

She relayed the scene, the degrading act of penetration and afterwards how the girl had taken his still hard organ in her mouth, fresh from her rectum and vagina, sucking it dry of the seminal fluid meant for impregnation.

'You saw the girl used, and you moistened,' he summed up the matter. 'As if readying yourself for the same treatment.'

'A girl, a female, cannot want that,' Tesra blurted, not caring if he struck her again for speaking out of turn.

The pirate held out his hand to be kissed. He might as easily have struck her with it, and they both knew it. 'You may beg for mercy.'

Tesra wanted to be strong, to take her punishment even though he might once again knock her to the deck, bringing blood to her mouth. She knew he would resist in her place, that if anyone were to capture him he would accept any torture, even death itself rather than disgrace himself in the presence of his enemies. But Marcellus was a man, different from herself. He did not seem to care what her opinion was of him, nor did he appear to burn for her touch as she did for his. Above all, she could not imagine him wanting or needing to please her the way she wanted to please him.

Tesra's heart slammed in her chest; something told her she was crossing a line, committing an act which would mark her, signaling once and for all her vulnerability, her dependence. And yet she could not resist placating him in this way. 'Forgive me,' she pressed her lips shyly, tentatively to his knuckles.

'More fervently,' he commanded.

Tesra's cunt burned under her fingertips, which she had not yet been allowed to remove from herself. 'Forgive me, sir,' she repeated, her voice a hot whisper.

'That is not how a captive kisses. You must make small nibbles; use your tongue, remind me that you are too small and insignificant a creature to warrant the anger of a pirate king. Suggest to me what other things, as a man, I would rather be doing with your recalcitrant body.'

'But you said there was to be no sex between us.' Tesra winced, realizing at once the enormity of her mistake. 'Sir, forgive me,' she sought to give his fingertips the suckling of their life, 'I should not have spoken.'

He withheld the hand she was so desperate to appease. 'You sound disappointed, my dear. Were you counting on being fucked today?'

'No! I mean... I... I don't know, sir.' He had her in a daze, confused, aroused, and uncertain what, if anything, she wanted from him.

'You've stopped masturbating, captive. Why do you insist on compounding your crimes?'

'I don't mean to, sir.' Tesra had tears in her eyes.

Marcellus was unmoved. 'Right hand in your cunt, left on your breast. Massage it heavily, manipulate the nipple.'

She was having a hard time staying upright. There was so much moisture now, starting to trickle down the insides of her thighs. If this were to go on much longer she was going to have another one of those explosions called orgasms.

'What did Vorra and the others do to you last night, captive?'

'They - they touched me. All over. They made me touch them with my tongue, between their legs.'

'Did you enjoy licking pussy?'

'No, sir. I mean, yes sir. Oh, sir,' she gasped, 'I don't know.'

'Are you lying to me, Tesra?'

The girl shuddered, on her knees before her captor. 'Sir... I'm going to...'

Marcellus found her back. 'You were asked a question, girl.' The whip slash sent her spasming.

'Yes... yes sir,' she toppled at his feet, writhing on the wooden deck. 'I lied... I did enjoy it, all of it. Servicing them, obeying their orders, crawling for them in the filthy hay just like they were my owners.'

Marcellus waited for the climax to subside. 'That is the last time,' he informed her, stepping heavily on the corona of her hair as he stood over her, 'that you will orgasm without permission. Is that clear?'

Tesra looked up at him in awe, the god he was rapidly becoming to her. 'Yes, sir.'

'You will crawl into my bed,' he told her. 'Facedown, ankles and wrists spread to their maximum. 'It's time I test the value of my prize.'

'Yes,' she repeated, the phrase seemingly tireless on her lips, 'sir.'

Vorra would have preferred any fate to this. Being called to the chambers of Rodrigo so early in the day, when the man was still sober, could only mean one thing. He intended to dispose of her, for whatever reasons suited him. The captain's second-in-command needed none, of course. Behind Marcellus his word was law. Having to answer to the handsome, able pirate king had made Rodrigo furious with jealousy, though, and the helpless slave girls were ever his target. The fact that the spoiled little bitch Drusia did not have to lick and kiss the arse of this man and to a lesser extent the slave keeper Montrego, was due to her special position as the captain's unofficial lapdog.

Vorra saw the knife thrust into the tabletop and fell at once to her belly. Slithering across the wooden deck, she covered the man's heavy black boots with soft stabs of her tongue. 'May this slave please you, master?' she pleaded throatily, seeking to dissuade him from whatever darker violence he had in mind. 'Let Vorra fetch your favorite bullwhip for you. Or will you allow her to beg for the privilege of master's cock in one of her unworthy holes?'

'Get up, bitch,' the man snarled. 'Or you'll be sporting with the sharks soon enough.'

Vorra rose gracefully to her feet, where she knew she stood half a chance of saving her life. 'Your slave is hot for you, master,' she purred, boldly guiding his hand between her legs to her sopping hole. It had always been this way for her - juicing at the first sign of strength in a man, displaying her readiness to obey and to please.

Rodrigo, hardly one to be distracted from his purpose by a pretty cunt, one among dozens, hundreds in the armada as a whole, seized the womb of the tall and once stately beauty. 'Your chatter is giving me a headache,' he snarled, forcing her onto tiptoes. 'You talk too much, Vorra. All you sluts do. Bothar has the right idea - the lot of you should be kept on hands and knees, barking for your supper.'

Vorra thought of Kasandra, whom Bothar had taken a shine to. As a result of the man's affections she was now deprived, in the men's presence at least, of every dignity as a human being. She peed on all fours, ate on all fours and took her fuckings and beatings on all fours as well. And yet to see her look into the eyes of the hard-faced, red-bearded master was to see nothing but utter love and devotion. This was a level of degradation Vorra would never slip to herself, namely falling in love with any of her masters. If she were to sink to that level she would have no hope, no rights ever again.

'I am an animal,' she acknowledged, espousing the beliefs of the second-in-command. 'I deserve only to be treated as one.'

'That is correct,' he rotated his hand, turning her to jelly. 'You are a domestic beast. Feel your arse, tell me what is there.'

She slid her fingers over the scars from the many whippings, knowing it was not these he wanted her to speak of, but rather the mark. 'I have a brand, master.'

'Do they brand human beings, Vorra?'

'No, master, only animals.'

'Domestic animals, that's right. Rodrigo's fingers were clenched tightly on Vorra's left nipple, plunging her into immediate, though silent agony. If there was one thing she knew from experience, it was that the cruel pirate lieutenant did not like to be interrupted while he was torturing a helpless slave girl. If he wanted screams, he would most certainly ask for them.

'Would you like me to stop, Vorra?'

'Whatever master wishes,' she gasped, her chest heaving.

'But if I gave you the choice,' he pressured. 'What would you pick?'

'For master to be strong,' she looked up into his eyes. 'To keep me in my place.'

'What is your place, Vorra?'

The slave's eyes glazed over. It was Rodrigo controlling her body now, dictating her responses as she moved against his hand, pushing herself closer to be loved, to be hurt. 'On master's leash,' she hissed. 'At master's feet. Crawling. Begging.'

'As a human being?'

'As an animal, master. As a bitch.'

'Get down, then, on all fours, bitch. And I will tell you why I had you brought here today.' Rodrigo released her, pushing her back.

Vorra assumed the position for her master, having no idea whether he would fuck her or whip her or both.

'We have a common enemy,' said he to the girl, choosing her cunt for his satisfaction.

'Yes, master,' she breathed as he filled her, giving her life and purpose.

'The captain,' he thrust himself into her vanquished canal. 'He denies us both; I my place as king and you your place as first among the slaves.'

'He favors Drusia, master.'

'The captain is not strong,' Rodrigo declared, clamping Vorra's hips so as to take her with the utmost brutality. 'He allows the slave bitch Drusia to wrap him round her finger. And now there is the new one. The gods alone know where he got her from or why he treats her like a piece of Talassian crystal. His only explanation is a story only an idiot would believe.'

'You are not an idiot, master,' she moaned. 'And you are strong. Very strong.'

'I should be king,' he decided, withdrawing himself to smack her arse with his cupped hand.

Vorra stretched to meet the blow. 'Yes, master. You alone are worthy. You are my king and my lord.'

'And you are a worthless liar,' he slammed his palm against her, the calloused skin impacting her with the ferocity of wood or leather. 'You speak what is required to save yourself.'

'Yes, master.' The girl did not point out his illogic, that if she were capable of deception, then she must surely be a creature of much greater sophistication than a brute beast. The fact was, it was Rodrigo who was the beast and she did not imagine for a moment that he was not capable of following through his threat to throw her to the sharks if she displeased him.

She'd seen it done before, most recently to a pretty little Iletian girl, barely

38

eighteen, taken as booty from an ill-fated betrothal galleon transporting her to her fiancé on an island further down the archipelago. The girl had been slow in obeying him, refusing to lick his bulbous cock in front of her captured crew. She must have been some sort of royalty, given her fine silks and seashell-studded tiara of bronze. Rodrigo had sheared the nuptial gown from her body with his bare hands and repeated the command.

Still she resisted. 'Mercy,' she begged, employing the Iletian words. 'I no understand.'

Rodrigo had not hesitated to lift her bodily, carrying her to the stern of the ship, tossing her like a sack of grain. It was a joke among the crew that whenever the man was at the helm the sharks followed closely, in anticipation of a good meal. The captain had been below at the time with Drusia. Perhaps there was something in what Rodrigo was saying; Marcellus was getting soft. And certainly Drusia was a spoiled cunt; there was no argument there either.

Vorra thought once more of the Iletian, a mere slip of a girl, naked and squirming, her incredibly long hair, silky black hanging down to the deck as Rodrigo carted her. And a moment later how she'd looked, her jade-green eyes wide with horror, terror on her shapely lips as he did the unthinkable.

'Please,' she had screamed from the water, her knowledge of the pirate's language showing a sudden and marked improvement. 'Masters, do not leave Mayleesha! Mayleesha will suck you! Mayleesha suck every man-cock! Mayleesha promise good fuck!'

The screaming could still be heard as the ship sailed away, a shark unto itself, the greatest predator in the deep.

'Come on my hand,' commanded Rodrigo, seizing her sex.

Vorra released herself instantly. Unlike a free woman, a slave did not choose the time and place of her orgasms. Nor was she afforded the luxury of gentle seduction, or even the dignity of being satisfied by a man's natural endowment as opposed to some object of his choosing. At first, when Vorra had been sold to a traveling carnival and minstrel show, it had been difficult to climax on command, like a trained seal. Gregov, the brilliant, mercurial and oft times vicious walker of high wires had taught her that art all too well.

A slave must surrender her will totally, turning it over, along with her body. Thus does she watch herself and get turned on by behaving as a shameless slut. To receive a command to come was a very sexy thing, in other words, something that in itself aroused a woman. Gregov had taken her body to soaring heights using this principle.

And he also lowered her to unimaginable depths, forcing her to beg for pain, to lick and kiss the edge of his knife, to rub her belly against the blade till she came and came and came.

Never once did he injure her, save for her pride. She became his beast in every sense of the word and had she the choice she would be unable to surrender her sleeping place in the small steel cage by his bedside for the dowry of a princess.

Vorra continued to shudder and shake, her juices pouring over Rodrigo's hand. The orgasm was for his pleasure not for hers. He did not have to tell her to look him in the eye. This was his way, total domination and overpowering will. If she felt pleasure, it was against her will, a suffering, even, that only marked her more fully as his property.

'On your knees, cunt.' He rose to his feet.

Vorra knelt up, knowing she must spread her legs as widely as her muscles would allow.

'Here is what you are going to do,' said the next in line for the throne of the pirates, the loose confederation of a dozen mighty ships, as he thrust his hand into her mouth to be cleaned. Vorra proceeded to suck him clean of her juices, her eyes set longingly on the erection he had not yet seen fit to spill inside her. 'I require information, my little pet. Concerning the yellow-haired slut. You will use every means at your disposal to learn who she really is and where she comes from. And you must do so in a way that will not reflect back on me, here or on my own ship. Is that clear?'

She nodded as best she could, the man's fingers gaping her jaws. Among the pirates Rodrigo's position was unique. As a captain he had his own vessel, but he also kept quarters here, on the flagship.

Satisfied, he withdrew his glistening hand, drying it on the top of her head. 'I am counting on you, slut,' said he, his manner and tone shifting to that deceptive softness the branded girl liked sometimes to pretend in her own mind was genuine affection for her. 'Do not disappoint me.'

He played the blade of the hunting knife over her cheeks. It was an instrument she knew well. Without being told she opened her mouth, sliding her tongue along the flat of it. It was a game Rodrigo was fond of. The first few times Vorra had pissed herself in fear, but she had re-learned to enjoy it, feeling as with Gregov that sense of total helplessness and sexual charge as the man made love to her with the killing metal.

'Fail me, Vorra,' he ran the point down her throat and between her quivering breasts, 'And I will devise a punishment that will leave you begging to be had by the sharks.'

Vorra arched her back, offering up her throbbing nipples. She was ready for him all over again. 'Yes, master.'

He touched them one by one, eliciting the most delicious female moans. Truly Vorra was fortunate to have a man this strong. If only he would take her for himself and make her his exclusive property. Willingly would she absorb his wrath, becoming his perfect victim in everything.

'The captain will not touch you again,' Rodrigo decided.

Her heart leaped at the sudden possibility. Did he want her after all? Was she one of the things he was jealous over? 'Master?'

He paused to drag the knife blade down her tummy, indicating how easily, by a mere twist of the wrist, he could slice her open. 'If he does, I will have you killed.'

'Yes, master.' Vorra's heart sank. It was hard to grasp the true meaning of these words. Was it a statement to her desirability, an admission to feelings on his part, or was it all part of his game with Marcellus? A men's game, where women were booty, pretty baubles to be fought for and awarded as prizes.

Rodrigo pushed her down to the deck of his cabin. There were no more words, only the fire in his eyes as he parted her thighs and fell on top of her, one animal upon another, smaller, defenseless one, and Vorra exploded with him, forgetting to obtain permission.

But Rodrigo was lenient with her, having exhausted himself in the furious rutting. It was a rare moment, almost tender as she lay beneath him, her soft body a humble pillow for his masculine form. As his penis finally softened and slipped from her, Vorra whimpered, wondering for the first time if she might be in love with the man.

A moment later he was asleep, one hand clutching and misshaping her breast, the other entwined in her hair. 'Sleep well, master,' she whispered, his head on her chest, ensuring her captivity beneath him for as long as he slumbered. 'Sweet dreams.'

Marcellus beheld the nude, golden-haired beauty spread-eagle on his bed. She was the very picture of male fantasy; her upturned bottom unbranded, unscarred, helpless to every predation; her back, virgin to the cat or long whip; her pussy, untouched by any mortal. The bonds that held her, silken cords from the boudoirs of the Talassian imperial court, only heightened the arousal factor. A lesser man would have taken his fill by now, claiming her maidenhood as his own. Marcellus, however, had a greater purpose. Or perhaps it was a lower one, more ignoble even than the potential ravishing of a captive nymph.

'You must concentrate harder,' said the pirate king, grazing his fingers incidentally over her swollen and exposed nether lips.

The light contact, following upon so much more of the same, an hour's worth of teasing to be precise, threw the facedown Tesra into yet another set of spasms.

'Oh please, sir,' she thrashed, 'do not touch me anymore.'

'Very well,' he offered graciously, 'I shall stop.'

A moment later she was writhing worse than ever, squirming her sweat-soaked body into the already wet sheets. 'Please, sir, touch me again...'

'I will not, Tesra, until you tell me why I have taken you prisoner.'

The tousled blonde curls tossed side to side. 'Sir, I do not know. Truly.'

He trailed a finger down her curved, sweat-glistening spine, enjoying the natural wonder of that dip between the girl's back and buttocks. Would there come a time, he wondered, when he would have the luxury of branding one of those cheeks, burning into her skin forever his ownership of her body and soul?

It was not a thought he could afford, though. He had a purpose for the girl and it was not to relieve his sexual pressures. Hold me fast, Nephisis, he prayed silently to the mighty lord of the sea. Grant me skill and wisdom to open this most trying of oysters, even as I resist its most distracting charms.

'Let us review, then,' he massaged her bottom, unable to resist the urge to mentally stake out the best place for branding. 'We have established in our conversation so far that I do not want ransom, isn't that right?'

'Yes, sir,' she attempted for the millionth time to free herself.

'And why is that?'

Tesra hesitated to repeat the insult he'd already fed her.

'I'm waiting,' he inserted a finger into her sex, deep enough to get her attention.

'Because I do not have enough value,' she gasped, 'to offset the trouble of a return trip to my island.'

'Good.' He impaled her more deeply. 'And what gives a woman her value?'

'The way she pleases a man; how much he wants to... to sport with her.'

'The word is "fuck", my dear. Really, your teachers did you a tremendous disservice in your education to have overlooked entirely relations between the sexes.'

Tesra clenched her fists. She seemed tired of being helpless, and yet this was scarcely the beginning. 'My teachers are the wisest seers in all the world,' she protested. 'By the hand of Persistrata, the sisters are given to know the mysteries of the heavens, to unlock the secrets of...' The anally impaled girl froze. 'That's it, isn't it? You've taken me in order to learn the secrets of the heavens. The ways of the sisterhood.'

Marcellus removed the finger and moved to the head of the bed. 'Don't be absurd,' he scoffed, turning her head and forcing her to lick it clean. 'The prattlings of a bunch of frigid women are of no use whatsoever to me. There is, however, something else you can do, my little yellow hair, something that does interest me enormously.'

Tesra sputtered under the humiliation of having to remove her own odor from his finger. 'Please, stop it... I already told you, I don't know what you're talking about.'

'Think about it,' he coaxed, drying himself on the back of her hair. 'A girl who can see into the navel of creation? Who can look up the skirts of the Mother of Life? Surely one so talented as you can help me locate a few fat treasure ships... preferably informing me of their courses a week or so before they set sail?'

Tesra had stilled herself. Turning her head as far as she could, she looked up into his eyes. The expression made him laugh.

'I need a break.' He slapped her arse good-naturedly. 'You won't mind hanging tight for a bit while I relieve myself?'

Marcellus strode to the door and called for Drusia. Yes, he was a genius. It was true. His plan was succeeding. And forcing the comely wench to watch him with the slave would be just the thing he needed to further break her spirit. A few more days of this and he'd have her in the palm of his hand.

And then the sky would be the limit. The riches of all the sea would be his for the taking.

Tesra was unable to walk. Mercifully, Marcellus allowed her to be carried back to the slave hold in the arms of one of his men, a tall olive-skinned man whose tongue had been cut out in a Talassian prison. The man had evidently suffered much as evidenced by the stoical expression and the green, glassy stare of his eyes. For some reason she felt safe in his arms - anonymous, somehow. Tucking her head in to his substantial chest she listened for his heartbeat, shutting out the sounds of the ship.

The pirate crew had come to life this night. Torches burned in the cold blackness of the open sky, pipes and high-pitched instruments were sounding and men's voices were lifting up to the very heavens. The pirates were singing songs, drinking rum and celebrating. One man, his speech much slurred, was belting out a tune about a girl named Amelia who grew addicted to the pleasures of a pirate's peg leg between her legs. She heard the cries of females, as well, which meant the slave girls were on deck for wench sport.

Drusia, of course, would be exempt, having been allowed to lie with Marcellus after her departure. In the last few hours she had copulated wildly with the man in every known position. Tesra had been made to witness it all from a position against the bulkhead, her arms shackled above her head. She'd determined not to show her own need or her jealousy, but it was so difficult. Why did Marcellus not touch her or penetrate her?

Tesra tried not to care. She did not want the pirate's touch. She did not want his cock, did not want to writhe and squirm, to excite and arouse and satisfy him like the little slut Drusia. No, Tesra wanted something noble, something just. She wanted escape. A chance to jump over the rail and swim for the nearest coastline, though the attempt might cost her life. Maybe the silent giant would help her. Perhaps he would want to keep her for himself, even. Should she ask, begging him to take her as his own captive? He might even be merciful and take her home, to her island, to her waiting sisters.

'Please, kind sir,' she murmured, as he was stepping over the body of a reclining dark-skinned girl, her body chained to the deck for the abuse of one and all. 'You can see I am held under duress, won't you help me?'

Just then an auburn-haired girl ran by, half screaming and half laughing, a drunken pirate hot on her tail, trying his best to spill rum on her welted body. Nearby another girl was on her knees, licking the glistening cunt of a sister slave, whose body had already been drenched in the powerful liquor. Behind the standing slave, a blonde like herself, was a one-eyed pirate, thrusting himself in and out of what must have been her nether hole. The look on her face was one of sheer bliss, though Tesra couldn't imagine the position was all that comfortable.

Meanwhile another man, a peg-legged fellow with a straggly black beard, stood over the kneeling girl, encouraging her with the whip to be both passionate and diligent in licking the blonde slave, who appeared now to be in the throes of a powerful orgasm.

Still another slave was suspended in a small cage, in which she could only squat. There was a chain attached to the top holding her at precisely the right level to accept the long stiff prick of Montrego, who was busy taunting her.

'You can suck better than that, Arabella,' he chided the slender auburn-haired girl, shivering and wet, 'or do you need another dunking?'

Arabella's mouth was stretched wide as she sought desperately to please her cruel master. Why were the men acting like this? Why did they insist on treating their females this way, simply because they were larger and stronger? This was not the will of the gods and goddesses; surely the First People, from the Time of the Beginning could not have behaved this way.

'If you help me,' she informed the mute, 'you will be rewarded. There is much gold on my island. And silver and diamonds, as well.' Tesra was surprised at how easy she was finding it to lie. Back home it would be impossible, not only because of the limits of her conscience but also on account of the powers of her teachers, who were able to see through dissimulations great and small. With men it was easy, even necessary to prevaricate. Her survival was at stake now, and she did intend to live, even to thrive until the time of her eventual, inevitable escape. The captain only thought he was conquering her, and he had a big surprise in store. They all did, any of them who thought they would beat her. She would endure all they forced on her; triumphing and turning it round as a power against them.

The mute laid her at his feet just long enough to open the slave hatch.

'Please,' begged Tesra, who only a moment ago had pledged to stay strong, 'do not put me back in that horrible slave hold. It is so terrible down there, and it frightens me so. Will you not have pity?'

Tesra, mortified, found herself kneeling before him, grabbing at his pantaloons, weak and servile as any slave. Fortunately for her he grabbed her before she could abase herself anymore. What more would she have done if he'd let her? Would she have offered her mouth for his use in exchange for her freedom, or maybe even her virgin sex?

At least I shall be alone down here, thought Tesra, seeking what consolations she could find in being locked once more in the filthy hold. Her joy was short-lived, however, as she heard a familiar voice, whispering behind her, like ice. 'Vorra,' she exhaled, not needing to see the woman to know her presence. 'I had thought everyone was...'

'Upstairs to be ravished?' she completed the thought. 'No,' she turned Tesra round gently but firmly. 'I'm afraid I'm being punished tonight. No hard man-cock for naughty Vorra tonight. It seems you, too, have been made to suffer. It's that little bitch Drusia, isn't it? She told the captain lies about me. Has she done the same to you?'

Tesra blinked back the tears. The cruel, raven-haired woman was the last one in the world she should be confiding in, but she was desperate and something in her tone seemed softer now, more sympathetic. Could it be they would be allies now that Vorra had been betrayed just as she was?

'She's with him now,' said the seer, so far from her island, locked in the belly of a gently swaying whale, cutting through the currents of seas hundreds of leagues from the Isle of Dreams. 'He let her sleep on his bed... he... he did things with her all day and I had to watch.'

Vorra took the girl in her arms. 'It's okay,' she soothed the suddenly sobbing girl. 'Tell Vorra all about it.'

'I was chained up,' Tesra explained, once Vorra had taken them to a place of relative comfort, a bale of clean hay against which they could sit, resting their backs under a slow-glowing lantern. 'Marcellus aroused me and then he abandoned me for her. My hands were overhead, my wrists crossed. I was nude, as I am now, totally helpless, and every chance Drusia got she would look over at me, blowing me kisses, letting me know that she was enjoying my suffering, and also how much Marcellus was enjoying her.'

'Drusia is a backstabbing bitch.' Vorra let the girl rest her head on her shoulders. 'She crawls to the captain to curry favor when behind his back she despises him. How I hate her! How I hate Marcellus, too. If Rodrigo were captain, if he held the kingship of pirates, it would not be like this.'

'Rodrigo is different?' she sniffled.

'Rodrigo is a real man,' Vorra stroked her blonde head. 'He knows what a woman needs and he gives it to her.'

'He is kind, then?'

Vorra laughed. 'You think a female needs a man who is weak like that, able to be twisted round her little finger? No, Rodrigo is strong. He teaches us that we are slaves and he is our master. He shows no mercy, no favoritism. We all crawl equally to him, we all lie as one beneath his sword.'

'You make it sound like something pleasant,' she complained.

'Is it not so where you come from, Tesra? Are the men on your Isle of Dreams so different?'

'There are no men at all,' Tesra explained. 'Only females.'

'But how do your people survive?' she asked, astonished. 'How are your females implanted with seed so as to grow new life?'

'We need no seed,' Tesra shook her head, grateful finally to meet one who seemed genuinely interested in life on her island. 'The goddess produces the new babies, all girls, of course, from out of the fire of Surasa, the Great White Volcano at the center of the island.'

Vorra laughed. 'You get babies from a volcano? That is the silliest thing I have ever heard. Babies come from here,' she said, placing her hand over Tesra's tummy. 'And when a man wishes to plant his seed the female bears young.'

Tesra flushed to have her sacred story so thoroughly ridiculed by an uneducated off-islander - a barbarian. 'Is it any more absurd then how things are done in your world?' she asked petulantly. 'With one half of the race holding the other in bondage, at war with itself?'

Vorra shook her head. 'Not all females are slaves. Many are free.'

'But your mother was not, nor are you.'

'That is true. To find truly free women you must go to the larger cities, to the places of wealth, such as Talassia.'

'Women there have power?'

'Not as men do, no. We are smaller, Tesra, we are not made equal. Surely this is obvious to you. A queen or princess may put on airs, but I promise you even she, in the privacy of the bedchamber, is subject to one male or other. Has she not legs to be spread like any other woman? A womb to be filled at his discretion? A back and arse to receive his discipline? No woman can be truly happy without these things, I promise you.'

Tesra fought the warmth generated by the light touch of Vorra to her neck as she spoke. 'We are happy,' Tesra said. 'On the Isle of Dreams we live in perfect harmony and bliss.'

'Do you?' Vorra whispered, inducing the girl to lay her head back on the hay. 'What is it like? Won't you tell me?'

Tesra went to her back, letting her hands fall to her side, palms up. It was wrong for her to be feeling even a tiny bit comfortable in the slave hold like this, and yet she was having difficulty resisting the growing sense of relaxation, even contentment. She did not belong in this place, subjugated and humiliated beyond belief. She was the fruit of the goddess, a talented seer, born to sing the praises of creation. A chill passed down her spine as she thought of the captain's words. He intended to use her powers to find treasure. What on earth could he mean? The words made no sense.

'The Isle of Dreams is a place of such wonder,' she began, sighing in anticipation of the very saying of the words, 'that even the goddess regards it as her favorite spot. Oh, Vorra, if only you could see it. The sky is blue as chalk, the mountains are white as the purest wool on top and green and luxuriant below. There are plants and flowers of every variety and great rocks of the most marvelous colors. Reds and blues and purples. The beach itself is made of these colors, for the sand comes from the rocks. The water is a dozen shades of blue and waves roll in night and day with such fervor that it is like the kiss of a grandmother to her granddaughter.'

'Like this?' Vorra kissed her, drawing the girl's lips up toward her own. It was a long, probing kiss, but not harsh and overpowering as the men gave.

'Not... exactly,' she replied, breathless.

'Go on, then,' Vorra encouraged. 'Teach me.'

'We are sisters on the island. There is no... physical love.'

Vorra kissed her navel, sending flutters through her belly. 'What on earth do you do, then?'

'We look upwards, and outwards. Oh, Vorra, you shouldn't do that.'

'Why not? Doesn't it feel good?'

'Yes, of course.'

Vorra touched the wet place between her legs. 'Are you related to a goddess?'

'We are, all of us.' Tesra began to writhe. 'The goddess formed us to share in her knowledge. To see with her eyes. To know all things. But it is a good power. Meant to be used in good ways. Not like the captain wants.'

'And what does Marcellus want?'

Tesra drew a ragged breath as the girl found her clit. 'He thinks he can find treasure through my visions. Gold, diamonds, I suppose. The whereabouts of ships, places he can steal from. I understand so little.'

'How strange. And could Marcellus really get this information from you?'

'I... I do not know,' the little blonde moaned. 'The world of men is new to me. I know not what I am capable of here.'

'You will do what men tell you. As do I and all the others.'

Tesra lifted herself against Vorra's hand, trying to increase the friction. 'I am not a slave,' she reminded her.

'All women are slaves,' said Vorra. 'Some are simply more honest about the matter. Do you think I hate the young man who stole my virginity and deprived me of my legacy? Do you think I would see him dead for tricking me into taking the brand, for allowing him to use me like a she-slut in the alley and sell me like an animal to be hauled off in chains to a traveling show? On the contrary, Tesra, I

46

owe him my life and were he here now I would beg for the honor of offering him what I could not then, namely my full and most passionate service based on what I have learned about my own slavery.

'I deserved to be stripped that day in the barn. By all rights he should have whipped me as well, for the crime of pretending to be something I was not, for the crime of acting like a free woman when all along I was nothing but a slave bitch, a piece of arse in need of a mark and a good beating.'

'I can't believe that,' said Tesra, the desperation and need thick in her voice. 'I refuse to, do you hear me?'

Vorra finished her off, subjecting her to a twisting, agonizing climax.

'We shall see,' she smiled down at the girl, exhausted in the hay. 'We shall see.'

He came for Vorra a short while later. None other than Rodrigo himself. Vorra crawled to him swiftly, allowing him to take her black hair in his fist. Half leading, half dragging her, he took her up the stairs, leaving Tesra alone.

In the dark she shuddered, feeling more alone and naked than she had ever been in her life. When the fur-covered creature brushed her leg she leaped to the top of the hay and began to scream. No one heard her and after a while she had no choice but to lie down, curled up on the bale. Above her, dimly she could hear the strains of the pirate's orgy. For a split second she was jealous of the slave girls, in the open air, drawing so much male interest.

What would it take to compete with the others? To make the pirates want her body enough to bring her up-top, to be put in the cage or chained on her back, to be whipped or fucked?

'Forgive me, Persistrata,' she whispered, unable to keep her hand from her already drenched pussy. 'I am too far from you now and too weak.'

Chapter 5

The girl was nearly ready. Over the past three days Marcellus had been stripping away her defenses, laying the groundwork for his attack, which would be both devastating and unexpected as lightning from a clear blue sky. Despite her seemingly miraculous origins, Tesra, the nymph of many names, had proven no different from any other female he'd ever dealt with. She was petty, jealous, laughably easy to read and born to lie at his feet.

In truth, he could have dispatched her of her pride and haughtiness on their very first encounter. Pretty, golden-haired Tesra could as easily have come aboard his ship a fucked wench as she had a whipped one. But that could have resulted in trauma, destroying the delicacies of her divinely inspired mind. She had powers, yes, and he had not fully gauged their depths, but she was also painfully human.

Though he had not shared the details with Rodrigo or the others, he did know a thing or two about the Isle of Dreams and its lovely inhabitants. The medallion was not all his grandfather had left him, nor was the ring. For behind the ruby lay a secret, one that would render Tesra his captive in a way she could not now dream.

He almost pitied the creature when she learned the truth, that so much of her pride and self-perceived divinity had been based upon a lie. A lie which he would expose this very day, in preparation for his assault upon the fortress of her mind.

At present the girl was enjoying her latest respite from his grueling training sessions. He observed her, at the prow, her long hair blowing in the wind. He hadn't a clue what went on behind those eyes - though soon he would. She looked delicious dressed as she was, wearing one of his shirts, belted about her waist like a short skirt. He knew well the curves of her body underneath, both by eye and by touch. She had orgasmed for him many times and she knew his sex as well, having enjoyed the privilege of viewing his sport with Drusia and also with Vorra. The latter had become somewhat sullen, and he'd noted she was being called more frequently into the company of Rodrigo.

As for his second-in-command, he seemed on the surface right enough, though Marcellus had in his gut a gnawing doubt. Rodrigo was anything if stoic and for the man to be so pleasant and quiet as he was now, keeping such a low profile, could only mean he was seeking allies among the others for a possible mutiny. Marcellus had just now sent Drusia and Vorra, respectively, to the most questionable captains, bearing bottles of his finest rum as a peace offering. Still, there was the very real possibility of trouble ahead.

All the more reason to press the future-seeing wench as soon as possible.

'The sea is calm today,' he observed, taking up a place directly behind her.

'Yes, sir,' said the girl, offering no resistance as he ran his hand against her hip.

'You seem a bit thinner.'

'Yes, sir.'

He made a mental note to put something a bit more fattening in her diet. For discipline's sake, and to keep her from losing her figure, he had kept her on a tight regimen, but even so he had allowed her some privileges. For the past two nights she had been allowed to sleep on the deck beside his bed, her neck chained to the foot of it.

'You are moist,' he observed, his fingers accessing her female lips.

'Yes,' said Tesra, a bit more huskily, leaning back ever so slightly against him. 'Sir.'

'Do you desire penetration?'

'As sir wishes.'

The question had been the same, four, five, ten times a day as he worked to increase her sexual responsiveness to almost unendurable levels. He was pleased to see how much more quickly she was responding to him with each encounter. Just now it had taken only the lightest of touches for her to open for him.

For a moment he listened to her heartbeat, confirming something he had suspected from her body language at the rail, the way she had seemed to him as she gazed out over the waters. 'You are troubled by something.'

Tesra said nothing.

Marcellus employed the universal leverage of master over slave, working her clitoris with his smallest finger, putting her heavy in need, though denying fulfillment. 'Tell me.'

'Please, sir, it is personal.'

The captain made her hurt in her need. 'Whose are you, captive?'

'Yours,' she slumped, her back against his chest, 'sir.'

He cupped her breast beneath the shirt with his other hand. 'Indeed. And whose breast is this?'

'Yours,' she conceded breathily, 'sir.'

'And this cunt?'

'Also... yours.'

'And your thoughts?' he continued the logic, devastating and brutal.

'My thoughts, too, sir,' she nodded, wanting to come on his hand. 'They are yours.'

He held her at bay. 'Tell me, then.'

'I dreamed last night I was back home on my island,' she replied, her words thickening to a gentle pant. 'I was a young girl again, on my way to see Velacera-be-na, the First Mother, she who helped me into Initiation, kissing my breast upon the sacred wounding.'

'I am not familiar with this ritual,' said the captain, determined to appropriate all that was in her mind for his possible later use.

'At the age of thirteen, sir, a sister is bled from the nipple, with the point of a gold claw on the finger of the First Mother. She drinks the blood which drips and then, into our mouths, in turn, is poured the sweet milk of consecration.'

'Interesting.'

This would be a simulation of breast milk, that which a normal woman produces. Though Tesra did not realize it, her little ritual was a symbolic reminder of her biological origins.

'Press your arse against my cock, Tesra, move against it and tell me the rest of the dream.'

It was a cruel command, for both of them.

'Y-yes, sir,' she quivered, her body visibly shaking with her dilemma.

Marcellus had become far more expert in resisting her charms. His awkward first attempts at training her, where he'd nearly mounted her like a mountain goat, were long passed. He no longer even needed Drusia to drain him constantly. He could now hold this girl fast, his hand supreme, his will over hers.

'I was climbing the carved stone stairs, up the great mountain of white crystal; Surasa, the white volcano,' said Tesra, her splendid firm cheeks fitting to his genitalia, inviting her further plundering. 'I was wearing the white robe of the initiate, attached at the neck and open from below the throat to the ankle, such that my body was exposed with every step. I wore the enta-sha, the body paint that is appropriate for this time. My hair was tied back tightly on my head. I was frightened, just as I had been at the time, in real life, but also excited. Somehow the journey took much longer this time and all around me there was thunder. I must have gotten very high, because banks of clouds made of whitest white were flying about me, though it was still quite bright out. At a certain point I recall looking down and seeing the sun below, and the moon as well. I thought this odd, but as one does in dreams, one keeps on, accepting whatever comes. The really strange part was that I was getting older as I climbed, so that by the time I reached the apex I was no longer thirteen, but the age I am now.'

'A grown woman.'

'Yes,' she reached back, daring to put her hands on his hips. 'Oh, sir, can't we please go back to your chambers?'

Marcellus clamped her nipple beneath the shirt. 'Were you given permission to touch me?'

'N-no,' she winced, a punished captive.

'Or to stop your story?' He seized the other.

'No,' she whimpered, the pain doubled, queerly mixed with the pleasure between her legs. 'Forgive me, sir. I reached the top of the mountain where there is a temple, open to the sun and stars, with a series of four columns, one to each of four winds. It is there one meets the First Mother. As did I, long ago.'

Marcellus chewed the girl's earlobe as he massaged the imprisoned nubs of her breasts, driving her mad. 'But it was different,' he guessed, 'in the dream than in reality?'

'Yes. When the First Mother turned to face me, from her place at the white marble altar, in her black hood and robe, it was not her, sir, who I saw. It was not Velacera-be-na.'

'Who then?' the captain demanded, abandoning her cunt and leaving her stranded.

'It... it was a man,' she cried, the horror of the dream intermingling with her current predicament.

Indeed, thought Marcellus, this was growing more curious by the moment. 'Did you know him?'

'No.' She shook her head. 'And I cannot even describe him. Black hair, black beard, very tiny eyes... beady eyes. He frightened me, sir.'

'Why is that, captive?'

'B-because,' she stammered, approaching a place of brokenness he had not expected at this juncture, 'he did not intend to initiate me as befitting a sister, but as something else.'

It did not take a seer to guess as what.

'What did he do with you, then?'

'I was laid upon the altar, in my robe that clasps only at the neck. I was laid out for him in the colors of my people, my body painted and splendidly beautiful. I was helpless to him, sir, and I remember looking in his eyes, questioning, wanting to know why. He merely laughed and drew a carved stone knife from his belt. He told me he would not kill me, so long as I cooperated.'

'Cooperated?' He licked cruelly at her throat. 'In what way?'

Tesra had caved in completely against him, requiring his strong body to support her. 'He intended to penetrate me, sir, with his male spear, and he told me that if I made it enjoyable for him he would allow me to live.'

'And did you?'

'I-I was scared to death, sir. I had no choice.'

'What was it he wanted specifically?'

50

'He wanted me to move for him on the stone altar, not to just lie like a wart on a beast as he put it. He wanted to warm himself in my mouth first and to have me wet between my legs when he entered me.'

'You did all these things?'

'I did, sir,' she moaned, the shame deep in her voice.

'Describe it in detail,' he demanded.

'First he climbed onto my face. He was naked under his robe and dirty. He stank like an animal and he had heavy swinging balls like an ox. He taunted me, asking me if I thought I was too good for this because I was a high and mighty seer. The whole time the knife was at my throat, pricking my skin. I promised him I was not too good and I proved it, taking each of his heavy, fetid ball-sacs into my mouth to lick and suck as though they were some sweet and luscious fruit.

'He called me a good girl, a good little whore, and I just wanted to be sick because his hairy man-arse was pressed against my breasts, smearing my beautiful sacred paint. The whole time I licked his sacs he stroked himself, getting his organ as large as possible in anticipation of stuffing it down my throat.

'"Beg for it," he said when he was ready. I asked him humbly to desecrate my mouth, pleading with this wild-eyed invader to use me for his pleasure. I nearly gagged from the stench and the overwhelming size. When I resisted he plugged my nose, forcing me to open wider. In and out he went, faster and faster till I thought he would explode then and there, shooting his foul seed down my throat. But he had other plans, involving my lower lips, which by then had become sopping, much to my shame and humiliation. Again he wanted me begging, as though I should need or enjoy such a thing. He wanted me to tell him what a whore and cunt I was, though the words meant nothing to me. He told me he was going to fill my womb and that I would become heavy with his child. I screamed at this point, but he was very strong and he had the knife. Besides, I was no longer able or wanting to resist. I wanted him inside me, I needed it and when his spear sank into me I cried out and wrapped my legs, begging him to fuck me harder, to shoot his load deep inside me, burning hot.

'The lightning flashed about me and thunder roared. I knew something was terribly wrong and as the man exploded in me and I around him, there came a hot white rain down from the sky, as if the gods were ejaculating on us from above. And then, just as he was finishing himself off, I began to feel it... in my belly.'

'What, Tesra, what did you feel?'

'The swelling,' she sobbed, her voice so pitiful that he turned her about to offer her an embrace. 'In my womb. I became great with the man-beast's child, just as he told me. Heavy and full, as if I were a cow or some other female animal.'

'It was but a dream, Tesra.'

By the windy breath of Nephisis she had turned the tables, forcing him into the position of her comforter, her defender and, if left unchecked, her virtual slave.

'To my chamber,' he announced, sweeping her off her feet. 'It is time for another lesson.'

A lesson in captivity, one that would change things between them. Forever.

Vorra moved steadily between the pair of pirate cocks, doing her best to split her time evenly. Captain Thrace, to her right, had been given the use of her for the day by Marcellus, though Rodrigo, to the left, he who was second only to the pirate king himself, could hardly be ignored. At present they sat at table, dividing a roasted pigeon with their stabbing knives. The unfed slave, naked and heavily chained on hands and knees, remained hopeful as she bobbed back and forth that they might deign to drop some small scraps to the deck.

It had been two days since she'd eaten, on account of Rodrigo's great anger that she'd not been able to meet again with Tesra since their initial encounter, which had yielded precious little that Rodrigo could use to his advantage. Vorra did not see how it was her fault, though, that Marcellus now kept the little blonde bitch by his side night and day like a poodle, but slaves were not given the chance to question the actions of their masters.

'I tell you, Thrace,' Rodrigo was saying, his mouth stuffed with the meat of the bird that only an hour ago had gotten itself caught in the main sail of Thrace's ship, the *Dread Endeavor*. 'The man is no longer right in the head. One worthless blonde cunt, that is all his latest folly has wrought. And do you think any of us will even get to taste the fresh meat, pathetic as it is? No, my noble friend. Look what you and I get - the stringy, worn out cunts like this one.'

Vorra dared not object as she deep-throated the thick-knobbed Captain Thrace.

'She's not so bad as all that,' Thrace came to her defense. 'Still, the point is well taken. We are not spineless worms to crawl in the dust our whole lives before some hereditary land-loving monarch. Our kings are made by steel, and so too are they brought down if they fail to deliver to us our life's blood.'

Out of the corner of her eye Vorra saw the tiny scrap of meat and gristle that Thrace had just now spit out onto the deck. Was it for her?

'Well said, Thrace. I myself, were I captain, would serve tirelessly to make us all filthy rich.'

'Such words,' he mused, 'could be interpreted as treason. Feed,' he snapped his fingers, giving Vorra permission.

Vorra dove for it, mouth to floor, eagerly devouring the pathetic bit of half chewed food.

'You spoil her,' Rodrigo complained.

'It makes them all the more eager, later on.'

Taking no chances, she showered Thrace's feet with kisses then scooted immediately to deep-throat Rodrigo's waiting penis, reassuring him that she was, in fact, totally unspoiled.

The man ejaculated quickly down her throat, neither acknowledging her presence nor in any way interrupting the flow of conversation. 'That's what the whip is for, my friend. But tell me this; is it treason to speak openly as a free man? Are we not pirates answerable only to the sword and the whims of Nephisis? What will you do, Thrace, when the day is done? Confront Marcellus as a man, eye to eye, or cower at his feet, licking in supplication like a slave?'

Vorra drank him down and then continued to suck till he was hard again. To leave a pirate's dick without permission, even after an orgasm, was not something a slave girl did idly, not unless she wanted to be separated swiftly from her tongue or even her pretty head.

'Your words bear thinking, Rodrigo. They do not fall on deaf ears.'

'That is all I ask,' he reached forward to clasp the man's arm, 'that you keep your eyes and ears open. Watch what occurs. Witness what Marcellus does, in comparison to what you and I know should be done.'

'We shall speak of this further,' agreed Thrace. 'But first you must return my property to me. Even if it be only mine for the day.'

Rodrigo kicked Vorra away from him. 'Go, bitch. Are you deaf as well as stupid?'

Not stupid, thought Vorra, and certainly not deaf. For it did not take a wise man or an astrologer to foresee that what was coming soon would be a bloody struggle, a battle for supremacy between sword-wielding men. But where in the midst of that would mere naked slaves such as her find safety?

Was there a goddess to whom she could pray? A goddess like the high and mighty one Tesra knew? Vorra continued to contemplate the matter as she finished off Captain Thrace, her lips and tongue bespeaking the only prayer a slave can know: that of absolute submission.

Tesra beheld uneasily the body of the naked male before her. 'I do not understand, sir,' said she to her captor. 'What it is I am to do.'

'The matter is simple enough,' replied Marcellus. 'You are to please the slave.'

Tesra attempted to hide her arousal, the uneasy stirrings which were becoming second nature to her in the clutches of the pirate king. 'P-please him how?'

Marcellus unfurled the whip. It was a snake, quick and black. Kissing the deck, it wanted more. Much more. 'You are not an ignorant female, Tesra. Your intelligence exceeds that of all the others, probably even that of Drusia here.' He gave a nod to the collared slut at his side, kneeling, head to his booted foot. 'Given this fact, I find it hard to believe you have not observed enough from the others to know what is expected of you now.'

Tesra continued to regard the statue-like male. The slave was strong and blonde like herself. He wore a cloth about his middle, originally white, now filthy gray. He clung to scraps of pride in his demeanor and stance, though perhaps this was only his training. Like the female slaves his body bore the mark of the whip. Was there a brand upon his buttocks, too?

There were few of the male slaves on the pirate ships. Most of those captured from among their enemies were slaughtered at once. The ones allowed to live were worked like dogs and kept in a state of terrible abasement. They performed the most grueling and dangerous labors of the ships and when they were not in service, they were kept in a special hold. Tesra had heard rumors that a female slave might be punished by being thrown in with these males, like an innocent lamb among wolves. It made her knees weak and her belly quiver to think what would be done to a female slave, how she would be richly used and put into subjugation by these creatures so long deprived of the natural sexual releases they obviously required.

'I... I do not know where to begin,' she said foolishly, blushing before the man, her nipples throbbing beneath his shirt, her thighs still moist. Only moments ago he had brought her back to his chambers in tears, cradled in his arms. She had expected softness and sympathy, or at the very least the physical relief she so badly needed. Instead this pair of slaves had been fetched, one male one female.

'Strip, captive.'

Tesra hesitated, amazed that she had so quickly developed modesty. Among her people there had been no taboos against nudity, no particular significance to the viewing of one another's flesh. She'd thought that a mark of the superiority of the sisterhood, now she wondered if it was not simply a function of their living as they did in complete segregation from males.

'Must I repeat myself, captive?'

'No, sir.' Tesra removed the garment quickly, knowing that if she did not he would not hesitate to use the whip on her, or any other means at his disposal. It had been two days since she'd required punishment and she did not wish it now.

The thought made her all the wetter. Was he training her to obey, like one of his slaves or pets?

'Drusia,' said he to the groveling, lovely female, 'kneel between the captive's legs.'

Drusia crawled on all fours, her face expressionless, her mind occupied, seemingly with nothing but the will of the cruel captain, a man whom, increasingly, Tesra was coming to think the brown-haired girl loved with an affection much deeper than mere slavery.

In fact Drusia's thoughts, or what she could read of them, were consumed with Marcellus; the details of his body, every facet of his being along with scads of facts concerning his moods and preferences and how to please the man. It was as if she were literally an extension of him and no matter how he might spurn her - which he did on a regular basis - she would never be capable of doing anything other than crawling back to him.

'Sir, if this is punishment, I pray reconsider. I promise I will be better in the future.'

'Hands on top of your head,' ordered the captain. 'Yellow hair.'

The derogatory term, one descriptive of the hair both on her head and between her thighs made her blush. 'Yes, sir.'

'I will have this done because it pleases me,' Marcellus informed her, his cock stirring visibly beneath his tight leather breeches. 'Just as I will have you lick and suck the cock of this right-less bond male, also for my pleasure.'

Tesra swooned to have the act put into words. The slave's penis, hard and throbbing, was going to be put between her lips, making sacrilege of that sacred place reserved for speech and song unto the goddess. A flash of humiliation crossed her mind as another thought occurred to her: was she in part piqued because she wanted to do this instead for Marcellus - to serve him and not his mere slave?

'You will not hold back,' said Marcellus as Drusia began to lap at her sopping sex.

'Y-yes,' she shuddered, feeling herself melt in the presence of this party of

54

barbarians, her body an open book, a sordid story of degraded seduction, 'sir.'

Sir. The word on her lips was sounding more and more natural, more and more representative of his status, his true power over her, absolute, uncompromising and even desired, as her heart desired blood, her lungs air. Was there another word, though, that she longed to say to Marcellus instead? A far stronger word which every time it fell from the lips of Drusia and the others in her presence made her hate the chained, sexually vibrant little slave sluts all the more?

How much she'd learned, she thought bitterly, from these arrogant, proud men. Hatred and jealousy, enmity against her oppressed sisters and all kinds of dark feelings within herself, feelings which threatened to break her apart the more she heard them echoed in the minds and bellies of the other girls.

Voices, bespeaking pain and yearning, along with a deep, deep desire to submit, a desire whose roots tunneled deeper than she could comprehend into the psyche. Could it be they ran to the very core of creation?

'Tell us what you are thinking,' Marcellus demanded as Tesra bucked her hips against the face and tongue of the kneeling slave, her fingers entwined in her hair.

'I... I want to feel a cock in me, sir,' she cried. 'I want to feel... your cock.'

'I do not copulate with free women,' he told her. 'Do you understand the implications?'

Implications? Yes, he was telling her that to follow her heart's desire - or rather her cunt's desire - she would have to beg and obtain his mastery over her. 'Sir, please, I can bear no more!'

'Drusia, come here.'

Tesra wailed in sudden need, her voice approaching that of a child. 'Sir, what are you doing?'

Marcellus patted the head of the slave girl whose face was covered in come. 'I have changed my mind,' he told Tesra. 'I am denying you the right to orgasm.'

Tesra's fingers gripped her scalp fiercely. Could she lower them? Was she allowed to throw herself on his mercy? 'Sir, tell me what I must do.'

Marcellus hauled Drusia onto his stiff cock, just now released by him from the opening at the front of his breeches. She made a slight gagging noise as he pushed his large, thick member to the back of her throat. 'I am tired of playing games with you, Tesra. I have been far too patient for far too long.'

Her heart thundered in her chest. She did not wish him to be angry with her. In fact, it terrified and pained her to think she'd displeased him in any way. Was this how low she was sinking? Had his subtle controls and so-called training come to this?

'I have done my best, sir, at every stage.'

'Lying cunt!' he snarled, tossing the hapless Drusia aside once more, flinging her by the hair to her belly practically at the feet of the male slave, who might as well have been carved in granite.

'Please, sir,' cowered Tesra, instinctively falling to her knees as he stormed towards her, fury writ in his clawed hands and wild eyes.

'Down!' he pointed imperiously to his feet.

Tesra collapsed to kiss them, grateful he had not struck her, grateful too that she was being given this chance to beg forgiveness.

'It is time you woke up, yellow-haired bitch,' said he to her, his hands on his hips, a million miles above her looking down. 'You think that being born on an island of dreams you may float all your life on illusions. Dreams are not real, nymph of too many names for her own good. From this point forward your name is Yellow Pelt. Say it.'

'I am Yellow Pelt,' she licked miserably, forming the abominable name as best she could with her parched lips and tongue. But what did he mean that her life was an illusion? Was he referring merely to her hidden sexual needs or was there something more?

'How was it you were born, again?' he asked her, 'Yellow Pelt.'

Still not daring to cease her ministrations completely, she alternated repeating her tale of autochthony while continuing to clean his boots. 'We are birthed from the sacred volcano. We come from the goddess, her divinity mixed with the life fluid of that woman who is to be our mother-teacher, she who was birthed from her mother-teacher.'

'Wrong, Yellow Pelt, that is a lie told to foolish little girls so they will not question the absurdity of life on an island of fools, of haughty bitches too proud to take their true place in creation at the mercy of men.'

A lie? How could he speak such blasphemy? How could he even know enough as a mere male to even address the subject?

'Beg to suck the cock of the slave,' Marcellus commanded her. 'Say with your own lips what I have already determined for you as your captor, the possessor of your body and soul.'

Tesra plunged fingers unbidden into her beckoning sex. 'I beg it,' she hissed the words, craving her own humiliation at least as much if not more than him. 'I beg to suck the man-dick of your slave. Please, captor, may I show you my desire, my readiness to suck?'

To suck you, she'd meant to say.

He removed her dismissively with his foot. 'Make it good and slow, Yellow Pelt. Begin at his toes and lick your way up. Give him a good bath with your tongue. Nephisis knows it is the first he'll have seen in two moons.'

Drusia laughed cruelly, drawing a harsh reprimand from the captain. 'Drusia is a naughty little slut,' she purred, offering him her arse. 'Please punish her while Yellow Pelt bathes your man-slave.'

'Come here,' he growled good-naturedly.

Tesra burned at the subsequent giggles and the sound of the girl shrieking as he tossed her noisily upon the bed.

'It should be you,' Marcellus was saying to her, 'abasing yourself like that.'

'But master can't part with his little Drusia, can he?' she taunted. 'Master can't bear to share her, even with a Talassian slave dog.'

A Talassian. By the goddess, Tesra cringed as she inched ever closer on hands and knees. Is that what this unearthly man was, with his long gold braids and soulless gray eyes? According to all she had discerned from the minds of everyone she'd encountered off the island, they were a bloodthirsty people possessing of a vast empire on land and sea under which suffered dozens of nations. But this man was yellow-haired and from the minds of those with experience, she'd garnered the Talassian men were generally dark-haired and kept their locks short. Perhaps he was already a slave when the pirates caught him, having been taken earlier from some other land by the forces of Talassia?

The stench of the slave grew overwhelming as she reached her objective. Will Marcellus not even watch me? she thought, her head lowering slowly, inevitably. Was he that insensitive and uncaring?

'Oh, master,' Drusia was saying far too theatrically for her to think it meant for anything but Tesra's own ears, 'how your touch reminds me, how it teaches me all over again my place.'

She pictured the girl using her body as the tiny weapon it was. Did the captain not know that Drusia had power over him, how far more often than he realized he was following her whims and not his own?

The Talassian slave's skin was surprisingly soft beneath the layers of dirt. With her saliva, working moisture into the pores, she was able to restore it to life, a small spot on his thigh. But at what cost? The smell and taste made her gag and retch.

'Slowly,' Marcellus reminded her, interrupting his nice little wench-fuck. 'And be thorough. The toes, the nails, all of it.'

Tesra groaned in misery. When she'd finished the tops of the feet Marcellus barked an order, impelling the slave to lift his feet one by one for her to clean the soles. Her loins burned as she sunk deeper and deeper into subjugation. Meanwhile Drusia screamed out her slave girl's pleasure as the pirate took her with brutal efficiency, rocking her tempting little body, a siren's trap to any and all males within a hundred miles' radius.

'She is good at this,' said Drusia as Tesra reached his calves, the skin below her a glistening trail of restored whiteness, the dirt and grime of ship slavery now re-posited neatly from his body onto her own face and tongue. 'Maybe she's had practice after all.'

'If I did not know better,' observed the pirate. 'I would think you were attempting to tease our little Yellow Pelt. Could it be my Drusia is jealous?'

'Never,' the girl hissed. 'I am ten times the woman she will ever be. Let me show you, master. Ravish me... now.'

The girl groaned, no doubt entered in one or the other orifice. Was she on all fours, on her back?

'If I hear your tongue again, girl,' he warned, his voice deep and predatory like a lion's, 'I shall take it for my own.'

'Yes,' she moaned, reduced now to nothing more than another subjugated female at the hands of her dominant male, 'my master.'

Drusia grunted in her taking. There was no dissimulation now. Marcellus was putting her back in line, disciplining her with his cock. Tesra, meanwhile, had reached the heavily calloused kneecaps. How this man must have suffered. Many of the scars she'd found on the backs of his legs and calves were too deep and jagged for the whip. Someone had tortured him. Deliberately. Would the pirates be so cruel or was it the mark of the Talassians?

With her initial revulsion passed, Tesra longed to press on. It was exciting her to be so servile, to be giving pleasure to a man whom all discounted as sub-human. Certainly it was not by virtue of his body. He was a strong man, in his way handsome. Would his penis be large? How would it taste?

Tesra mingled her licks with kisses; shy, communicative of her newness to this form of contact. How many women had he had this way? How long had it been? Was there a lover he'd left home somewhere - or a wife, as it was called in the minds of these people?

She gave a little gasp of wonder as she lifted the loincloth with one hand. He was well endowed, very male and very hard. Licking her lips, restoring what moisture she could, she moved her head in to deliver what Marcellus had commanded of her.

'No,' cried the pirate king suddenly, 'that is enough.'

The slave himself stepped back, breaking the near contact, and left once more in the lurch Tesra turned her head towards her mercurial captor.

'Away,' he was telling the equally frustrated Drusia. 'Leave us alone. Take the other slave with you. I am done.'

'But master,' Drusia reached for him as he rose to his feet, cock still stiff and ready, 'your little girl will please you more. Please do not abandon her.'

'You may sport with the other one if you are so desperate to have your hole filled.' Once more he spoke in the unknown language, and this time the male slave moved with obvious eagerness, scooping up the squealing, very unhappy Drusia.

'Let go of me, you animal!' she squealed. 'You don't touch me, I belong to my master.'

'Take her,' he said to the male slave, this time in the common tongue of the pirates. 'Beat her and then fuck her. Do so on deck, in plain view that it may be known she is merely another slave, subject to my cruelties.'

Tesra was too shocked to gloat. 'Sir,' said she when the girl had been carried kicking and screaming over the shoulder of the suddenly fortunate male. 'Am I to assume that you desire to be intimate with me, as a man is to a woman?'

'No,' he retrieved the whip from the floor, shaking it out, 'you may assume that you are to be punished. On your hands and knees,' he commanded. 'Arse in the air.'

The whipping was unlike anything Tesra had experienced in her life. On the deck, when she'd been chained to the main mast, she'd experienced some suffering, but not the concentrated viciousness of Marcellus' blows. Unlike the crop, which was a short burn and sting, the long whip was like fire, being dragged over her skin. He seemed to know just where to strike her too, on her back, her calves, the very crack or her arse to cause the greatest agony. It did not help that she was covered in sweat, that of herself and the male slave who had dripped upon her in his heat.

'Please, sir!' she cried, till her voice no longer sounded coherent to her own ears. 'I beg mercy.'

'Well?' he demanded at last, pushing her down to her throbbing back, redoubling her torture. 'What have you to say for yourself now?'

'I do not know,' she sobbed, broken before him, as aroused as she was terrified. 'I only wish to please you, sir. Do not be angry with me... do not be angry with... Yellow Pelt.'

By the goddess she'd said it, acknowledging what she was to him, a thatch of golden fur, a sleek pet for his amusement - and his cruelty. What was next after such an admission? She dare not imagine.

'Use me,' begged the captive, spreading her virgin legs, beckoning him with her untried tunnel, that secret place no female of her island should ever speak of. 'Have me as you do Drusia and Vorra.'

Marcellus' face danced with emotion, subtle, perhaps to the untrained eye, but somehow readable to her. He wanted her. He needed her. He was afraid of her. She lay there, watching the man as he scrambled for his sword, discarded on the large oak table where he sometimes drank with Rodrigo and the others. 'Submit,' he demanded, pointing the drawn blade down at her belly.

He was over her, astride her hips, his cock and balls yet exposed and straining. She drew in her breath, seeing if the blade would take up its place at the depression of her retracted stomach.

It did. With one slice, he could cut her open.

'I submit, my captor.'

'Offer yourself to be my slave.'

'I am,' she testified, eyes unblinking, 'your slave. If you will have me.'

He shook his head, the answer somehow unsatisfactory. 'You do not know of what you speak.'

'Teach me,' she arched her back, wincing as the pointed tip pricked her skin, drawing forth a drop of blood.

The pirate, tricked into wounding her further, growled. He did not like this game, as he called it, any more than the others.

'It is time,' he bent to grasp her head, 'to teach you.'

Marcellus placed his body upon hers, not for sexual contact but for mental; his purpose simply to effect the grip of his hands on her skull, the touch of his forehead to hers, the rest of her body immobilized beneath the weight of him, which was perfect for the task at hand. The moment had come, and as he'd expected, it was in the throes of her sexual heat. Tesra's mind - Yellow Pelt's mind - seemed to be activated by desire, especially that for submission. Which made for a dangerous game given how much he himself seemed to be desiring her as well.

He told himself that everything so far was according to plan, that he was not behaving erratically, but only with deep cunning in an effort to unbalance and ultimately upend her defenses. Marcellus the pirate king was not captivated by the yellow-pelted slut, he was acting in his own best interest. Greed. Pure and simple. Which is why he was going to do what he had to now, penetrating her mind, cunt-like to his cock.

'Listen to me, Yellow Pelt. Yes, that's it. Look deep into my eyes. Trust me, girl. Let me in. Let me take you where we need to go.'

She was trying to shake her head, but there was nowhere for her to go.

59

By the gods she was a stubborn one. He'd have to employ other means. It would mean risking physical penetration, but what choice did he have? Did he even want one if there was? Could he resist this much temptation? The luscious virgin, for days having begged him to do what any man would kill for the chance to do?

She moaned as he sank his cock into her belly, full and satisfying. No man had been there. He was the first, and he would be the last, as well. This was a prize he would never share, even at the cost of his own life.

'Yield, Tesra, do not fight me.'

She clutched at him with fierce but unresisting strength. Truly she was a delight; her cunt as good as he'd imagined it and better. Just the merest seepage of blood and then pure honey, tight, the channel made by her precious goddess to be his vessel. And the tits, sculpted for his mouth, made to be nibbled, suckled, the tips so convenient to control and tease and punish.

'Have I your attention now?'

'Yes,' she looked up at him, eyes wide as her breeched cunt and full of wonder, 'sir.'

He still had hold of her head. 'We are going for a ride,' he told her, though this was not exactly what he'd planned. They were supposed to connect in mind only, not in flesh. Tesra moaned, already climaxing. He followed the waves, in her eyes, in her body and then, miraculously, he was with her, upon the ocean, the depthless blue robe of Nephisis, laid long ago over the rocky dry earth to give life. They were skimming the surface together, hand in hand, no ship beneath them. Remarkable: this sailing without a vessel. He knew not the place, nor could he identify it clearly as day or night. There were stars and a moon, but the black was bright and glowing as if it were midday.

They were flying, in the seer's mind. He had gained access, at long last. Now to steer them both, to teach her how to use this power in the world of men - to his advantage. Tesra wanted to look up, to contemplate, or else to dive below, but his purpose was different. Abandoning his place beside her, still in the dream world, he mounted her, climbing her bare back as though she were a great flying bird. Willing the device to appear, he manufactured a bit and bridle for the girl to wear. She balked, but there was little she could do, not with her body so deep in the throes of submission. If he wished to imagine her seer's spirit in bondage of this type, then she must live with it.

Round her middle he made appear the leather strap, cinching it tight. Tesra was saddled now and he would dig at her sides with spurs to direct her. The last thing he needed was the whip, small and sleek, appropriate for disciplining a flighted filly.

Tesra learned quickly who was master of her powers. When she attempted to soar to her ridiculous goddess she won a pretty set of lashes to her exposed hip and thigh. Her attempt at a dive met with a cruel reigning in that left her neck sore and twisted.

'Are you ready to cooperate?' he asked.

The inner Tesra nodded her bridled head obediently, desperately. 'Yes, oh yes,' moaned the outer Tesra, at the mercy of his power to orgasm her pussy on the deck of his cabin, 'my master.'

Master. She'd called him master.

Marcellus held back the roiling orgasm. If he overwhelmed her too completely she would no longer be a seer but merely another mindless cunt like the cuddly Drusia. 'Pay attention, slut. We are flying.'

She reached for him and he denied her. 'Take me,' he demanded, 'where I want to go.'

Tesra sprouted wings. He used her like a falcon, her every flap covering hundreds, thousands of miles for them. No longer limited by time, he flipped through days and weeks, the sea below them shrinking to a circle, a whirl of storm. The names and manifests of ships appeared in the blue, the chatter of conversation filled his ears, the talk of governors and admirals, the whole of Talassia's government and planning sliced open for him, sheared like an anthill. He could even see the emperor, alone, contemplating his own future.

The future, yes, this was it. The girl was taking him there. He'd managed to redirect her esoteric powers to concrete ends. Speaking of which, there was a wall ahead. A living wall of golden water - another thing he had not anticipated. 'Turn!' he cried. 'We are going to crash!'

At the last possible second she did, but not before her wings were caught in the swirl of the endless waterfall. They were both plunging now, perhaps to their death, but Marcellus did not care. From out of the thin air he had seized what he wanted. The information. The only kind of vision that mattered to a pirate.

A Talassian treasure fleet was preparing to sail. Out of the harbor of the imperial capital itself, bound for Cartishia, far to the east, loaded with gifts and women for this potential new ally of the ever-expanding empire. There was a princess, too, daughter of the dreaded Emperor Teranos, destined to be his emissary, and bride to the aging monarch of that faraway island nation.

It was to be heavily guarded, but three-quarters of the way to its destination it must pass through a narrow strait, a waterway walled by high rocks allowing the passage of but one ship at a time. Marcellus, the king of pirates, would split the fleet at this juncture, demolish the flotilla of naval escorts and take the treasure galleons.

'Sir,' cried Tesra, whether out loud or in her mind he did not know, 'help me!'

He clutched at her, keeping her close as they careened to earth for a landing. She was about to make him the richest pirate who ever lived and there was no way he was going to lose her now.

Chapter 6

'This is madness,' grumbled Rodrigo, passing the spyglass back to the king of pirates. 'Half the Talassian navy must be out there.'

Marcellus examined once more the tiny, rounded image with its specks and dots, a scale model reflective of a view much larger, a space of half a mile, encompassing the reality of the situation. 'So too is half the Talassian treasury,' he countered. 'Look there,' he pointed to the enemy fleet, from which they were well hidden at the moment behind the mighty, teeth-like cliffs. 'It is as I said. Already they are reconfiguring single file. They will pass this way.'

Rodrigo took back the glass confirming the accuracy of the prediction. The Talassians were going to attempt to sail through the Strait of the Barracuda, rather than take the longer, safer way round the archipelago.

'The emperor must be in great need of this new alliance,' Marcellus speculated. 'Perhaps there is more truth than rumor to this supposed rebellion by his generals.'

'And your little sea witch told you this too, I suppose?'

'It requires no witchcraft, Rodrigo, to see what is to be done. They will put the galleons in the middle, exposing the warships to the front and rear. We shall wait till the last of the galleons has entered the strait, block the remaining man-o-wars behind and pick off the ones in front leaving the treasure ships completely unprotected.'

'If you accomplish this,' mused Rodrigo, 'your name shall be added to the annals, as one of the great brigand kings of all time.'

'I wish only to add gold,' he clapped the shoulder of the man whom he still held out hope to call friend. 'To your coffers and mine.'

'My sword,' pledged Rodrigo. 'For blood.'

'You are my arm,' confirmed Marcellus.

'And you my heart,' saluted Rodrigo, leaving the king alone upon the deck of his ship, first among pirates, lord of predators. He could only hope the plan would succeed. Tesra had been able to provide little in the way of detail subsequent to his first vision. His use of her mind had impacted upon her more severely than he'd expected. Upon awakening himself from the crash he'd found her still unconscious, barely breathing. Nursing her in his own bed he finally succeeded in getting her to open her eyes just yesterday. Two weeks had passed in which the pirate fleet had been sailing at a murderous pace, all the while preparing for the raid of their lives, a venture which would see them all rich as the emperor or dead as the skeletons of the deep where their ships would swiftly be dispatched.

Marcellus was a skilled warrior as well as a decent tactician and he had the element of surprise. Half the crews of each ship had been dispatched to positions high upon the rocks. From this vantage point they would serve the dual purpose of harassing and disabling the warships while leaping down upon the galleons to seize control. The other half would be employed in hit and run tactics, manning the much streamlined fighting ships, which had the advantage of speed over the heavy Talassian warships.

The difficult part - one of many, actually - would be determining at what point to engage the choke point, blocking the pass with the great floating sheaves of fire and smoke to be thrown down from the height of the rocks. Once deployed, these would cut the front half of the Talassian fleet from the warships behind. The sooner this was done, of course, the fewer ships to deal with after. But if the treasure ships were interspersed they might have to risk losing treasure to minimize the danger. There was also the problem of cutting off their own ships, leaving them to the mercy of the muchly angered Talassian navy to the rear.

Marcellus had prayed much to Nephisis, who, as is well known by all who travail the seas, favors the free men, the buccaneers who make their living from the sea, rather than the arrogant empire builders who seek to tread upon the ocean beneath them as though it were some road laid for their benefit. Such men would as soon pave the mighty seas with stone, burying over the pirates and all other denizens of the deep than they would pay one iota of homage to great bearded Nephisis, he of the quick eyes and jolly laugh.

'To you, noble Lord of the Sea,' he raised his sword, the polished metal gleaming off the rays of the shining sun. 'Goes the day, the victory and the spoils thereof.'

Tesra turned her head weakly towards the door, the effort taking all her energy.

'Vorra and I have been sent to take care of you,' announced Drusia, sounding anything but caring. 'While the men are occupied.'

'Where is Marcellus?' she managed, her eyes darting back and forth between the two gleaming-eyed girls just now entering the captain's quarters.

'He's getting ready to fight your little battle,' Vorra sat on the edge of the bed.

'Quite the little fortune teller, aren't you?' Drusia sat on the opposite side.

'What are you saying?' She tried to sit up. 'Marcellus has told me nothing of a battle.'

Drusia pushed her back down, rather abruptly. 'What a pity,' she mocked. 'With the two of you being on a first name basis and all.'

Tesra tried to remember. Dimly, she had seen Marcellus yesterday. He sat where Vorra was, feeding her broth, telling her everything would be all right. She had taken some kind of a fall. In a dream, of all things. He'd explained to her about the ship, reminding her of her own kidnapping, but it hadn't seemed so horrible anymore, not compared to the other thing, the plunging in her mind, the crashing. A chill came over her as she remembered. Marcellus had seized possession of her dreamscape, forcing her to convey him over the plains of the known and unknown. He'd harnessed her in leather, forcing her, bitted and enslaved to carry him on her back, the wings of her mind carrying them whither he would go. But he had not sought to fly over the inner space for its right purpose of worship. He wished profit. He had sought to be as a god himself, and in so doing had forced her into the wall.

The Wall of the Unknowable. The impenetrable barrier that no mortal may cross.

'Let me go.' She tried once more to regain her freedom.

Marcellus had broken a law, whether he realized it or not, and there was to be punishment, not from the Talassians but from a far greater power. Unless she warned him. But the two slaves held the much-depleted Tesra down with ease.

'You're like a little doll,' Vorra stroked her hair. 'A yellow-pelted doll.' As if on cue Drusia pulled the sheet down, exposing the girl's naked body.

'What are you doing?' asked Tesra warily, other memories returning to her, of things done to her before by these women.

'We're going to find some ways to pass the time,' Drusia said, lifting the girl's limp wrist and tying it with the cord. 'Since we're locked in here, thanks to you.'

'Locked in,' she mumbled as one arm and then the other was drawn taut over her head and secured to the head of the bed. 'What do you mean?'

'We're locked in,' Vorra opened her legs, placing them wide apart. 'While we wait the outcome of the battle.'

'It's a foregone conclusion, actually.' Drusia produced the nasty-looking silver clamps. 'Since your good friend Marcellus has signed our death warrants.'

The clamps were for Tesra's nipples. The girls applied them one by one, carefully, mercilessly on the already peaked nubs. The pain ripped through her, hurting like nothing she had ever known. 'Please,' she begged. 'I am not well.'

Vorra was busy working on Tesra's clitoris, making her wet enough to receive the large wooden shaft, fashioned in the shape and size of a penis. 'You'll feel a lot worse when the Talassians blow this ship out from under us.'

'Pray it's only that,' said Drusia somberly, adding a fresh twist of anguish to each captive nub. 'Better an eternity at the bottom of the ocean than even a single day as a slave of Talassia.'

'Drusia knows what she's talking about,' Vorra confirmed, surprisingly calm as she began to push the device into Tesra's defenseless sex. 'She was a slave on one of their galleys. Isn't that true, Drusia?'

Drusia licked her lips in anticipation of kissing Tesra. 'I begged to die,' she confirmed. 'On one occasion I chewed my own arm bloody and jumped into the water hoping to attract the sharks. For my punishment I was given to the ship's dogs for a night. Do you know what Talassian dogs are trained to do with slave girls, little fortuneteller? I'll give you a clue. They are all male and they are not interested in playing fetch.'

'Tell her about the beatings, Drusia. With the whip of nails.'

'Shut up, Vorra,' she snapped. 'Before I forget that we are supposed to be getting along right now.'

Vorra took out her anger on Tesra, plugging her fully with the wooden cock. 'I'll take you on any day,' she challenged. 'King's bitch.'

'At least I am the bitch of the king,' Drusia taunted, her lips brushing the moaning Tesra, 'and not one of his underlings.'

'I hate you,' said Vorra, fucking Tesra all the harder.

Drusia made no response, her tongue now fully inserted in Tesra's mouth, having easily breeched her slack and pouting lips. Beware my king, she thought. If you can hear my mind, then stop before it is too late. Stealing the knowledge of the future was one thing, but to act upon it, this was tantamount to desecration, an open defilement of what is holy and orderly. For such a sin a man can only die, and in the worst possible way.

'Pay attention!' Drusia slapped her face, drawing her back to the pain. 'I'm not going to bother abusing you if you're not even going to pay attention.'

'Yes,' said Tesra submissively, opening herself to the girls' tortures, the petty teasing and taunting mixed with the very real agony of the clamps and shaft, 'I obey.'

'Of course you do.' Vorra thrust the device to the hilt, only to pull it all the way out. 'Now beg me to fuck you.'

'Do it,' Drusia pulled at the clamps, which unlike the discrete attack of the whip brought a hell that had no beginning, no ending.

'Please,' grunted the nymph from deep in her throat, her own needs compounding the duress, 'fuck me.'

'Fuck me, mistress,' Vorra corrected.

'We are both your mistresses,' Drusia pulled the clamps toward her, pointing Tesra's breasts to the back wall.

'Oh, please,' she bucked her hips, fearing she would tear the ropes, or else the nipples from her own breasts, 'fuck me, mistresses.'

'Only the lowest of slaves comes like this,' Drusia told her. 'You do know that?'

Vorra thrust the artificial cock in and out, fast and deep. 'Beg to come, slave.'

'I beg... to... come... mistresses.'

Vorra rested the shaft against her clit. 'Work for it.'

Tesra did not need to be told twice. Like a madwoman she impaled herself, spasming and writhing, her own personal earthquake. The slaves watched, mocking, sneering. Tesra was beyond caring, beyond preserving any shred of dignity. She'd have done anything, said anything just for this relief.

They allowed her minimal recovery time afterward. Pulling the shaft free of her sex, Vorra handed it to Drusia who put it to her lips, making clear what it was she was to do next. 'You're our little slave, aren't you? The slave of slaves. Little Yellow-Pelt, King's new pet.'

Tesra opened wide, taking the hard, slick object to the back of her throat. It tasted of female sex - hers and others. How many girls had yielded to this device, their precious love-giving power cruelly exploited by a mockery of human anatomy? For a moment she lamented her gaping pussy, but Vorra had no intention of leaving her alone. As soon as the wood was gone she replaced it with her tongue, at once roiling the girl with yet more unwanted orgasms.

'Slut,' Drusia kept repeating, as if the words did not apply as well to her. 'Hot-cunted little slave slut.'

'Yes,' Tesra confessed, astounded that such a confession could come to mind much less reach her lips. 'I am a hot-cunted little slut.' But not a slave. Never a slave. Desperately she clung to this idea as the women continued to have their way with her, turning her in all positions, ultimately forcing her to please them as they climbed one by one onto her face. It was while she was servicing Drusia this way, licking this glistening cunt of which Marcellus was so fond that she heard the first of the cannonballs.

It's begun, she thought. Too late now for redemption. For win or lose this battle, Marcellus was doomed to lose the war.

'Hard to starboard!' shouted Marcellus. 'Do not let them escape!'

The fat galleon was no match for the corsair. Like a hawk bearing down upon its prey the pirate ship *Treasure Dream* closed the gap down to nothing, its hull scraping satisfyingly against the heavy treasure ship. There was a shout of joy from the pirates as the first wave went over the edge, overwhelming the small number of Talassian marines stationed onboard. Slitting their throats and leaving them for the fearsome sharks, noble sea dogs of Nephisis, they made their way into the hold to find their booty.

'Second wave, hold!' commanded the pirate king, barely restraining the drooling pirates. It was a problem, of course, occupying so many treasure galleons at once; their ranks stretched thin as it was. Immediately turning the wheel he dispatched them to the next ship, an even larger one that at the moment was spinning in the water, slowly, leaning heavily to one side.

It was going to sink on them!

'Signal to Rodrigo!' he shouted to the flag-bearer. 'Tell him to intercept. We don't want to give the old man of the sea this much gold!'

Though in truth they owed this much to the god and more. The plan could not have gone better. Not only had they bottled up every last one of the treasure ships and disabled the five intermingled warships, they had actually succeeded in sinking two others behind and running the rest off. Marcellus doubted they would be that scared of the pirates, but it was quite likely in the melee, with so much smoke and fire that the admirals had assumed themselves under attack from some much larger force; perhaps the fleet of the mighty Alliance of the Serpentine City States rumored to be unhappy with the massive tributes levied by the new emperor, or even some rebel faction of their own forces.

Indeed, it was this psychological element upon which he'd counted to win the day against such overwhelming odds, but regardless, the booty now belonged to the piracy. A bit more mopping up, securing the various drifting vessels, finding adequate transport for all the gold and so forth and they would be home free, the open sea ahead of them, the nearest Talassian naval station some six days' sail or better behind.

Surely this would satisfy his critics, Rodrigo chief among them. There would be women aplenty now, and he himself, if he wished, could trade yellow-hair for some luscious Talassian court slave, or even the submitted body of one of its ladies - the princess herself if she had managed to be among the survivors.

For some reason, though, Marcellus, king of pirates, did not wish to do this. He was growing rather fond of the irritating and quirky seer. A dangerous emotion for a pirate, to be sure. It was one thing to favor a slut like Drusia who wore a brand on her arse and who could be as easily traded or disposed of as a pair of boots, but to fawn upon a free girl, even a captive, that was asking to become captive himself. Pirates had no mates. This was a known fact. His father had none, nor had his grandfather. Their women were concubines, used for sex, to bear children or give pleasure as the case might be. His grandfather had been the greatest whoremonger on the high seas. He was well into his nineties and still sporting with hapless wenches, making them squeal and beg in delight. Likewise he had kept his slaves in line, mastering women half and ultimately a fourth his age with a will of iron, his shriveled flesh conquering their nubile curves with devastating efficiency.

It was Marcellus' grandfather who'd been led to the Isle of Dreamers. He'd half joked it was his libido led him there, to that place invisible to all who sail, untouchable to all who plant flags in the name of cities and nations. Young Marcellus had heard the story so many times that he had it memorized. The way the old man had seen the far off lights, glowing green, beckoning, after the shipwreck in which his crew had all been lost. Clinging desperately to a rum barrel

66

he kicked with all his might, following its call, like some mysterious lighthouse.

He'd collapsed of exhaustion on the shore, scarcely sure if he'd lived or died and gone to the lands of the next world. The next thing he remembered there were hands at his face, delicate female hands, and murmuring voices, curious. They were young and they had no clothing. He was instantly hard at the sight of them under the light of the moon, mixed with the eerie white and green light from the mountain behind them. They wore shell necklaces, their bodies were perfect and beautiful and he wanted more than anything to be putting them to his pleasure, using them as the comely wenches they were.

'Not yet,' said a new voice, that of an older woman, her face and body concealed behind a black robe and hood. 'They must first be prepared. Then you may have them. As many as you like.' Thus was Marcellus' grandfather introduced to the Isle of Dreams. That place where there are no males and where children, laughably, are said to be born from thin air.

He impregnated a dozen of them in the next two days. The efficiency of his seeding was due to the old woman's insistence that every load be deposited in the womb of one of the females, though in preparation he was allowed to make use of their other orifices. At first the girls were frightened and had to be held down by the others, but after a while they grew eager, literally begging to be chosen for implantation. The old woman gave him herbs in a foul-tasting beverage, which aided in his prowess. Through its influence he was able to stay hard almost continuously and his ejaculations numbered two, even three times an hour.

One of the more interesting aspects of the process was how, after being seeded, the girls were tied down on their back, their hips elevated above their head. The old woman explained that this would help the seed to penetrate, thereby enslaving the womb. The woman had measuring devices of some sort and was able to tell instantly if he'd been effective. If he had not he would mount again, the nubile body still in bondage. Some required multiple attempts, and these he grew the most acquainted with. One of them, afterwards, did not wish to leave his side.

The impregnations took place in a cave, beside an underground river, very similar by its description to the spot where Marcellus had warmed the insolent, pretty arse of Tesra prior to bringing her to his ship. It had occurred to him at that point the girl might even be his own half cousin, a generation removed, though the odds were remote.

According to his grandfather, neither he nor the females were supposed to remember what had transpired. There was magic surrounding the event, and presumably the old woman, as well as the others of her kind who came to help in the final stages, must have been quite powerful as to be able to control the pregnancies and the sex of the babies, so that no unwanted males would be born. The spell was cast on him in his sleep. The fact that he remembered must have been a sign of its failure.

Among the things he recalled was the leader explaining how men were brought periodically for this purpose, and how the females were going to be sequestered for the duration of their pregnancy so as to conceal the truth. Some nine months to the day then, after the sailor's departure, there would a ceremony of deliverance, the goddess being praised for another seemingly miraculous group of appearing babies, their mothers smiling, another spell having rendered them completely ignorant of the fact that the squirming, tiny girls so safely ensconced in their maternal arms had just a short while ago resided completely inside them, in the very chamber once flooded by the sailor's seed.

What had struck Marcellus' grandfather most in all this, the incredible sexual experiences aside, was what he had felt when the old woman touched his brain seeking to erase his memories. Though it had come to him only as a dim recollection when he'd awakened, he was quite sure that through the old woman he had touched the pulse of creation itself, seeing it by means of an inner eye, ever circling, never blinking.

'It's the pirate blood in my veins, boy,' he would say, 'kept me forgetting it all.'

To his dying day he remained convinced that he would somehow return and that by this power he would become the richest, most powerful pirate who ever lived. Marcellus' own father inherited the mad dream, though he seemed never quite fully convinced of the reality of the quest. A somber, melancholic man, given to fits of temper, Marcellus' father kept the best of himself for the rum, his one true friend. A fierce fighter and able leader he did prosper, though he remained largely alone till the day he died. Marcellus scarcely spoke a dozen words to him in the last decade of his life and his last words were a curse, condemning both his own father and Nephisis for giving him a yearning he could never satisfy.

The legacy came in turn to Marcellus, his only son, who combined the best traits of his father and grandfather and had used them well, catapulting himself all the way to the kingship. A title that, if for no other reason, he had earned here and now on account of this battle.

'Majesty,' called Montrego, limping upon his one twisted leg, his body fit as a fiddle nonetheless, 'we have located the Talassian flagship. Its colors had been taken down to disguise its identity.' This was a not uncommon occurrence in the game of pirate and prey.

'Indeed, and what have you to report?'

'We have the princess, sire, bearing her weight in Scornian gems.'

Marcellus nodded. 'Excellent.'

The gems of Scornia, dug from the black mountains were so rare as to be found in veins of white silver, their color so brilliant that a single one of them, blue, purple, green or red could light the sky for half a mile.

'And the wench herself; is she as easy on the eyes as her dowry?'

'Hard to say, sir. She is rather heavily clothed, as are her handmaidens.'

'We shall attend to that oversight shortly, eh?' Marcellus grinned, giving the man a hearty slap on the shoulder.

'By the Sea Lord, we shall,' the gnarled pirate chortled. 'And won't that just be a kick in the crotch to the emperor.'

'I'd say we've grabbed his balls good, and given them a healthy twist.'

'Shall I bring the wench aboard?'

'Yes. And have the yellow-hair brought up as well. I think she should find this instructional.'

The prospect of having the delicate Tesra observe the brutal enslavement of the Talassian women stirred the king mightily, though once again it made him wonder if we were becoming too fixated on her.

Perhaps, he mused, he would do well to put her to the iron today as well as the others.

'Breathe a word of this to the men,' whispered Drusia in her ear, replacing the cover over Tesra's much exploited body, 'and we shall do worse to you later on. Is that clear?'

'Yes, mistress.'

'One more kiss goodbye.' Vorra held the shaft to Tesra's lips, and she did so, obediently, passionately.

'Hide that thing, you imbecile.' Drusia shot dagger eyes at her fellow slave. 'Do you want us to end up drawn and quartered?'

Vorra frowned but did as she was told, stuffing the device under the mattress.

'Get a move on, sluts.' One of the men poked his head in the doorway. 'The king wants the yellow-hair on deck. Right away.'

'Bitch,' Drusia sneered at Vorra, grabbing one of Tesra's arms.

'King's toy,' Vorra retorted, taking the other, and one woman on each arm they dragged her out of bed.

'Move it,' Vorra shoved her in the back as soon as her feet were planted, and Tesra stumbled forward.

'My legs are so weak,' she complained.

'Oh stop being so dramatic.' Drusia smacked her naked arse. 'You don't have to deal with a tenth what we do. Sleeping up here in luxury, laying in a bed all day.'

Vorra yanked her by the hair to the door. 'One day you'll be back in the hold, then you'll learn your place again.'

'Why are you doing this?' she cried. 'Didn't I already submit to you?'

'And you think that's the end?' Drusia scoffed, the girl's naiveté amusing her greatly. 'It's only the beginning, slut. Submission is like blood to a shark; one little smell and you want more and more. Why do you think men enjoy owning us year after year without becoming bored?'

'I never bore the masters,' said Vorra. 'I know how to please them.'

'Bully for you, Vorra. Now help me get her up the stairs.'

The sunlight was overwhelming, as was the sensation of the open air on her sallow cheeks. Tesra wanted to cry at the feel of it, of being outside once again. Though it might not be her beloved island she was once again under the sky of the goddess, wrapped in the cloak of roaring ocean. Even the boat, with its gentle swaying seemed to reinforce her joy in being alive, given a second chance after her near death at the edge of the Wall.

But what was this? They were far from alone on the deck. In fact, she had never seen it so crowded. To one side stood the pirates and the slaves. Some men she knew from Marcellus' ship and others she took to be captains from the other vessels. The men all stood proudly, though their faces and bodies bore the signs of recent exertion from the battle. The girls were on their knees, heads to the deck, as was fitting females of their station.

On the other side of the boat, looking more than a little wary and afraid, stood a party of richly dressed females accompanied by a small party of men, two dressed rather foppishly in velvet, feathered hats and high velvet boots with curled toes. Three others looked to be soldiers, in mail vests, heavy strapped boots and tight leather breeches, uniform blue, though they were at present weaponless.

'Ah, my little Yellow Pelt,' the king proclaimed. 'Just the person I was waiting for. Now we can begin. Drusia, Vorra, kneel with the others. Tesra, come here.' He snapped his fingers, and handed her his cloak, wrapping it about her shivering, naked shoulders.

'You will never get away with this,' said one of the females, dressed in a long red gown covered in a cloak of green, her hair elaborately trussed, dark rivulets running down the sides of her face. 'My father will see you all impaled from the walls of Talas City if you do not release me at once.'

'Clearly,' noted Marcellus, 'you are Teranos' daughter. I recognize the bark.'

'Wait until you encounter the bite,' she threatened.

'Is that any way to speak to your future husband?' mocked the pirate king.

'What nonsense is this?' She stiffened, her black eyes seething with contempt. 'I am destined for the king of Cartishia.'

'You are destined,' Marcellus scooped one of the gems from the barrel full of them, 'for whomever sees fit to collect your dowry. And at present that is me. And, of course, this man as well.'

He tossed the yellow coin-size jewel to Montrego, who caught it, blowing the girl a kiss.

'Now you are his,' Marcellus declared. 'And,' he threw a blue one to the man next to him, 'his as well.'

There was laughter among the crew as he threw them each a glass stone of Scarnia. The symbolism, Tesra suspected was important both to the pirates and the Talassian woman herself.

'You are mad. Have you any idea of the value of those gems?'

Marcellus threw a handful over the edge into the ocean. 'Greater, I suspect than you yourself would fetch in any slave market.'

'Guards,' said the princess, her voice more shrill than regal. 'Charge at them. Kill them all.'

The three soldiers held their ground, eyes darting back and forth at the grinning, predatory faces of their captors.

'Your highness,' said one of the velvet-wearing fops, a quivering mutton-chopped man with red hair, 'it may not be in our best interest to anger them any further.'

'Be silent, Torixar!' She stamped her foot, small and dainty in the sandal. 'Or I shall have your bare behind scoured with rods... again.'

The fop lowered his eyes, clearly embarrassed in front of the pirates. 'Yes, highness,' he muttered.

'Trillonodon,' said the princess to the other fop, a taller man with a red-feathered cap. 'Remove my outer gloves that I may address these men more comfortably.'

70

'Do not,' said Marcellus to the man, his hand already poised to pull the cloth from the girl's small, arrogantly proffered hand. Trillonodon looked at the pirate king. 'Onboard my ship males do not serve females. Females serve males.'

'This is absurd.' The princess stomped her foot once more. 'I will have no more of it, do you hear me? I am Ameliadora Versatia Hyronomia Crysalos, fourteenth daughter of His Imperial Majesty, Teradon the Fourth, supreme overlord of all Talassia as well as—'

'The fourteenth?' Marcellus interrupted. 'Do you hear that, lads? The bastard is so cheap he won't even expend a daughter in the single digits! Best gnaw a bite from those gems and make sure they are real. Perhaps the girl is a scullery maid for all that.'

'Guards!' she shrieked, grabbing at their sleeves. 'Why are you not defending my honor? Go and kill them, give up your lives for my honor, you simpletons!'

The soldiers ignored her, their eyes still poised on the pirates. These were warriors, and if and when they fought would be on their own terms.

'You,' said Marcellus to the one called Trillonodon. 'Tell the princess to cease insulting her men-at-arms or else you will be required to cuff her quite soundly.'

'I - I could not, sir,' stammered the fop, turning pale.

'Very well,' Marcellus nodded. 'Montrego, kill him.'

The thrown knife was in the heart of Trillonodon before he could draw a protesting breath.

'Torixar,' said the pirate king to the first fop as the second collapsed dead onto the deck, 'convey that same message to the princess.'

He did so, his voice shaking.

'How dare you speak to me that way!' she cried. 'I shall have you skinned alive. I demand you fall and kiss my foot at once, begging forgiveness.'

'Silence her,' warned Marcellus, 'or you shall die with your friend.'

Torixar pleaded with Ameliadora to be silent, but her refusal earned the velvet-hatted man a pike through his midsection, thick enough to skewer him.

'Who is senior among you?' Marcellus asked the three soldiers.

'I, sir,' stepped forward a man with a thick scar, from his left ear across to his mouth.

'Silence her,' the pirate king commanded.

'Princess Ameliadora, I can give but one warning,' the soldier said, his face darkly edged.

Princess Ameliadora looked him full in the eye and spit upon his face. 'Here is what I think of your cowardice,' said she.

The soldier struck her across the face, hard. The maids gasped, stepping back. The princess was stunned, looking at the blood on her hand from the corner of her mouth.

'Tell her now,' instructed Marcellus to his willing mouthpiece, 'that she is not to speak without permission again, and if she does so she will be flogged. She is to nod if she understands.'

The soldier repeated the words, though obviously she knew them already. Promptly, though warily, she gave her assent.

'Her handmaidens are to take their clothes off now, for our inspection,' Marcellus said, still not deigning to speak to her directly.

'Do it,' Ameliadora snapped at the huddled girls, more than happy, it seemed, to sacrifice her servants.

The handmaidens clutched at their robes, clearly terrified to be naked in front of all these men, most of whom had stiff cocks visible beneath their breeches.

The senior soldier stepped forward. 'Shall we strip them for you, sir?' he asked Marcellus.

'The decision is theirs. If they wish to live they must find one of my men to claim their naked flesh, in two minutes' time.'

Two minutes. Tesra felt the clamping in her heart and between her legs. These sheltered servants of a haughty, spoiled princess had the span of just a hundred and twenty seconds to successfully offer themselves up as pleasure slaves to the horny, bloodthirsty crew.

'Come on, girls,' called one, a bit bolder than her sister servants, 'you heard him. What choice do we have? Do you want to die? I for one would willingly spread my legs and suck in order to live!'

She was a redhead, like Kasandra, only lusher with fuller breasts. 'Does anyone want these?' She cupped them blatantly. 'Or this?'

This was the space between her nether lips held clinically, desperately apart.

'I don't know, whore,' called a gravelly voice from somewhere in the crowd. 'But I'd be happy to take a free sample.'

There was laughter from among the men. The girl shivered, knowing she was being exploited, but having no choice she went to him. After giving a good grope and thrusting his hand hard between her thighs, he pushed her away. 'Not hot enough,' he said.

Immediately she accepted an offer from another to have him try out the feel of her arse under his spanking hand. Meanwhile, a luscious blonde had stepped out of her dress and undergarments and was heeding calls from the crowd to dance for them.

'Are you wet, slut?' called a man.

She touched herself, her eyes flitting shut as she writhed before the boatload of lusty brigands. 'Yes,' she announced, to her shame, 'I am.'

'Hurry girls, encouraged a brunette to the last two, shaking herself free of the cumbersome clothes. She was a hot one, with a fine body clearly built for a man's discipline and heavy usage. Immediately two of the drunker sailors began to fight over her protruding breasts and bottom.

The remaining pair panicked as the pirate king announced that there was just one minute left for them to prostitute themselves or face the fate of the other Talassians. 'Please,' wailed one, tripping over her half torn robes, falling flat on her face, 'take me, someone.' She had lovely raven curls, though as she crawled about on the dirty deck it was clear they would not remain pristine for long.

The last one, a stocky girl with large aureoles and thick pussy lips practically threw herself at the men, landing in the arms of the mute pirate, who seemed content with his bounty, throwing her bodily over his shoulder.

Meanwhile the redhead and the blonde were being made to take turns on their knees at the cock of one crafty fellow who told them he needed more evidence to 'make up his mind'.

'Time,' called Marcellus as the redhead was taking her turn.

The blonde cried out in panic but a nearby brigand took pity, dragging her by the hair to his feet, where she fell to kissing and licking them ardently.

'Thank you, master,' panted she, again and again, the nature of her new status having been made more than clear to her already.

'Thank you, master,' murmured the other girls in turn, appreciative of the men who had saved their lives.

The only one not speaking was the stunning brunette, she who had been born for the collar, more so than any of the others. Her mouth, as it turned out was occupied, as was her cunt, the two drunken sailors having devised a unique compromise to share her charms. The girl moaned softly, eyes closed, her body well exposed and on its way to full exploitation as she knelt for them on hands and knees. It was a position she would grow accustomed to, along with dozens of others appropriate for that unique brand of animal known as the female slave.

'Fetch the branding iron,' called Marcellus, satisfied with the new crop of slaves.

'Disgusting,' sniffed Ameliadora haughtily. 'You are sluts,' she pronounced. 'All of you; worthless sluts.'

'Indeed?' The pirate king raised his brow. 'And suppose I were to give you the same option?'

The princess turned pale beneath her fine hairdo, the make-up a sudden contrast to the ghastly white. 'You wouldn't dare,' she said, though there was a good deal less starch in her voice than in the beginning.

'Or,' he proposed alternatively, 'I could give you that same amount of time to please your own soldiers with your naked charms such that one of them will claim you.'

Ameliadora backed away from her guards, seeing them no longer as her servants, beholden to her father, but as men, larger and stronger than her who might, at any time, take from her what they wished.

'You have no idea of the ransom I would bring,' said the princess to her captor, her demeanor indicative now of real fear. 'My father would carve you half the empire for my safe return, or the weight of your ship in gold.'

'For daughter number fourteen? I think not.' He shook his head. 'Not even for daughter number one. It is well known that among your people a captured female is considered already forfeit to slavery. Should you return, even now, your own father would have you stripped, branded and raped.'

'I have the blood of the House of my fathers. I am sacred to my people. There is a temple to me on the Isle of Ciros. Did you know that?'

'No,' Marcellus smiled, 'I did not. Perhaps now it shall be a temple for slaves.'

Ameliadora, proud and regal, fell to her knees. 'Please, sir, do not do this to me. I am not like them. I am different. I do not deserve this.'

'Different?' he repeated, clearly toying with her. 'And how exactly do you mean that, noble princess?'

'I am not a slut,' she said eagerly, seeing her opportunity to escape at her servants' expense. 'They are little bitches; that's why they were my virtual slaves. See how disgusting they are now? Like animals?'

Tesra could hardly miss the rutting as the handmaidens and their new masters, as starved for love as many of the pirates themselves, fell into one another, expressing their primal carnal natures. Male and female, dominator and dominated. Interestingly, Bothar had managed to discover the new redhead and was at present mounting her from behind, his teeth dug firmly into her neck. The girl was spasming, in helpless orgasm as he rode her to his bliss. Soon enough this new girl would wear the collar and bark for him and eat from a dish at his feet. And the others at the feet of other masters; the little dancing blonde, the raven-haired girl and the brunette, taking on one and all.

'And you are not like that?' asked Marcellus.

'No, not at all.' Ameliadora shook her head vigorously. 'On the blood of my people, I swear it.'

'You would not be averse then to a small test?'

'A test?' She hesitated. 'Of what kind?'

'To see if you are a lady,' he replied. 'Or only another slut.'

'I know of no such test,' said the princess warily.

'I do.' He held up his index finger. 'Resist this, overcome it and you shall have your freedom.'

Ameliadora, fourteenth daughter of the emperor, the most powerful man in the whole of the world, regarded her captor, her lovely brow creased. 'That one finger?' she clarified. 'That is all you offer to challenge my resolve? My womanly purity?'

Tesra cringed, knowing full well what could be done with this single digit applied to the right, or wrong place.

'I am a simple man,' he shrugged. 'A mere brigand. Perhaps not right in the head.'

The princess was on her feet, having fallen completely for his trap. 'Let us get this over with; I wish to be on my way before sunset. You will, of course, provide me armed escort to the nearest outpost of Talassia?'

'It will be my pleasure,' he bowed with deceptive gentility, ushering her towards his cabin, 'highness.'

Tesra watched them descend the stairs, her heart sick with jealousy, her loins thick with need. In a fit of desperation she begged a sailor for his touch. He cuffed her harshly, annoyed at being distracted from his pursuit of another girl, the blonde handmaiden, the lithe slut with the yellow curls whose steamy dancing was driving half the crew to distraction.

'What's the matter?' Vorra towered over her, the comely wench herself having been thrown over in favor of the newcomers. 'Is special little Tesra not feeling so special anymore? Welcome to our world, bitch.'

Tesra wept at the girl's feet, wetting them with tears. She wanted Marcellus. She wanted to go home. She wanted to wake up and find it was all a dream, that she had in reality taken her swim unmolested that morning and crawled back out of the pool and laid on the rocks for a sound sleep, like a lizard baking in the sun.

What visions she would have to tell her compatriots, then, and the mother seers, too. Visions of the men-creatures and the beasts they keep for food as well as their pets.

And she would tell them about the slave girls, and they would laugh, because no such thing could be possible in reality, that men-beasts could own females and chain them and drive them like dogs, even marking their skins with red-hot irons.

'You there, Vorra,' shouted Montrego. 'Bring Yellow Pelt over here to the iron.'

'With pleasure.' The larger girl collected a wad of her hair for leverage.

Tesra was dragged this way across the deck, her flesh scraping the wood, her pride shattered. 'No, please,' she was crying. 'Don't bring me any closer. I don't want to see anymore. Don't show me the brandings! I cannot bear it!'

Montrego put her to her knees, pulling her wrists tightly behind her back. 'Who said anything about watching, cunt? You're participating. That's right, my little flower, you're getting branded along with the rest of them. Captain's orders.'

Her heart gripped with fear. It couldn't be true.

'And you'll go last.' He pushed her to the back of the line. 'Just to build the suspense for you.'

Tesra swooned at the sight of the glowing hot metal, fixed with the insignia of the pirate code as it kissed the skin of the first victim, the brunette, perfect in body and submissive soul, her body in repose over the branding barrel. Crackling and hissing the metal ate its way into her soft, defenseless bottom cheek, marking it, and her forever. The girl's moans and screams rose high into the air, mingling with the cry of the wind and the sound of shining sunbeams.

Tesra passed out.

But Montrego did not allow her to stay this way. Dousing her with briny, ice-cold seawater, he restored her to a state of enlivened terror. 'The king says you watch it all, cunt.'

Meanwhile a slash of the broad whip brought the moaning, thrashing brunette to her senses. 'Get up, slave, and make room for another.'

Painfully the new slave crawled, her splendid figure and natural sensuality now completely owned by the king and his minions, and she was already being fitted for the iron collar as the blonde was put into place over the branding barrel.

'Isn't there any other way?' she was bargaining. 'I'll have sex with whoever you tell me to - in any position.'

'You'll do that anyway, cunt.' Montrego lashed her limbs into place. 'And this little mark is our insurance.'

'But how,' she wanted to know, 'will I ever find a husband now?'

'I wouldn't concern myself with that.' Montrego pressed the branding iron expertly into place. 'It's masters you'll be having now.'

The blonde's skin hissed under the merciless heat. Just four more girls and then Tesra. And after that, the collar and more degradation. Already the brunette was being had again, while a second pirate was yanking hard on a chain attached to her collar, insuring the maximum depth of his penis in her rectum.

Other men were there, too, drawn like a moth to a flame. One was masturbating over her buttocks, readying himself to spill onto the fresh wound. A second was taking aim at her back, where she'd been whipped.

'Persistrata,' Tesra announced skyward, 'take me now. Bring me to the world beyond death, only spare me this ultimate degradation.'

'Pray to this,' said a pirate, offering his thick member. 'This is the only god a slave need ever know.'

Tesra gulped his seed in a few thrusts, her eyes still glued to the terrible procession. The branding completed, the blonde was now crawling to her collar and ravishment while the redhead was being fitted for arse marking.

Opening her mind, Tesra sought to reach Marcellus, but she sensed nothing. Even the thoughts of these others seemed silent to her now. I am dead, she thought, dead to my powers, dead to my people and dead to my pride.

'Not bad.' He tousled her hair, wiping his dick against her cheek.

'Thank you,' she whispered, hating herself for her servility, 'sir.'

'Next,' called Montrego, as yet another slave came forward - one fewer now between Tesra's quivering skin and the sizzling hot iron.

Chapter 7

'I assume,' Ameliadora watched him bolt the door to his cabin, 'that you will touch me intimately.'

Marcellus took his time, allowing the anticipation to build. 'You are not as naïve as I thought, princess. Can it be you have had experience with matters of the loins?'

'You mean heart,' she corrected. 'In court all affairs twixt male and female are referred to as based in the heart.'

'Indeed,' he brushed her cheek, employing but the one finger. 'We shall reach there soon enough. Tell me, Ameliadora, have you ever been with a man?'

'No, though there are many who have desired to do so.'

'And you discouraged them?'

'I toyed with them, amusing myself at their expense.'

The finger was at her chin, and pushing he arched her neck. 'You would look well in a collar, Ameliadora.'

'And you would look well hanging from a gallows.'

'You are a cold one,' he mused. 'Ivory-white on the outside, but beneath... I wonder.'

'Wonder all you like, you shall never find out,' she challenged.

'Remove the covering from your head,' he told her, 'and release your hair.'

'That was not part of the bargain.'

'I have the right to touch you, where and how I wish. Are you afraid that I will seduce you so easily?'

'I fear nothing,' flashed the eyes of the emperor's daughter, 'and no man.' Haughtily, she undid her elaborate covering, finally allowing long tresses of midnight black to pour down her back. 'There,' said she to him, 'you have what you wish. Can you handle it?'

'You are proud of your hair, I gather.'

She shook out the radiant curls. 'I have one handmaiden whose sole job it is to comb it, for two hours at a time, ten thousand strokes. She must count them and if she misses I beat her with the hairbrush on her bare bottom.'

Marcellus ran his finger over her lips. 'Your handmaids serve a different purpose now.'

Her cheeks reddened, but she did not retreat from his teasing. 'Bring that finger closer and I shall bite it.'

'Animals bite,' observed the pirate king, 'not ladies.'

Ameliadora, having been bested yet again, moved to slap him, but Marcellus grabbed her wrist. 'I am not the animal,' she fought to free herself, 'you are.'

He let her go. 'Disrobe, princess. The time for female chatter is done.'

'No one sees naked the daughter of the emperor.'

'Not even the men you like to tease?'

'When I have proved my virtue to you,' she restrained herself from trying to slap him again, 'you will be very sorry.'

'As you will be yourself if you do not remove your clothing.'

'I do so,' she informed him, working at the fastenings behind her back, 'under duress.'

'Duly noted.'

It took some time to remove all the layers of her elaborate garments, but at last she stood before him, just as the gods had formed her. Truly the princess was beautiful by any standard. If the other thirteen daughters of the emperor were this attractive, he was indeed a wealthy man. How much better she looked now, though, her porcelain-white skin, smooth and bare and vulnerable, her long mane of hair hanging suggestively nearly to her waist.

'You desire me,' Ameliadora said, her smugness more than a little obvious. 'Just as the others do. I am the most beautiful girl at court. Every male wants me, from the stable hands to my father's own councilors and dukes.'

'You are a pretty enough girl,' he acknowledged. 'Then again, so are most of the females chained in my hold. A nice pair of tits and a round arse is less special than you think. I suspect it is your father's money and power that makes you so popular at court.'

'Arrogant pig! Lying thieving pirate! I will see you rot in my father's dungeon, I will—'

Ameliadora, the pretty, conceited little wench went at him with her tiny fists and once again met overwhelming male resistance, and with the king's hand in her hair, holding her fast, she was completely stymied.

'Now it is time,' he told her, 'for the test.'

Ameliadora's eyes conveyed volumes. She seemed not at all certain of the finger as it approached her bowed body, intimately surveying the possibilities for contact - and maybe, too, for abuse.

'Kiss it,' he pushed the finger to her lips. Ameliadora closed her eyes, trembling, but did so, and a moment later she gasped as he touched her nipple. 'Do you play with yourself, princess?'

'No, never.'

He flicked it. 'Is that the truth?'

'Ow,' she wailed. 'All right, it's true, I play with myself.'

Marcellus smiled; quite certain she would never again lie to him. 'And what do you imagine when you are touching yourself?'

His finger slid down her tummy, like fire and ice at once, making her moan and shiver. The girl was a hot one and would give much pleasure to her masters in the future, whoever owned her.

'Please, do not make me...' She attempted to thrash her head, her words dissolving as he began to finger her clitoris.

'You will tell me,' the pirate persisted, scraping his fingernail in such a way as to turn her insides to jelly.

Ameliadora's knees buckled. 'I think of men. Strong men, having their way with me.'

'Be more specific,' he continued working her to a lather, 'which men and what do they do to you that arouses you so?'

'My guards. Those strong soldiers I stand beside each day and who must defend me with their lives,' she said, the confession oozing from her soul like the moisture from her cunt. 'I imagine that things are different, that they are free to do with me as they wish.'

'And what do they wish, do you suppose?'

'I've seen the look in their eyes. They would want to have me, to strip me of my clothes, to use me as a whore. To put me through paces as a bitch, making me spread my legs for them, making me...'

'Say it,' he coaxed the suddenly resistant girl.

'I... I... oh, please, I am going to climax.'

'You will not.' He pulled back. 'Not until I say so. Now answer the question; what do they make you do?'

'I have to... to suck them,' wept the fourteenth daughter of the Talassian emperor. 'On my knees, and when they shoot their seed I must take it in my mouth and swallow it or else they will beat me. With whips or rods.'

'This does not sound like the sort of treatment imposed upon a free woman,' he speculated.

'No, it is not.' She blinked back the tears.

'Nor even that due to a whore who is paid for her services.'

'That is just it; no free woman deserves or wants such things.'

There was horror on her face, but also deep need.

'Perhaps you are another sort of woman.'

Ameliadora resumed her useless struggles, her body still under his complete and utter control. 'No, I am not; I am a princess, of the blood of the royal house of Talassia.'

'Would you like my finger, royal princess,' he asked pleasantly, 'back inside your royal cunt?'

'Yes, oh yes!' Her eyes lit up as she answered without thinking, without gauging the ramifications in their game, a form of human chess, as it were, with her body being the board.

'Beg for it.'

She came to her senses. 'No, I cannot... I will not.'

He released her, allowing her to fall helplessly at his feet. 'Go then; I release you.'

She looked up at him through disheveled hair, her fine make-up ruined, her body flush with the evidence of sexual play. 'What manner of trick is this?'

'None, Princess Ameliadora, I am setting you free. You have resisted me. The bet is won. I shall provide you escort home. Now if you will excuse me, I grow weary.'

She watched in visible disbelief as her imperious captor retired to his bed, reclining upon it, and in a matter of moments, fingers interlaced beneath his head, he was snoring.

As he knew she would she remained in the room, watching him, and eventually she made her approach. 'Are you sleeping?'

He swatted at the voice in his ear like a mosquito.

'Captor,' said she a bit more loudly.

'Why,' he opened one eye, 'are you yet here?'

'I was hoping,' she replied, recovering what dignity she could, 'that we might make love first.'

He shook his head. 'I am not a Talassian noble nor one of your fantasy guards. Go home, princess. You do not belong here.'

The princess' expression softened. 'Please?'

'I do not make love to free women.'

'As a whore, then.'

'I cannot afford your beauty. You said so yourself. Besides, pirates do not pay for what they can take.'

'Then take me,' she shook out her raven curls boldly, 'pirate.'

'If I take you,' he warned, 'you will not be as you are now.'

Ameliadora's hand was at her cunt. She was too far gone; too caught up in what she thought was just another game. What the proud beauty did not know was that the rules were no longer of her own making. 'I do not care,' she breathed, bending to touch him. 'I only want to be fucked. By you.'

He seized her wrist in a grip of iron, denying her the right. 'There is a whip on the wall,' he told her. 'Go and fetch it.'

The girl smiled catlike, her eyes narrow slits of desire. Marcellus did not think she had a clue what was to follow, but she soon would.

'Do you like my arse?' she paraded for him, moving to do his will.

'You will return on all fours,' he replied, 'the whip between your teeth.'

The dark-haired, white-skinned princess obeyed, crawling prettily for him, naturally, the way a female does upon approaching a male to whom she wants to submit. Taking the whip from her mouth he tapped her arse, the one she was so proud of.

'On the bed. Remain on all fours. Facing the wall.'

Marcellus gave her five light stripes, more an aphrodisiac for himself than a genuine introduction to corporal punishment. That would come later for the girl, following her branding. Nevertheless, for a spoiled girl such as she it was a heavy load indeed. Clutching the sheets with her fingernails, sobbing and shaking, she begged him the whole time to stop.

She did not, however, move to rise or defend herself. Again Marcellus found this natural behavior, the female seeking, whether or not she knew it, some proof of the male's power over her, a visible sign that he was both capable and worthy of her domination. The pirate king had never in all his experience seen a girl who was not softened, made wetter and more ready by mild abuse at the hands of her lover. What else was one to make of the female body, after all? The way it yielded so perfectly. Nipples tightening before a man's eyes, begging to be pinched and hurt. The curve of the back, drawing the attention to the arse, that wonderful expanse of unmarked territory that cannot help but give a man ideas. And her limbs, more slender than his, so easily fitted for cuffs, and the graceful throat round which he yearns to lock his collar and affix his leash.

Such a pretty bouncing thing she is, breasts in his face, intelligent eyes, laughing mouth, skin sweet smelling. Like a rabbit to be hunted. A fleece to be had. The man is her hunter, and she his prey. But it is not her death he desires, the flesh from her bones, but only her subjugation, her domestication, that he might coral her like any other animal. And she, for her part, must accept whatever comes, for it is not only her lot but also her desire. No woman can respect a man if he is not strong with her, if he gives her own way instead of stamping his own upon her. Of this power, too, she needs signs.

Drusia was never hotter than after a night chained in the punishment hole, never more ardent than after being forced to submit to the male slaves or to take upon her flesh an undeserved beating. This is how it was between them and why it would never change. Freedom, Drusia had told him once, was unbecoming a woman, as well as frustrating and confusing for males. Perhaps she was right. Which was why he had given the order for Tesra - Yellow Pelt - to be branded. That she might know the peace of slavery, and he himself might no longer be tormented by his conflicting feelings for her. Besides, as his property it would be more clearly understood now that her visions belonged to him so that when it was time to use in the search for more treasure - and that time would come sooner rather than later - there would be no lingering doubts as to whom those powers belonged.

Besides, a woman looked better branded. It was a pleasant sight, and good to the touch. Often while penetrating her he would run his hand over Drusia's brand, pressing his thumb into her hot flesh, reminding them both of her perpetual sexual captivity. The orgasms were good this way. Very good.

'No man has been here,' said Ameliadora, panting, feeling him at the doorway to her virgin lips. 'It is a gift I give to you, my pirate.'

'No,' Marcellus thrust himself to the hilt, showing no mercy, 'it is a pleasure I take.'

The spasms hit her almost at once, the cruelty of his words seeming to arouse her as much as the feeling of his cock in her wet, virgin hole. Though he did not lose control Marcellus felt something of the heat of the moment, finding release from the tension of battle in the princess' warm depths. She was a more than adequate vessel, as well as a willing proxy as he continued to wrestle with this troubling matter of Tesra.

Was he doing right in marking her a slave? Might this traumatize her all over again? And why had he opted for such a draconian move when only yesterday he was fawning on her, nursing her back to health?

'Submit,' demanded the pirate king, forcing the sweat-soaked head of the woman down into the sheet.

'I submit,' came the reply. 'I am yours.'

'Your slave,' he completed for her.

Ameliadora tensed, as if to fight, but there was no serious resistance left. They both knew where this would end, for it was what they both had wanted all along. 'I am your slave,' she moaned, the largest orgasm yet overtaking her.

Marcellus emptied himself into her womb, thinking as he did of his grandfather and how that infernally lucky young pirate had once had his way with the maidens on the Isle of Dreams, coming at will into their bound bodies, possessing them again and again till each was found to be with child. How many daughters did the man count for himself this way? And how many granddaughters? And what of the other pirates who'd found their way to the island to be pressed into this rather unusual service? Did any of them remember their bliss? If so, they would have ached in their hearts and never again been satisfied with life, just as was the case with his grandfather.

For it seemed that sadness followed a man's visit to the place, and that any who touched its shores inevitably suffered melancholy afterwards. Himself included.

Marcellus was on his back now, contemplating. The freshly conquered slave was crawling onto his lap, licking his thigh, trying to interest him in having another go.

'Leave me,' he brushed her away, though in truth the delicious girl could arouse him again in short order. 'I am no longer in the mood.'

'Sir?' She looked at him quizzically.

'Are you deaf? I said to go away.'

'B-but where?' she asked in a small voice, the vista of her future opening for her quite suddenly and uncertainly.

'You might find Montrego for starters,' he shrugged, 'and have him brand you. After that you can cool your heels in the slave hold.'

The girl's blood drained from her face.

'Must I repeat an order, slave? Was the one whipping not sufficient?'

Ameliadora looked as though she might faint. 'It was, sir, but please, how can I... how can I face them?'

'Face who, girl?'

'My handmaidens.' She shuddered. 'They shall see me like this, no better than they.'

'And are you better than them, slut?'

She swallowed hard. 'No, sir.'

'Then I suggest you go and begin your new life among your fellow slaves, thankful that you have been given this chance to live.'

'Yes,' she said weakly. 'Thank you, sir.'

Marcellus watched the departing arse, less haughty in its undulation than before, though twice as delicious for being marked and possessed. He could only imagine the revenge that would be meted on it, too, by her former servants once they got the princess in their grip in the slave hold below.

Was Tesra down there by now? Or was she yet being used, as was the custom following a girl's branding. He should not care, but he did. Rising sulkily from the bed he retrieved the bottle of rum, taking a healthy gulp. After this followed another, and then another. By the third the room was spinning.

Strange, he thought, that the liquor should affect him so quickly. He must be more tired than he realized, or else he was growing old like his father and grandfather. Intending to sit in the chair he leaned forward, only to fall headlong to the floor, the bottle crashing beside him with a splash of dark brown liquid. It was like the vision, plunging back to earth, only now it was real.

Knowing himself to be poisoned, using his last conscious breath, the pirate king called out her name. It was her life he feared for the most. Having brought her here, into such danger, he would not now abandon her to his enemies.

'Forgive me,' he whispered, his voice cracked and fading, 'my nymph of many names.'

Never had a female come so close to the iron and escaped. Her tummy already pushed down on the barrel, Tesra could feel the heat of it, burning her even through the intervening air. A matter of inches, a few seconds more and her world would be fire and terror and burnt flesh.

But it was Rodrigo who intervened, much to the surprise of everyone, the blonde nymph most of all.

'There is a change of plans,' said the king's second. 'The yellow-haired slut does not kiss the iron this day.'

'On whose authority?' demanded Montrego.

Tesra heard the smooth, clean sound of metal sliding on metal, a blade withdrawn from a scabbard.

'The authority of steel,' said Rodrigo, the threat backed by the drawing of other blades, many, sharp and vicious.

'You defy the will of the king,' the outnumbered Montrego observed, though he had backed away, giving clear indication he was willing to negotiate.

Rodrigo hauled Tesra to her feet. 'Perhaps,' he concurred. 'Then again, it may be that I am merely concerned to see, before it is too late, if the king has changed his mind on this matter.'

'He has been behaving strangely of late,' Montrego agreed, accepting the subtle invitation to resolve the matter without bloodshed. 'It would be wise to confirm the matter with him.'

'The king is sleeping heavily,' said Rodrigo, his words seeming to carry some meaning Tesra did not comprehend. 'He may well sleep till morning.'

'I see.' Montrego nodded significantly. 'Perhaps you should settle the matter with him... in the morning. Keeping the girl of course, in the mean time.'

Rodrigo was already slapping her in irons, hands behind her back. 'I had not thought of that, Montrego,' he said, though clearly he had. 'I accept your suggestion.'

'What is going on?' demanded Tesra, her relief at not being branded suddenly overcome by her rising alarm over the safety of the king. 'I demand to know. Where is Marcellus?'

Rodrigo wasted no words. Grabbing her by the throat he squeezed, just hard enough for her to see how easily he could choke the life out of her. 'Listen to me carefully, bitch, and we will get along just fine. I happen to have need of your body right now, but not your tongue. If it wags again I will cut it out. Got it?'

Tesra, on tiptoes and gasping for air, was not at liberty to give much response. But apparently her desperate gurgles were sufficient as he released her back down to her heels.

'Do not I think I spared you the branding out of any sort of mercy or pity,' said the hawkeyed, shaven-headed pirate, attaching the leather collar rudely to her neck. 'It is simply that I must have you clear-headed tonight. By morning, I assure you, it will be a different story.'

Rodrigo was tightening it too much, but Tesra dared not tell him. However slim her life chances were now, and they seemed slim indeed, they lay in the hands of this man, the cruel lieutenant of her pirate king.

'Tonight, my precious cunt,' he attached the leash and stroked her cheek in mock affection, 'we shall make sweet love together, like you and Marcellus under the moonlight. How do I love thee,' he slapped her breasts, one after the other with vicious swats. 'Let me count the ways.

'Behold,' he called dramatically to the crew, those few still congregated on the deck, variously engaged in wenching, rumming and treasure barrel diving, 'I am your king; and this is my mermaid queen.'

There were peels of laughter, raucous and very male, the hostility, danger and treason thick in their voices as they egged on the sarcastic Rodrigo.

'Oh, witch queen,' Rodrigo knelt before the chained, leashed wench as though she were a goddess, 'pray tell, where am I to find treasure upon the high seas? Tell me. What is it you say? I must ask your magic muff? Very well, then.'

The pirates were egging him on, enjoying richly this lampooning of their king, the mercurial, of late oddly fixated Marcellus.

Tesra bit hard on her lip. He was actually doing it, pretending to speak into her yellow tuft, his tongue dipping teasingly between her thighs. At first glance it might seem a submissive posture for the man, but there was no mistaking his confidence, his power. Even in this position, Tesra was his victim.

'Ahoy, mateys!' he exclaimed with great relish, having engaged in a brief and hilarious conversation rendering Tesra weak and desperate with desire. 'The muff speaks to me. It tells me where to look! Honor the muff, oh my brothers, worship it!'

Tesra fell forward against him as he left her on the brink of orgasm.

'Listen up, you swags,' he lifted her, flinging her over his back. 'Listen to the magic muff that has dragged us halfway across the deep.'

The crew was closing in.

'The muff,' Rodrigo kept on saying, spinning her about so as to display her backside and sex. 'Pay it homage, let it rule your life!'

'Honor this!' a man smacked her hard with the flat of his hand.

'And this!' cried another.

Tesra's elevated buttocks were greeted by a hail of spanks. The feeling was sweetly painful, the touch of skin on skin proving deliciously erotic, all the more so for the very real pain she was enduring.

'That's it, lads. Show the slut what we think of her wrapping the king round her clit! Show him how we deal with cunts that talk and give orders.'

The worst part of her ordeal, as he spun her about, lifting and lowering her like a toy, was that she dared not scream out under the assault. A man like Rodrigo would not hesitate to slice off her tongue or any other part of her that interfered with his purposes.

'Enough,' he said at last. 'It is time I took the sea slut and taught her some manners.'

'Three cheers for Rodrigo, our next king!' called a man, sounding like a plant.

There was some hesitation; the laughter subsided, there was now the more sober question as to Marcellus' whereabouts and how he might respond to this little escapade.

'Three cheers,' the man repeated, as men strategically placed on the deck drew swords, and the pirates responded warily.

Tesra fought back blind panic. Was Marcellus truly dead? Could there be any other meaning?

Rodrigo was not gentle with her. Tossing her into the rowboat he seemed oblivious to the integrity of her person. Fortunately she landed on her bottom, her chained hands helping to steady her.

Jumping in after her he pushed off from Marcellus' ship with one of his powerful legs. They were bound for his own ship, named appropriately, *Dark Mayhem*. Slave girls lived in terror of this vessel, for it was said there was no mercy for females there.

Indeed, as he lifted her onto the deck she could sense the oppression, palpable in the air. Two chained girls, heavily weighted in irons, their bodies covered in slash-like scars and wounds, knelt scrubbing the wood with primitive brushes. The bucket was filthy with black water, as was their skin. Upon seeing their master both girls fell to their bellies in obeisance. They remained so as he passed, Tesra's hair clumped in his hands, her body stooped beside him.

She tried to keep up, but it was difficult with her bound hands. When she finally fell he twisted her to her back and dragged her along on her buttocks. From the main mast a third girl watched, her body wrapped in chain, attached to the wood from ankle to throat. There was no telling how long she had been there. Tesra noted the sign, *I am a willful cunt.* Her body was not so willful now, it seemed.

A fourth girl was literally hanging upside down by her ankles over the deck. Tresses of long dark hair swayed in the twilight breeze. Her hands an inch from the deck, she too bore an inscription, inked onto her belly. *I am a proud slave.*

Rodrigo's cabin, just below the ship's wheel, was already occupied.

'That will be all, Vanya,' said the man to the female busily licking the floor.

Tesra regarded her with fascinated horror. She'd been scrubbing the entire filthy surface with her tongue, dipping it over and over in a bucket of water. Moreover, she was completely shaved, her head shorn of all hair.

Vanya did not rise her to feet; pausing to kiss the master's boot - and to sniff at Tesra - she shuffled from the captain's quarters, no questions asked. It was only when Tesra saw the hindquarters that she noticed the protruding tail, a finely brushed mop attached to an anal plug.

'I am not going to beat around the bush,' said Rodrigo to Tesra when the miserable creature had closed the door behind her with her nose. 'I have arranged this little meeting tonight to try your powers for myself. I'm quite sure it will all prove a hoax, but I've never been a man to take anyone else's word on anything - least of all something that might make me rich.'

Looking at him piteously, she awaited permission to speak.

'You will tell me how he does it,' Rodrigo continued. 'How he gets in your mind or whatever other nonsense is supposedly involved.'

'If you don't even believe in it,' said Tesra, finding herself unable to resist speaking out of turn now, in spite of all his threats. 'How will you know it when you see it?'

'That's a very good question,' he agreed. 'And the answer is quite simple. I shall take your testimony. And as is the case with any slave, I shall do so by means of torture.'

'T-torture?'

'Y-yes,' Rodrigo mimicked. 'N-now go and stand by that m-machine.'

Tesra did so, filling with wicked dread at the sight of it. In shape it was a vertical wedge, the apex of it fitted with a cylindrical shaft, the size of a very large man or a small elephant.

'Get on it,' he commanded, indicating in particular the simulated penis.

'I will not fit,' she protested.

'Then you had best lubricate yourself and pray you stretch,' he undid the shackles, freeing her hands, 'because at the count of five I shall rain down leather upon you like the vengeance of the war god.'

One look at the uncoiled whip was enough. Horrid as it might be to endure penetration by a stick of wood, she could not tolerate another hard punishment, no matter how much she might deserve it.

'I'll do it,' she said, seeing that he was already fixing to use the thing on her. 'Please, don't beat me.'

Tesra mounted the saddle-like wedge, lining the tip of the well-worn shaft up with her swollen nether lips. The thing was so massive, and she was so tender as of yet from her experience with Vorra and Drusia. But the whip proved excellent incentive. One bite of its lightning quick tongue and she was down on it, violated, brutally stuffed.

'Marcellus has been most negligent in your training,' observed the man, turning an ominous looking crank at the far side of the device. 'You are a lax and lazy slut, a dishonor to your master.'

'I am not his slave,' she said, most foolishly risking his further fury. 'I am his free captive.'

'A free captive?' He laughed. 'Now there is an absurdity typical of the mind of a mere female.'

Rodrigo activated the primitive mechanism, now fully wound, and at once the shaft began to move up and down, slowly and cunningly.

'The rules are simple,' the pirate explained as the machine commenced pummeling her. 'If you move your arse, or lift it in any way to avoid the shaft, you receive a lash. In the meantime you will answer my questions.'

The wooden cock felt good inside Tesra, very good. It knew all her secret places and its shape was perfect. And yet it wasn't quite fast enough, nor was it quite as vigorous as it could have been. The urge to move against it, to rub herself, was growing; but this would mean displacing her bottom.

'You seem a little too comfortable,' he observed, and made the shaft rise higher. She would have to take more of it, and deeper. It was too much. She wanted to lift herself to find relief, just for a second. But then it went down again, leaving her empty. A second later it was back up, moving in and out. She moaned. It was too confusing. She couldn't sit still.

The whip sliced at her back in merciless slow motion, a leather demon opening her, bearing her soul. Down she went again, onto the false penis. But already it wanted her to move and play. She needed to fuck it; her cunt demanded it. If she could raise herself, just for a second, it would be all right.

'Who are you, really?' he demanded, unleashing the leather snake a second time.

'I am Tesra,' she wailed. 'Born of Persistrata, the goddess of the Isle of Dreams.'

'Lying cunt!'

The shaft was attacking her. She could not hold out.

'Sir, please, let me lift my hips, if only for a moment.'

He lashed at her like an animal. 'You are a witch,' he accused. 'You suck the life from a man's penis. You cast spells, like you did on Marcellus. Before he met you he was a man - you made him a slave.'

'I have done nothing.' She arched her back, squeezing the muscles of her vagina in an effort to regulate the flood of sensations, the pour of liquid over the wedge.

'You can't see the future,' he told her. 'All you know is how to obey simple commands. Stay. Sit. Suck. You're like any other bitch, aren't you?'

'Sir... I... no, I mean, yes.' Tesra writhed, trancelike, nearly dislodging herself entirely from the juice-soaked seat. In the time it took her to resume her position of cunt-filled subjugation she'd earned two fresh stripes, one each across her heaving breasts. She had wanted to protect them with her hands, but she needed those to keep herself upright on the cunningly created intercourse machine.

'You cunts go just as crazy for this contraption as you do a man,' he declared disparagingly. 'Only goes to prove you are animals, capable of no free thought, no refinement.'

'Yes... please... I'll do what you say, anything, just let me go.' Tesra was climaxing on the shaft, wet and helpless, a mass of surrendered need.

'How did you find him the treasure fleet? Tell me!' Rodrigo whipped her full on the thigh, even as she bucked uncontrollably and the words came from deep in her throat, a low groan.

'He touched me... he put his hands on my head... he was in me, and on me... I let him... do it...'

Tesra sucked at the air, her lungs starved, her breasts rising as she inhaled. Like a woman demon possessed she grabbed them, holding them like Marcellus would if he were here. Blessed Persistrata let him not be dead.

Abruptly the shaft stopped its motions.

'Since everything that comes out of your mouth is nonsense, you don't need to speak,' Rodrigo decided, holding up the leather gag with the built in shaft, a much smaller version of the one she was currently sitting on.

Tesra opened obediently, taking the foul-tasting object into her mouth. It was designed both to silence and humiliate a woman, for at the same time she was rendered mute she was also forced to suckle the artificial penis, the drool from her actions meandering down to her throat and breasts.

'Now,' he lifted her unceremoniously by the hips, 'it's time to see if you've been lying to me. And I truly hope you have not, because I have far, far better means of torture at my disposal. Trust me, sea witch, compared to my slave hold, that of Marcellus is a royal boudoir.'

Tesra clawed at the wedge, her cunt muscles clutching. She did not wish to leave the shaft now, for it had claimed her and it was making her hornier and hornier, like an alley cat wanting to rub and fuck and fuck some more. Tesra, beyond all manner of degradation, endured the sting of his laughter as he put her on the floor on her back.

'If only Marcellus could see his little prize now. You'll excuse me if I don't use the bed. Personally, I believe slaves should be used on the floor or in the dirt at all times. Keeps them humble, don't you think?'

Tesra pleaded with her eyes. Let him do what he wished to her, but if it was not too late, let him spare the pirate king.

'This is what Marcellus should have done from the beginning.' He opened his breeches to reveal a stubby, thick-veined organ. 'Open your legs, wide.' He kicked the thighs of the gagged girl. 'This,' he said, descending to claim her in one swift and imperious motion, 'is what separates a man from a woman. A man abused will rise to anger, prepared to fight. A woman will oil herself for capitulation.'

He was referring to the slick canal that received him to the hilt. Tesra fought the roiling spasms induced as he settled himself. If she did not control herself she would orgasm for the pig at any moment.

'Lock your ankles behind me,' he commanded. 'You will be holding back nothing this night.' Tesra did as she was told. His arse was hard beneath her heels and as she pressed his buttocks he gave her an extra deep thrust, enough to induce whimpers from her imprisoned mouth. 'Look at me, cunt.' Tesra did not want to open her eyes, did not want to regard this man for whom she was a mere object of contempt, a rude little animal in need of his brutal training. But she was his captive now, in every sense of the word, and when he dug his fingers into her defenseless breasts she knew she must obey lest he go on hurting and hurting her. Regarding him she felt instantly violated, in a way no mere physical penetration could manage.

'You are nothing special to me,' said he, as if this were some surprise. 'I have beat down women twice as strong and clever as you. Any tricks, any attempt to play with my mind when we connect and I will smash you like an insect. Nod if you comprehend.'

Tesra was losing herself already in those eyes, narrow and depthless, unspeakably cruel. Agreeing to her own mental ravishment she gave him the affirmation he needed.

'See?' he sneered. 'What took your pirate king days to accomplish I did in an hour. You are mine now, little bitch, as simple as that.'

The smile was pure gloat, undisguised malevolent glee. How much the man must hate Marcellus, she thought. How jealous he must be of the more handsome, stronger and more able king, to whom everything came so easily - women, power, treasure. No wonder he couldn't bear the thought of Marcellus having his own personal genie, to grant wishes and find him wealth untold. Truly this man would stop at nothing to destroy the king, and she feared in fact that he might already have done so.

'Hearing no objections,' he relayed, obviously enjoying his own bad joke, 'let's begin this little mind meeting, shall we?' He spit into both his hands before pressing them to the sides of her head. Unlike Marcellus there was no finesse, no real passion in his touch. Only a cold grappling for power, the muscles in his fingers calculating just how hard to clench, restraining themselves, but just barely, from busting open her skull like a ripe melon. Right away she could feel his rude attempt to batter at the lining of her mind. If she did not let him in he might well destroy them both, blowing their brains to pieces. But if she did let him in, then she would be at his mercy, as much inside as out.

In the end Tesra had no choice, for he was also using his cock on her as well, turning her physical body to mush. Finding herself in a white room, in a long white gown, she awaited him, her eyes fixed on the open door. It was a vision place, a place of her inner life. Rodrigo's boots tromped down the hall, closing perilously. She could feel wetness between her thighs in anticipation. Bracing herself, she stood for him.

He entered dressed all in black, boots and silk shirt, vest and pants. The sword at his belt gleamed like polished silver. His gloves were fine calfskin, reaching nearly to his elbows. Without hesitation he marched up to her, struck her across the face and knocked her to his feet.

'Get up,' he said coldly.

Barefoot in her sheer gown, wounded and degraded, she rose shakily to her knees.

'All the way,' said he, his cold voice echoing off the walls of the bare, windowless room.

Tesra stood and he hit her again, harder.

'Get up,' he repeated. This time she required help, but as soon as he had restored her teetering onto her feet, he knocked her down once more.

This time, when he merely unfastened the black pants, she was grateful, and moving to her knees she took him deep.

Rodrigo's hands went to her head, in the dream just as they had in reality. Tesra made no never mind as he played with her hair, patting and stroking. She kept on sucking, knowing this was where she belonged, that before such a man as this she could never stand as equal. A pang of sadness passed through her as she thought how Marcellus had taught her something similar.

'Concentrate, bitch.' Rodrigo's voice came to her as a loud boom, an echo, internally and externally. Eyes within eyes she shut herself, spreading the wings of vision. She was the bird again, soaring, bridled, the man on her back. But unlike with Marcellus she was not in daylight, not in open air.

By the gods she should have anticipated this! Rodrigo's mind was too filled with hate to sustain the ethereal air of the heavens. They were plummeting straight down into darkness, to the infernal pit of dragons.

'Let go,' she cried out to him, mind to mind. 'You are going to kill us both.'

'A vision,' he gasped madly. 'I will not release you till you give me a vision.'

Her wings were tearing. The air was heating as they spiraled down, down to the edge of a vortex from which nothing could escape, neither divine nor mortal.

'A vision of what?' she cried. 'You are rich. What more do you want?'

'The future,' he demanded, his voice thick and hot with greed, his eyes blind with the stupidity of a wounded animal. 'Mine. And his.'

He meant the pirate king. So Marcellus was alive after all. Could she reach him somehow, even from here? Could he help her escape, physically or mentally?

'Obey me, bitch!' Rodrigo was shouting, his voice as shrill and ultimately powerless as was his petty and undisciplined mind. 'Show me the future!'

The future. That which no man should see. The veil. The Wall. He wanted to cross it, just as Marcellus had. Only his way was straight down to hell. Praying she would be able to pull back in time, she braced herself.

'Yes!' cried Rodrigo. 'By the gods,' he dug his spurs into her side, 'yes!'

There were explosions around them and the blooming of fires. All manner of strange creatures copulating and devouring one another in the air, while in the midst of this claws rose, seeking to rip them to shreds.

She thought they were dead, but at the last possible second Tesra kissed the sky, and they were allowed to swoop free of the tornadic winds of the underworld. But not before they saw something that was perhaps worse than hell.

'You will speak of this to no one.' Rodrigo released her afterwards from the leather gag. 'As you have no doubt guessed, Marcellus is not dead. I merely drugged his rum. But next time, if you even hint of what took place between us, I shall kill him outright.'

'Yes,' said Tesra, numb and bruised, 'I understand.'

It hurt her jaw to say the words, and also her heart. She was going to have to betray her love to save him.

Her love.

Is that what he was to her? How had he leaped to that category from that of captor? Had Rodrigo's venom been so severe as to inspire in her sympathy for the arrogant, domineering, wild-eyed king of pirates?

'Events will transpire tomorrow,' he continued, much hidden behind his dark eyes. 'Contradict me in nothing, accept everything, and you and he both shall live.'

'But,' spoke Tesra out of turn, 'if I am not allowed to warn him, then who will?'

'The job is mine. I am his second.'

Tesra's heart pounded in her chest. She was still reeling from what they had envisioned, and it did not take a seer to see that Rodrigo intended to use this information, concerning not his own fate, but that of Marcellus himself.

'I must warn him,' she defied, attempting to brush past. 'I cannot let him die.'

Rodrigo struck her across the back of the head with the hilt of his sword. 'And I,' said he with cold calculation, 'cannot let you live.'

Chapter 8

Marcellus awoke feeling as though there were hundred pound rocks pressing upon his skull, a quarry full, dumped on top of him in his sleep. Rolling to one side of his bed he saw the rum-stained floor and remembered. 'Rodrigo!' he cried, calling for his second.

'I am here!' The man dashed into the room, having been quite close at hand. 'Thank the gods you have survived. We thought you might not.'

The pirate king brushed away the slave girl's attempting to mop his brow with a damp cloth. 'I want the man or men responsible.' He sat up, gritting his teeth against the whirling pain in his skull. 'It was an attempt on my life, that much is clear.' By the beard of Nephisis, he'd never had such a hangover in his life.

'Pardon, excellency,' bowed his underling, second among the captains and his comrade-in-arms for nearly eight seasons, 'but it was no man attempted to poison you.'

'Not a man?' he scoffed. 'What then do you suggest? A ghost? A demon rose from the deep? Really, Rodrigo, I am as pious as the next man, but when it comes to matters of life and death I must trust in what I see with my own eyes, not some ancient sea tales.'

'Then trust this.' Rodrigo snapped his fingers dramatically, gesturing to the silent pirate beside him, a member of his own crew. He nodded and left, returning a few minutes later with the nymph.

Tesra was led in by two guards. Her mouth was gagged, she was chained and she bore the evidence of a whipping, quite recent from the redness of the welts decorating her breasts, thighs and buttocks.

The pirate king tensed at once. 'What is the meaning of this, Rodrigo?'

'We have already apprehended the would-be assassin, sir, and as I said, it is not a man.' Rodrigo pulled her forward. 'Behold the proof.'

Marcellus, his own hand cold and bloodless, examined that of the blonde nymph. Under the fingernails he could see the residue, quite plainly. A white powder, of the sort used in death potions. Almost as an afterthought he noted her as yet unmarked buttock. 'I ordered her branded. Why was this not done?'

'Therein lies further evidence of her treachery, majesty. It seems she was in cahoots with Montrego. He managed to hide her from the iron in the general melee, intent on saving her as his own bride. It was he who helped her poison your rum using powder easily concealed in any number of her orifices.

Marcellus pondered these things. Truly it was a bit overwhelming to think such things so early in the day, especially with his head splitting open as it was. 'Fetch Montrego,' he instructed. 'I must hear his side of the story.'

'Alas, that is not possible, majesty. It seems, in attempting to escape, the man was consumed by sharks.'

How convenient.

'Tesra,' said the king to the prisoner, 'look me in the eye. Are Rodrigo's words true? Did you attempt to kill me?'

'Yes,' she replied without hesitation. 'I did.'

He regarded her, the dispassionate eyes, the luxuriant body he had helped her to understand and appreciate. He'd taught her many things. Could murder be one of them?

'Do you know what is done to assassins - even unsuccessful ones?'

'No, but I assume their fate is not pleasant,' she said mechanically.

'That would be an understatement.'

'Sir,' Rodrigo interjected, sounding far too obsequious for Marcellus' comfort, 'there is more. The girl tried to seduce me as well. She wished to use me as a vessel, through which to dispel her visions.'

'I do not intend to execute her.' He forestalled anymore arguments from Rodrigo along this line. 'A king who has such fear of a mere female that he cannot master her except in death is no king at all. I sentence her to the hangman's daughter. See to it that the arrangements are made.'

Rodrigo pursed his lips, the fury simmering just below the surface. Soon, all too soon, Marcellus reasoned, he must face this man, hand to hand. In the meantime he must think. And prepare.

'Yellow Pelt,' he said to the condemned woman. 'I have ordered you to face the ordeal of the hangman's daughter. Are you aware of such a sentence?'

'No, sir.'

'It is, essentially, a punishment at the hands of my crew, your body bound on a special device and muchly scourged.'

'I see,' she replied thinly.

'The hangman's daughter is essentially a rack,' he continued, studying her facial expressions, or lack thereof. 'Adjustable, from which a prisoner may be stretched or otherwise positioned for abuse. The condemned approaches it on hands and knees, passing the feet of a dozen or more men, each of whom, in turn, will have the opportunity to whip and fuck her for as long as they wish.'

Marcellus waited for a reaction. Hearing and seeing none, he continued.

'As for the name, itself it is a very old piece of pirate lore, supposedly referring to an incident in which a comely wench, the daughter of a hangman, allowed herself to be seduced by a condemned pirate, eventually helping him get free of the dungeon in which he was being held by the captain.

'In true pirate fashion, the stalwart buccaneer betrayed his rescuer. Having enjoyed the fruits of his prize, he left her bound and naked on the stone floor, the evidence of his having of her written all over her face, quite literally. He had tricked her all along, of course, for she had been promised an honorable marriage and much gold.

'Finding his come-soaked, despoiled daughter hogtied on her belly, the father was furious. Devising what he felt to be a suitable punishment for the randy girl, he had her strung up on a rack where she was soundly whipped and then had by his men, each in turn. Afterwards, humiliated and fully broken, she was made to crawl from man to man, a full line of them, that she might beg one to accept her as his slave. Blubbering, she kissed the feet of each, desperate for a master lest her father kill her outright. None would take her and in the end it was the hangman himself who plunged the blade into her chest.'

Tesra looked as though she might faint if not supported by the two guards.

'Having heard all this, do you wish to appeal the sentence?'

'No,' she whispered, all spark gone from her, along with the fight he had come to love so well, 'I do not.'

Who was she protecting? Surely she was not in league with Rodrigo. Who else, then? Her wretched goddess?

Marcellus regarded the rising and falling of her chest, the visible buds of her nipples. The little slut was aroused, just like any common slave anticipating her ordeal. Was the matter so simple after all? Was she really just one more female born to suffer at his hands?

'Prepare her,' he said to the guards, feeling somehow cheated. 'We shall carry out the sentence at once.'

Tesra knew she should not be aroused by what was to come, and yet clearly she was; her thighs slick and wet as she crawled catlike across the deck of Marcellus' ship.

With each step it only grew worse, for with every pair of pirate feet, with every new set of boots, there was represented in her mind one more rock hard penis to fill her helpless sex, one more pair of hands to maul her flesh, to wield a whip on her bare skin.

By the time Tesra reached the hangman's daughter she could hardly hold herself up. What she wanted more than anything was to collapse on her front and have someone pick her up. But a quick slash of the short stiff whip to her exposed bottom reminded her she must get up and put herself in place.

The cuffs were snug leather, set far apart, one each for her wrists and ankles. Another strap ran around her waist, securing her to the center of the wooden frame. At first she did not see the reason for this last accessory, but as the rack began to lift off the deck she saw it was to keep her steady. With her arms and legs spread-eagled like this Tesra was totally helpless and vulnerable, and the feeling only added to her sexual arousal.

'The sentence of hangman's daughter has been imposed,' called a thin, dark-bearded pirate, apparently having taken Montrego's place. 'Think ye it just?'

'Aye,' called the hoary lot, as if they might say otherwise.

'What say the prisoner?' he said now, speaking words belonging to some ritual or other. 'Be it just according to she?'

Was Tesra supposed to speak on her own behalf? If so, they would be sorely disappointed, for she had been sworn - nay bullied and blackmailed - to muteness on this and many other topics regarding recent events onboard ship. Much as she hated to put herself in this position, she could not allow Rodrigo to harm Marcellus and if her torture and her silence could save him, then so be it. She could only hope the man would honor his end of the bargain, as she was about to honor hers.

The first man delivered a few quick flogs with the cat o' nine tails, then announced his intention to penetrate her. Tesra assumed he would have to take her standing from behind, but as it turned out the rack was collapsible, pivoting on points midway up the side of the frame. Thus could she bend to any angle, above or below the horizontal.

Choosing a position of maximum openness, the pirate let Tesra's bottom hang higher than her head, and stepping between her swinging legs, he grabbed them for support then pushed himself inside her. 'By the salty sea,' he growled, 'I've been waiting to do this for a long time.'

Jackknifed as she was there was little for Tesra to do but hang there, her hair sweeping the soggy deck, waiting for the man to finish with her. She felt nothing but frustration as he climaxed, for while she was more than ready he had taken no interest whatsoever in reciprocation.

It was the same with the second man, who beat the soles of her feet with a thin wooden rod of some kind and then went round front for her mouth. Setting the height of her face exactly at the level of his crotch, with her body at the horizontal, he greedily stuffed himself between her lips, using her mouth more or less as one would use a vagina.

'Mmm!' he exclaimed, handling her ears to keep her on task. 'That's it, you little bitch, drink it down.'

Tesra choked on the creamy load, and when a bit of it dribbled down her chin afterward he made her lick it along with the entirely of his cock, and his balls.

The next man didn't even wait for the first to dismiss himself. Taking advantage of the well whipped, upwardly sloping curve, he made for Tesra's rear hole, which at this point was still virgin.

She protested and received five sharp blows from the stinging, razor-thin riding crop, the one she was growing to dread most. Tesra had no idea who was hitting her, whether it was the man who wanted her bottom or another. In any event, she was made to beg for the very thing she had just squealed over. 'Please,' she pleaded huskily, the unbidden words in her mouth tasting like an invader's penis, 'use my arse.'

'Fuck me hard,' elaborated the new man, the words obviously to be repeated by her. 'Use my tight, unworthy arsehole.'

Tesra said all that, flush and spasming over the new depths they were pushing her to, and the pirate obliged, breaching her without benefit of either anal foreplay or lubrication.

'Oh...' she groaned, 'this can't be happening. This can't be—'

Tesra blinked and a fresh penis was staring her in the face, demanding entry. The last man had finished himself off and was already replaced. She took it to the hilt, whereupon she found herself partaking in the novelty of double penetration, a male dominating her in front and back both. Now if only someone were attending to her loins, left forgotten and burning. Was it appropriate to plead to be fucked on the hangman's daughter? Was it allowable to cry out, either in pleasure or pain?

And which was she feeling? The physical sensation aside, there was the great weight on her heart, the burden she now carried, worrying about Marcellus but also seeking, as always, to be free. Might it be in her interest to seek alliance with any of the captured Talassians? Would she fare better under their administration? Given the native cruelty of the now tamed Ameliadora, she doubted it. Then again, could anything be worse than what she was living now? Better, perhaps, an honest slave in Talassia, a brand on her thigh, than her current existence, neither slave nor free, here nor there.

The arse man finished, yielding to another.

'The bitch is hot as a forge!' declared a showman type, plumbing her with his fingers. He had the pirates chanting as he teased her opening with his uncircumcised head. 'Shall I?' he called.

'You have our blessing,' cried a bald man with an eye patch, and the others laughed.

Oh yes, by the goddess, she thought, do it please.

'Do you think the slut wants it bad enough?'

'Do it,' she moaned out loud, 'fuck me, sir, please.'

He sank his erection into her. 'Oh I will, bitch,' he grunted, 'don't you worry.'

'Here,' someone handed him a whip, 'flog her at the same time.'

The crowd pleaser whipped her in time to his pelvic thrusts, the long cords biting into her flesh in exact duplication of the pummeling of her sex. Tesra was out of her mind, wanting to take them all on, coming and coming and coming. On and on it went, the crowd pleaser milking his turn for all it was worth. Sweat dripped and trickled over her fevered flesh. Tesra's new orgasm was like a creature all its own, with claws digging at her back. Eyes sealed tightly shut she retreated, or rather imploded, to the interior worlds Marcellus had helped her to open up. Could she soar even now, she wondered, on her own, in the midst of all this, her breasts weighed by gravity, nipples burning to be plucked and squeezed, perspiration seeping, wounds gaping, men coming, one upon another?

By the goddess, they were switching again. A new man for her cunt and another for her arse. But not before she was briefly put upright, to be whipped, fore and aft, breasts and buttocks. Then came two more. And two more after that.

Tesra's dark world flashed into light. Oh, goddess, there it was again, the terrible vision. Marcellus being struck down by a mighty hand, metal gloved, the spiked fingers themselves the size of a man, and on the back of the hand the stylized eagle, a world in its talons and sprigs of laurel.

The insignia of Talassia.

This is what she and Rodrigo had seen - or rather, foreseen. The death of the pirate king at the hands of the emperor himself - he who in the Talassian language was called the dragar.

'Oh, goddess,' she cried in unspoken voice as yet another man exploded down her throat, a second following suit in her womb, 'let it not be writ in stone. Let it be undone.'

Stone, her mind echoed. Like the rock of a tomb. Like the great walls of the dragar's palace. The veil lifted and she saw it. She, Tesra, would be going to that ominous gray castle, and soon.

A voice laughed in the background of her mind, mocking her as she stood upon a nameless plain before a colorless sky, the sun invisible, its rays giving no warmth. 'There is much to be learned, my child,' it said. 'And soon you will know it all.'

It was the dragar's voice; she was sure of it, though she'd never met the man. Up to a few days ago, in fact, she had never even known of his existence. How had he breached her mind like this? Could the dreaded emperor already be here, laying a trap, possessing and burrowing into her mind as these others took her body?

Tesra lost consciousness, this last thought pressing upon her soul. It had all been too much for any one mortal to bear. 'By the foam of the sea dog!' she heard a pirate call as from the end of a tunnel. 'She's gone!'

'Fetch a bucket of sea water and wake her up,' suggested one. 'Then we'll start all over again.'

'Please, my lord,' cowered Vorra, her head to the man's feet, 'spare my life.' She could hear the breathing of Rodrigo, the low growl as he stood above her, the curved blade in his hand thirsty for blood. Having found her waiting for him in his cabin he'd flown into a rage, blaming her for something the king had done.

'Up,' he commanded, inducing her instant obedience as she placed herself back on her heels for his inspection, legs apart. 'Have you any idea how much I hate them both?' he said.

'You mean the yellow hair, master?' she supplied helpfully, the point of the sword beneath her chin, lifting her head back painfully. 'And the king?'

'Of course.' He pricked her, drawing a drop of blood. 'Who else? Somehow she's bewitched him again, and he has refused to execute her.'

'But, master,' she offered, a bit hoarse, 'won't this give you another chance to learn what you need from the girl so as to defeat him?'

'She tells me nothing. I've seen him die, in a dream, at the hands of the dragar. That could mean almost anything. His hands number in the thousands across the seas. And what has she shown of my life? Nothing, that's what.'

'Master, you do not need prophecy. You are strong enough to take care of your own fate.'

'Such a pretty little pet.' He softened, as always taken by her flattery and submissive beauty.

Vorra offered no resistance as he flicked the blade over her nipples, then rested it at her belly button. 'Abuse me, master,' she begged. 'Release your anger upon the body of your slave. Trample her and crush her beneath your will.'

Rodrigo grinned, as always diverted from his mental calculations by the immediate offer of sexual mastery. 'Kiss the blade,' he commanded. 'Make love to it.'

The command was not new to Vorra, but it never failed to fill her with a thrill of expectation. Some nights she would awaken in a cold sweat, dreaming of how her life had hung in the balance on so many occasions, her flesh dancing the razor's edge of life and death, blood and sex.

One wrong move and the sharp instrument would slice her wide open. On the other hand, if she were seen to hold back, to seek to maintain some scrap of pride or prudence, he was as liable to slit her from throat to cunt.

To begin with she kissed the flat of the blade, softly, lovingly, her lips pressed to the killing metal, the blood of a hundred, a thousand, having washed over its surface. Next she ran her tongue across it, boldly, pricking the very end of the outstretched blade with her tongue. What better proof than this of woman's weakness and man's strength? Next she put the blade to her cheek, encouraging him to caress her face, to trace the lines.

Now she put it to her breasts, her palms on either side of the deadly metal, guiding it into place. If it were possible she would want him to fuck her this way, the sword for the prick. As it was she contorted herself prettily, abasing her naked body so as to maximize the contact - creative, potentially deadly but also sensually stimulating like nothing else she'd ever experienced. 'Please, master,' she begged, 'use me.'

'I will dispose of them both,' he was saying, obsessed as always with Marcellus and his little consort. 'Next time I won't just put him to sleep. And the little blonde, I'll have her thrown to the sharks.' Vorra whimpered with need. 'Then again,' he mused, deigning to stuff himself in the girl's mouth, 'the vision might be true. Marcellus could be doomed already, in which case I need only sit back and wait.'

She agreed with him, of course, though she could no longer say so given her present position.

How could it be that the girl only grew more beautiful with every degradation? In fact, standing before him now, wet with sea foam, her ravished body cleansed but not healed, she had never seemed to the pirate king more desirable.

'You look like a drowned rat.' He tossed her a cloth, and Tesra clutched it to her breast, shivering. 'If you had asked mercy,' he told her, 'I would have given it.'

'Even after I tried to kill you?' Her teeth chattered.

Marcellus shook his head. 'But you did not try to kill me.'

'How do you know this?'

'I simply do.' He shrugged, letting slide her failure to call him 'sir'. 'Just as I know you are hiding something from me. Something you have seen and are afraid to share with me.'

'No,' she shook her sopping blonde curls too quickly, 'nothing.'

'Must I beat the information from you?' He reached for his belt. 'Or fuck it out of you?'

'As sir wishes.'

He smiled wryly. 'You are stubborn enough to be a pirate. Come here.'

Marcellus placed his hands on her head, right where they stood. 'No games this time. You will open your mind to me. Without hesitation.'

The nymph resisted only briefly. Whether it was his own will having strengthened or hers weakened he was not sure, but he found himself sifting her thoughts in short order. Indeed, it was true what he'd suspected. Rodrigo was the poisoner. Only it was not an attempt to kill him, merely to drug him so he would have unencumbered access to Tesra for the night. The clumsy oaf had wanted a vision all his own, something to cement his hold over a mutinous crew, a group of men too ungrateful and greedy to appreciate what they'd just been handed.

So what had she shown him? Had he mounted and bridled her, riding her moth-like body across the horizons of her mind? No, the clod was too clumsy, too dark and too impenetrably selfish. By the god's own eyes, how had he missed seeing this himself, how black was Rodrigo's heart? Or had it been a recent development, a gradual rotting away of good wood as oft happens at sea to untreated lumber?

Tesra was squirming, wanting to break free. He bent and touched his forehead to hers. At once he was in the white room with her. Rodrigo was coming, dressed in black. The king stiffened in fury to watch him hit the defenseless girl again and again. This was not discipline, not training, but simple bullying. Now she was appeasing him as a female, on her knees, placating with her warm mouth. By the foamy brow of Nephisis the girl was hot in her submission. But he mustn't be distracted. He must delve deeper, to see what they had seen.

The whirlwind, yes. This he knew. Tesra and he had already ridden its crest. But what was different? The madman Rodrigo was pulling her down, that was it. Not letting go. He was forcing a vision, demanding she show him the future, the fate of two kings, one in reality, one in desire.

He himself was the real one, and now Marcellus saw his own image as in a perfect mirror, carved crystal, living and breathing. So delicate and real.

And then he beheld the hand, swooping in from the sky like a hawk, then a cloud, filling the horizon. The tiny king has no chance. He is smashed by the glove, the fist of iron, the mail of black metal with no kinks, no weakness, no mercy.

For a second, a brief second, he beholds the emblem, the crest. It is that of Talassia. The royal seal.

So this is what the girl feared - his own death at the hands of the dragar.

Marcellus laughed out loud, a deep, terrifying sound, like the lion fresh from the kill, the mighty panther tearing at the throat of its enemy. In part it was a war cry, but there was also in it great irony. The sea nymph had sought to protect him from this vision, and yet what pirate king of the high seas did not foresee his own potential end at the hands of his foes on a constant basis? Day and night he stared death in the face. It was his friend, his consort, and at times his whore. This is what made him strong, what made him king. A man like Rodrigo would never understand that in a hundred years.

'Show me something else, wench,' he demanded. 'Show me something I do not already know.'

The wall. She was trying to telegraph to him something about a wall. About going someplace he should not go. Marcellus scowled. He was tired of boundaries. Tired of being patient with the delicacies of her feminine soul. Was he a timid old woman or a brigand's brigand?

Thrusting his fingers into Tesra's wet cunt, which was as always open and ready for him, he manipulated her to jelly. The other hand still on her forehead, fingers spread, he posed the question, one that would eliminate this pussyfooting forever.

Show me his greatest treasure, he asked. Reveal to me what I can steal from the dragar that will shame and reduce him above all else.

A flash of light followed. The inner dawn. A woman revealed herself. A goddess, radiant and red-haired, her curls like unfurled fire.

'Yes,' he cried out loud, laughing as he kissed Tesra once on the forehead, her body floating before him, 'I understand.'

Chapter 9

The pirate king had gone insane. This was the only explanation Tesra could find for the mission they were now undertaking. What logical objective, after all, could there be in raiding such a pitiful island, which by the man's own account to her contained nothing more than a volcano, a few rocks and hovels, a handful of domestic animals, some stray grass and some ragtag shepherds?

To make matters worse they'd sailed for days on end to find this particular place, at harrowing speed, first with the fleet then in Marcellus' own ship, and finally in this one small boat under cover of night, the treacherous Rodrigo rowing along with two others as the king sat at the prow training his spyglass upon... nothing.

Her worst fear was that Rodrigo had only come along so as to murder the king as soon as they set foot ashore on the desolate place. And in his current state Tesra wasn't all too sure Marcellus would know to stop him. Indeed, even since that day on the ship, when the king had pulled from his mind some secret vision which even she did not know of, he had been different, like a man walking on clouds, more like a monk or priest than a pirate. Had the gift of inner dawn driven his male mind into madness? It seemed a strong possibility.

He was not himself. He had not touched her, had not disciplined her, not even when she'd attempted deliberately to provoke him. Spilling the wine in his lap had merely made him laugh, and arguing petulantly about his slovenliness only made him wink and pinch her cheek. Like some lovesick fool. Or one of the fops from the court of Princess Ameliadora.

Even Drusia had become disgusted with him. It was rumored she'd crawled to Rodrigo begging to be his slut. The number two pirate, for his part, seemed to be enjoying every minute of Marcellus' newfound weakness. Surely a mutiny was close at hand, if not already underway. Despite the wealth the king had brought, he was no longer a leader and Tesra doubted seriously the man would even have a kingship to return to when this disastrous mission was said and done.

'Is it not beautiful?' he asked Tesra, offering her the spyglass for a look at the night-shrouded mountain, which every few centuries or so poured out torrents of hot lava, destroying the island's one and only village.

She declined, preferring to scan the horizon for other dangers, ones not seen with eyes of flesh or glass. Something was wrong out there. Very wrong.

'The stars have never seemed so bright to me,' he sighed. 'Like hand-painted gems upon a carpet of midnight. Isn't that so, Rodrigo?'

'The gods are full of mystery, majesty.'

Marcellus sat at the prow, leaning forward on the first bench, his back straight, his noble brow level with the craggy, black-shadowed cliffs just behind the moonlit waves. The light sea breeze had caught the torrents of his hair, making him look even more possessed. 'We are playthings to the gods, Rodrigo. Never forget that.'

Tesra, wearing a cast off shirt and downsized breeches, her hair tied back in a bow, clung to his arm. 'Turn around, my king. This will not go well in this place. I sense danger.'

'Playthings,' he reminded her sweetly, touching her cheek. 'That is all we are.'

He is mad, thought Tesra. Of this there is no doubt.

The tiny boat dredged itself upon the sand. The beach was rough, the grains dark and crystalline. The volcano lay in front of them, and behind that the gnarled trees and gritty soil in which the inhabitants made their livelihood.

There was and would be nothing here. Nothing good, at any rate.

'We must reach the top of the volcano before dawn,' said the king, stepping first into the lapping water, an inch deep.

'As you say,' Rodrigo intoned flatly.

Did the man expect anything here? Had Marcellus confided something in him? Whatever it was, it lay dead ahead.

'A precaution,' said Marcellus, clapping the iron onto Tesra's wrist, the other end of the chain wound about his fist.

She shuddered at the intimacy. How long since he'd confined her like this, consigning her to metal, fixing her for ravishment? Lately he'd imposed on her a torture far greater than iron and leather - namely that of neglect, knowing that his lust was being spilled again and again elsewhere. Into the slut Drusia and that new pet, the ever horny former princess. 'My lord,' she whispered, reaching for him with her lips.

He accepted the kiss, briefly, allowing her to open her lips against him. Between her legs she burned, from fear and need and confusion. From an island such as this he had taken her, wrongly, and now he was returning her to one, having stolen her heart and hidden it in one of his chests, a pirate's lock upon the handle.

And all that from their one union, the one encounter, her seer's eye submitted, her lithe body given over to the predations of the first and strongest man she would ever know. Did he not know she was his, that she would be to him consort, whore or even slave? What was wrong with her that he had rejected her, refusing to use her during the ritual of the hangman's daughter or any time afterward?

It was the pirate king who broke the contact first. For a split second, in his dark green eyes, she thought she saw a flash of pain. The one and only such trace of human weakness she'd ever seen in the man. What was this place, to draw him out so?

'Why have you brought me here?' she asked instead. She remained at arm's length, immobilized, her arms in his grip. He had not wanted the kiss to go on, nor had he wanted to face the inevitable consequences, her in the sand, the thin garment torn from her body, her legs parted rudely, his spear plummeting her sex as though it belonged to him, which indeed it did by right of conquest.

'I was told to,' he said simply. 'By your goddess.'

Tesra's mouth dropped open. To her knowledge the man did not even believe in her. Why then would Persistrata speak to the pirate king and not to her?

Rodrigo drew his sword. 'We must go now. The dawn approaches.'

Marcellus nodded, stoic, almost lifeless. His own sword, she noted, remained at his waist.

'My lord,' she blurted, feeling the hot breath of Rodrigo at her back, 'do not do this. He will kill you before we reach the top.'

'No, Yellow Pelt, he will not. I die at the hand of the dragar, remember?'

'Marcellus,' she wept, her knees buckling, 'we must stop!'

He lifted her into his arms, cradling her. 'No, my nymph, we must go on.'

The trail was steep but not impossible. Many feet had trodden here before; indeed it was a sacred path, for the stone had been carved, yielding itself to stairs, crudely cut and weathered over time. Tesra thought she knew this mountain upon closer inspection. Was it some vision of her own or one transcribed to her by her teachers as a hatchling? Twice as they climbed Marcellus nearly lost his footing, but he would not set her down. On both occasions Rodrigo held him up from behind; actions that seemed to belie her theory that the man was planning to kill him. And yet there was no mistaking Rodrigo's real intent, unchanged since the moment she'd met him.

'My lord,' she addressed him, employing the term she had chosen on her own, 'I can walk.'

'No, you cannot,' he countered. 'Because I am carrying you.'

For the first time it occurred to her that the pirate king might be planning to toss her down into the fiery depths as some sort of sacrifice. This seemed the sort of thing his own god would demand, being a bloodthirsty male deity, but he had hardly imagined such a thing coming from a goddess.

The heat could be felt as they ascended. Was the volcano already active? From what Marcellus had told her it was due. But there was no predicting such things with complete accuracy. Huddling close against the underside of his chin she was secretly glad of being cradled. How protected this man made her feel! Such a strange sensation, it was too, to have needs and feelings awakened and satisfied all by this same creature, her sea beast who had stolen her so long ago it seemed, from the Pool of Reflection, that naïve puddle of her girlhood.

At the very top of the volcano the mountain had been chopped flat, the expanse consisting of some several hundred square feet and providing a platform for worshippers - or perhaps practitioners of human sacrifice. Setting her down gently on her feet, he unbuckled his sword.

'We must pray now,' Marcellus said, kneeling upon the dark rock.

Rodrigo frowned slightly then followed suit, the posture coming awkwardly to him, on one knee. Tesra complied as well, as did the two other pirates. She herself used the time to implore Persistrata, from whom she had not heard since leaving the Isle of Dreams. It displeased her that the diving being might speak to him instead. Subconsciously she moved against him, hip to hip. For the first time in her life, Tesra felt afraid.

'Enough,' the pirate king announced, breaking the trance. 'Let us complete our business.' His business consisted of reaching beneath his cloak to extract a velvet bag. The first of the two objects she did not know. It was a circle of bronze, a medallion of some kind. Without ceremony he kissed it, then set it on the ground at his feet.

The next item she knew all too well. 'The ring!' she exclaimed, recognizing the ruby gem that had magically opened the rocks of the pool allowing her kidnapping. He held the ruby aloft and for a moment she thought he was going to toss it, but then, out of nowhere, came a great black bird. Wings clapping like thunder the bird seized the ring, swallowed it whole and flew away.

'Marcellus,' she whispered, despairing of how she would ever return home without it. 'What have you done?'

'I have stolen,' he answered her, his face unlit with an eerie smile, strangely calm, 'that which is most precious to the dragar.' His words made no sense to her. They walked back down the mountain in total silence, all but the pirate king clueless as to what this journey had been for.

The soldiers were waiting for them at the base of the cliff when the party returned, a large number of them, maybe thirty, having hidden themselves behind the rocks in readiness for ambush. Another fifty or more, Talassian marines, encircled from behind.

'Lay down your weapons,' called their commander, a vice-admiral by the crest in his helmet, 'and live.'

Tesra doubted any of them would live. The pirate king offered no resistance. Setting her down he followed instructions, kneeling, hands behind his back. Rodrigo and the other two remained standing.

'I have followed my side of the bargain,' said he to the Talassian admiral. 'I have delivered them both. The pirate king and the seer. A thousand talents; that is your side.'

Indifferently the admiral waved his troops in to seize the other three pirates. 'Arrest them all. It is for the governor to sort out.'

'What of the wench, sir?'

Tesra squirmed as a grinning Talassian lifted her by the waist off the ground.

'She is not to be touched. By order of the emperor himself.' There was grumbling among the men, who seemed intent on her despoilment. 'There will be plenty of time for that later, lads,' said he, ominously to the marines.

Tesra stood with the pirate company, awaiting audience with the governor of the province in which they had been captured. The hall was enormous, the ceilings vaulted as high as the sky, the marble columns as thick as the great trees she had seen in visions of the man-forests of the north. The whole of the chamber was painted in various bold colors, trimmed in gold. To the nymph it seemed as if she'd died and gone to the hall of the gods, and yet she had been given to understand that this palace was the seat of only one small district of the Talassian empire, and not a very important one at that. What then would the emperor's palace look like?

Tesra had attempted to stay close to Marcellus as they were transported here, first by boat and then over land in a horse-drawn cart. The man had shunned her, not deigning either to touch her or speak so much as a word to her. It was as if she had died to him the moment the ring had been spirited away.

Rodrigo, on the other hand, had been quite vocal, much to the irritation of their captors. As a result he'd earned a gag in his mouth, a leather slave bridle sized for a male. All five of their party was nude, having been immediately stripped, and they also bore shackles. Tesra assumed this was standard treatment for Talassian prisoners.

The governor's audience hall was a beehive of activity at the moment, the center of which was the throne, a golden chair set high on a dais on which sat a balding, jowled man with a paunch wearing a purple and green robe, layered and trimmed in gold. He had small eyes and a hawkish nose. Round him several other richly dressed men, their dandyish appearance reminding him of the princess' courtiers, were bobbing their heads up and down, whispering things here and their into the man's ears. But he seemed bored.

There were a number of cases to be presented, and lots of onlookers, curious to see Talassian justice in action. The men and women visitors stood to the sides of the throne, leaving a wide pathway for the petitioners. Their clothes were quite elegant, the females donning garments similar to, though not as elaborate as the one Ameliadora was wearing the day of her capture. They smiled readily, chattering softly back and forth. The men, by contrast, were stoical, scabbarded swords at their belts, their heads covered in velvet feathered hats, their legs in stockings and breeches gathered tightly below the knee.

There were also slaves, male and female both, identified by their nude or near nude bodies as well as by the collars on their throats, in polished gold and silver. Many of them, wearing leashes, knelt beside masters, while others served the governor. A pair of them, young auburn beauties with proud breasts, stood behind him, waving his portly body continuously with fans. Tesra wondered what else the pretty slaves were required to do for the man.

'Your excellency,' called a man in a long blue robe, bearded with a silver medallion around his neck. 'If you please, a case of domestic discord presented for your wisdom and settlement.'

'How many more of these are there?' the governor wanted to know, snapping his finger for a slave bearing a tray of delicacies. 'Isn't it lunch yet?'

'Nearly, excellency,' bowed the man. 'Just these two matters,' he indicated the young couple before him and, to the right, the naked company of pirates, 'and we shall have done the emperor's business for the morning.'

Tesra thought there was in the bearded man's words a subtle reminder that they both answered to a higher, and no doubt more brutal authority.

'Very well,' he sighed as the naked, kneeling slave offered him the tray of tiny pastries and wrapped meats. 'But I warn you, I am cranky now and my decisions will reflect that.'

The young couple was brought forward. The man wore a brocaded tunic in pale orange, boots and breeches. The girl was very pretty, with long dark hair combed over her delicate shoulders. The green gown she wore revealed an ample bosom tapering to a trim waist. Tesra thought her to be around her own age, though the worry on her finely shaped face made her seem possessing of additional years.

The blond man, by contrast, seemed supremely confident, anxious even to get on with things. It was he who pushed the girl forward, hand at the small of her back, into the presence of the boisterously chewing governor.

'Well?' the governor spit through an overfull mouth. 'Has either of you a tongue or not?' .

The young man looked at the bearded magistrate, who nodded significantly, indicating he should speak first. 'Excellency,' the young man began, his voice reflecting the polish of a public speaker, 'I am Mintalar, of the merchants, apprentice to Vasiliar for three years now. And this,' he pointed with ill-disguised contempt at the lovely female, 'is the whore of a slut who used to be my wife.'

The governor snapped his fingers. A new girl, slender as a child, ran to him and knelt, head bowed. 'I gather,' the governor proceeded to wipe his greasy hands on her long, silky blonde hair, 'that you are seeking a divorce. If so, you must have grounds.'

'The whore cheated on me, excellency. She spread her slut legs for other men.'

'And you witnessed this?' He pushed the soiled girl down to his golden-sandaled feet where she set about licking reverently.

The question seemed to throw him. 'Witness, sir? Well not literally, though it's plain enough, ask anyone around. She screws them left and right. I am away, you see, sir, buying merchandise, and that is when she desecrates our marriage. I even hear tell she lies with them in my own bed. Can you imagine, sir?'

The governor snatched the silver food tray from the first slave and tossed it over his shoulder, barely missing the head of one of his guards. 'So she is left alone for long periods of time,' he observed. 'How then do you fulfill your marriage responsibilities?'

'Excellency?'

'Her cunt,' he retorted sharply. 'When do you satisfy your wife's cunt?'

'I - I - well, it's often enough, sir,' he sputtered.

The governor maneuvered the head of the serving slave to the opening in his robe, conveniently placed at his crotch, and Tesra could see now why he did not want her holding the tray any longer.

'Really, merchant?' he chortled, settling back to enjoy the twin sets of lips, one on his sandaled toes and one on his stubby cock. 'And how often do you suppose that is?'

The merchant stared dumbounded.

'You,' he addressed the wife. 'What is your name?'

'I am Serena, excellency.'

The girl's voice was soft and shy, precisely as one would expect.

'Serena,' he nodded approvingly. 'Very well, Serena, tell the court how often you require sexual relief.'

Her head was lowered, her hands crossed in front of her. 'Daily,' she whispered.

Tesra marveled at her honesty, the clear, pink blush on her face.

'You see!' the young merchant cried in triumph. 'She is a slut, just as I said!'

'Merchant,' said the governor, shifting in his seat, 'if you again speak out of turn I shall have your balls fed to my hunting dogs.'

The blood drained from the young man's face.

'Serena,' the governor continued, 'how do you obtain sexual relief?'

'I touch myself,' said she, again amazing Tesra with her forthright display. At first she'd thought the woman foolish, or simple, but as she considered the matter it could be she was quite brilliant. Clearly in a court such as this it did little good to hide anything - especially as a woman.

'How often?'

'Three, sometimes four times a day.'

'And what do you imagine when you do this?'

'My husband,' said she softly. 'Inside me, mastering me.'

'Have you given your body to any others since your marriage?'

'No, excellency.'

The young merchant held his tongue.

'How then do you explain your husband's suspicions and the rumors he claims to have heard?'

'If it please your excellency,' she offered, her eyes still focused on her dainty feet, 'I have been told there are women who are jealous of me, and they spread lies.'

'Jealous, why?'

'Men find me pleasing to behold,' said she without a trace of vanity.

'You, merchant.' The governor's tone was darker, far less patient as he shifted back his attentions. 'Why did you marry this woman?'

"W-why?" He swallowed. Clearly events were not unfolding at all how he had imagined. 'Because I loved her?' It came out as a question.

'Because you wanted to make others jealous,' the governor supplied, playfully stroking the head of the subservient girl at his loins. 'You enjoy beautiful things, but you don't know how to take care of them. A woman is a bit more complex a possession than a vase, young fellow, or even a horse, no?'

The merchant was silent.

'You have no grounds for divorce,' said the governor to him. 'She, however, has them against you.'

'Excellency?'

'You have not satisfied her. You are husband in name only. Serena, if you wish to be free of this man I shall grant it, along with compensation of three quarters of his wealth, including all that he will earn for the rest of his days.'

'Excellency,' the man pleaded, falling to his knees, 'have mercy!'

'Get up,' the governor snarled. 'You are a pathetic example of manhood. Serena, what is your wish?'

'I do not wish to divorce my husband.' She was looking him in the eye for the first time. 'I love him, your excellency.'

The young man drew a sharp breath as though this were news to him.

'In that case there is to be no divorce. Merchant, you shall remain this woman's husband and serve her every need, or I shall see to it that you are dealt with most unpleasantly.'

'B-but, sir, you do not know what she might ask of me. How can you give a woman such power?'

Now it was Serena's turn to fall to her knees. 'Husband, I ask nothing but to serve you. Keep me, my lord, as your own.'

He did not appear to comprehend.

'Be my master,' she clarified, lowering herself with exquisite grace to kiss his feet, 'and make me your slave.'

'Merchant,' the governor said throatily, his interest in justice overcome with other needs, 'order your slave to strip for the court.'

'Excellency,' he protested, 'she is my wife.'

'She has declared herself to be in bondage in front of witnesses. You must now treat her accordingly.'

'Serena,' he begged, 'don't do this.'

'I am yours,' she repeated, 'master.'

'I am waiting,' said the governor.

'T-take off your clothes, Serena,' the young man said weakly.

The raven-haired woman began unlacing her dress from behind. A moment later it slipped from her shoulders, revealing delightfully peaked breasts beneath a thin chemise. Stepping from the dress and slippers she stood before her husband now in only the diaphanous silk, so little to cover her modesty.

'Tear the garment from her body,' the governor commanded.

The young man's fingers trembled as he clutched at the neckline. Serena beheld him with joy, drawing a tiny breath as the material gave way in his hands.

'Strike her. Knock her to the floor.'

'Excellency, please!'

Swords were placed at the merchant's throat, and half-heartedly he slapped her. She licked her lips, clearly wanting more.

'Harder!'

He delivered another smack, the adrenaline kicking in. 'Kneel,' ordered he between clenched teeth.

'Yes,' said Serena, 'master.'

'Whip her,' the governor commanded.

The leather device was handed the merchant by one of the guards. Serena, meanwhile, was put in position, head to marble floor.

'You will make her scream, merchant, or I shall have it done to you in her place.'

The merchant's blow was stiff, awkward, but the smack on the girl's buttocks was still sufficient to raise a welt.

'I have struck you,' he said in astonishment. 'I have whipped my own wife.'

'Not your wife,' she corrected. 'Your slave, master.'

Serena received a second lash, greater than the first. For a pair of novices they seemed to learn quickly so that by the time he threw down the whip, exhausted, they were both sweating and breathing heavily, the merchant, clothed, standing and relishing his power, the former free woman Serena on her belly, her naked body in anguish, her will and spirit deliciously broken.

'Tell me,' the governor wanted to know, 'how did that feel, my fine young fellow?'

'Oh, sir,' he crooned, 'it was indescribable. I never dreamed such a feeling could exist. I promise you, sir, I will never forget what I have learned, nor will I ever neglect my duty as a slave owner, or - should I choose to have a new wife in addition - as a husband.'

'Another satisfied customer,' said the governor blandly.

'A hundred thanks to you, sir.' The man bowed obsequiously.

'Not necessary.' He shook his head, a bit too pleasantly to be believed. The governor waited till he had lifted the slave and taken her into his arms to let drop the other shoe. 'There is the matter of the fee, however.'

The merchant, already facing the double bronze doors, tall as a cedar, stopped dead in his tracks. 'A fee, excellency?' He whirled on his heels.

'For my services.' He pretended to study the tips of his wine-stained nails. 'You owe me one slave girl. That is my standard fee for dispensation of wisdom in cases such as this.'

His shoulders drooped near as much as his countenance. 'But, sir,' he wailed, his heart broken yet again, 'please no, I beg you!'

The soldiers took the girl, who offered no resistance.

'I did warn you,' the governor reminded, 'that you would not like my decision.'

'Be gone, imbecile,' snarled the guard captain, 'and be thankful you haven't lost your head. What kind of idiot brings his woman troubles to the palace?'

The merchant blubbered as he stumbled, spears at his back. The great bronze doors opened and closed and the man was gone.

Serena, kneeling at the feet of her new master, to her great credit, remained nonplussed.

'You have said you require frequent sexual relief.'

'Yes, excellency,' she replied.

'Then you shall have it... serving my guards. You may thank me for my generosity.'

'Thank you, master,' said the slave Serena, her whip-lashed body tremoring very slightly. 'You are kind to a slave.'

'Abuse her well,' said the governor to the captain as he led her away, though Tesra suspected the young woman would be found by the governor's men to be both warm and willing... even as she herself was warm and willing after witnessing the scene.

'Bring forth the next case,' called the bearded man, wasting no time. 'The last of the day.'

Marcellus alone seemed to be without trepidation. With measured steps, oblivious to the prodding spears, he took up his place in the line up. Tesra managed to stay beside him, trying as much as possible to melt into his tower-like strength.

'Remove the gags and manacles,' ordered the governor.

'Excellency,' yammered Rodrigo as soon as he was free to speak, 'I am not with these others. It is I who informed the admiralty of the whereabouts of the brigand, the wanted and dangerous Marcellus, here.'

The governor appraised him, as if determining if the man could really be this stupid. 'And what, pray tell, is your own occupation which has led you to perform such an outstanding public service to his imperial majesty?'

Rodrigo's face tensed, his mind no doubt looking for a way out of the trap the fat man had sprung so effortlessly. 'I am... or rather I *was* a pirate, excellency, however I have turned over a new leaf and—'

'Enough.' The governor raised a pudgy, jewel-encrusted hand. 'You, girl,' he addressed the woman still slavering at his dick, 'go and please that man over there, the public servant.'

Never had a man, least of all the predatory Rodrigo, seemed less anxious to receive fellatio. 'His excellency is very generous,' he said nervously.

'Not at all.' He put the other slave to his glistening, saliva-coated cock. 'It is not for nothing I am considered a saint among my people.' The new girl did not miss a beat, offering the back of her throat as readily as had her dispatched sister in chains. 'Incidentally,' remarked the governor, 'you have not been granted permission to ejaculate. If you should come into the slave's mouth, thereby soiling my property, I shall follow through on my promise to that last cretin and feed your testicles to my dogs.'

Rodrigo's face paled, the fullness of his dilemma upon him. If this slave slut were any good at all at serving masters, which she almost certainly was, it would be next to impossible for him to restrain himself. Helpless and terrified he had no choice but to let the slave draw his pulsing organ deep to the back of her throat.

'You,' the governor pointed to Marcellus, 'what is your story?'

Tesra winced, knowing the man would sink his own ship in a heartbeat.

'I am Marcellus,' he said with predictable bombast. 'King of pirates. Scourge of the seas. Sworn enemy of the dragar and all who sail beneath his flag.'

'I see,' the governor mused. 'Well at least we know where the man stands, don't we?' There was dry laughter from among the courtiers, and at this point one of the bobbing, feathered fops bent low to his ear. A second, not wanting to be left out, followed suit upon the other ear. The governor nodded, and one of the men immediately departed out the back door of the chamber.

'And what of you two?' He indicated the remaining pirates. 'To whose camp do you belong? The one man navy or the sniveling traitor?'

Rodrigo stiffened, opening his mouth to protest, but a sword pressed to his neck discouraged him.

'I serve Marcellus,' said the one proudly. 'If he will have me.'

'I, too,' said the other.

'Both these men,' vouched Marcellus to the governor, 'are mine.'

'Well, well, your kingdom seems to be growing. From one to three. Perhaps the empire needs tremble yet. What of the last member of your party, though? Am I to assume she is your queen?'

'Not a queen, excellency,' Tesra spoke for herself, 'but a daughter of Persistrata, a daughter of the sisterhood, born under divine sign.'

The governor pursed his lips. 'I should have guessed. And I suppose you, too, are intent on overthrowing our empire?'

'No, sir,' she clasped Marcellus' hand, against the man's will, 'I seek to go home. I seek for us all to go home.'

'I have no home,' Marcellus rejected her, 'but the sea.'

'Oh, I think we can remedy that,' he grunted, expelling himself at last in the slave girl's mouth. 'As it so happens I have lots of space in my dungeon.'

She continued to lick him till he dismissed her, allowing her to crawl on hands and knees to a water dish beside the throne. Happily she lapped at it, the sheer servility of it making Tesra tense and wet.

Rodrigo meanwhile was grimacing, holding back as long as he could against the devilish little tongue. To orgasm like this, in front of enemies would, she gathered, be itself an act of shame.

'I will not be going to your dungeon,' defied Marcellus, once again showing monumental imprudence.

'Oh? And why exactly is that?'

'I am too important for you. The dragar himself will deal with me, and even he will want me dead, not merely imprisoned.'

The hall was tense and silent, and Tesra did not think many who spoke this way to the impetuous governor lived to tell the tale.

'My dear friend,' he laughed, seemingly genuinely amused behind his cold and clever eyes, 'do you not see that you have just signed your death warrant?'

She had not intended to intercede on his behalf, certainly not to rush forward, falling on her face before the dais. Nevertheless, this is where she found herself a few moments later. 'Spare him!' she begged. 'Kill me instead.'

The guards lifted her like a rag doll.

'Excellency?' enquired the captain holding the short stabbing blade to her throat.

'No,' he shook his head, 'not just yet. I should like to amuse myself a bit first. Girl, you say that you would trade your life for the pirate's?'

'Willingly, sir.'

'And what of your honor?'

'She has none,' blurted Rodrigo. 'She is the whore of Marcellus, worse than a slave.'

The governor snapped his fingers, signaling to the captain, who in turn removed the sucking slut from Rodrigo. The man was visibly relieved at first, but he quickly saw that he had jumped from the frying pan into the fire.

'Hand him your knife,' said the governor to the guard captain, and the soldier placed the pearl-handled dagger in the very reluctant hand of Rodrigo.

'Kill yourself,' said the governor, as though he had ordered him merely to lace up a pair of boots.

Rodrigo snorted, the sound masking panicked laughter. 'You can't be serious.'

The governor shrugged, lacing his fingers on his formidable lap. 'You are a servant of his Imperial Highness, are you not? You said so yourself. What better way to serve him than by eliminating, personally, a notorious pirate?'

The knife clanked to the marble floor. 'Excellency, I have held up my end of the bargain. I was promised gold, and a position high in the admiralty.'

'And you will have both,' said the governor. 'The gold I shall place in your coffin personally. As for height, I shall see to it your bones are bleached in the sunlight, upon the highest mountain I can find.'

Rodrigo let the words sink in, his lip tremoring. 'You have betrayed me,' he accused. 'You will face the justice of the gods.'

'Happily,' he laughed, 'will I face the penalty for removing the likes of you from this world.'

Rodrigo made it all of two steps before the guards cut him down. Tesra did not turn to look, not even when the red blood seeped across the floor and between her feet.

'Now,' the governor announced more cheerily, 'to the entertainment. You, young goddess, step forward.' Tesra did so, the sarcasm hardly lost on her. 'You will lie upon this very floor,' he indicated, 'spreading your legs for whichever man wishes to have you. If you endure all takers, then I will not put your pirate king to death.'

Now it was Marcellus' turn to speak. 'Do not do this, Tesra. He hasn't the power to kill me; he is only playing with you.'

The nymph regarded the bloodthirsty governor and his soldiers. Perhaps Marcellus was right, but who knew? There was much to consider, not least of which was the general shame of behaving before all these fine ladies and gentlemen in a way that would mark her inarguably as a whore. The lowest sort of bitch, really, for unlike a slave she could not even claim that she was being forced. It should be a horrible thing to contemplate, but something about this idea, that she was voluntarily relegating herself to such a place - and in full witness of the handsome pirate who had been so thoroughly ignoring her - aroused her beyond belief.

Marcellus would be enraged. Marcellus would feel helpless. Marcellus would be jealous.

'I will do it,' she decided, 'for my own reasons.'

Her pussy was wet, the lips slick and ready. All in the audience chamber could see, too, the way her nipples were stiff, how her face was flush and her breathing heavy. No longer a proud daughter of Persistrata, she was a creature of men now, a needful slut, begging for the touch of the roughest man, longing to be filled with hot, hard cock, and yes, to be abused as well. What would they do with her? Would they be allowed to whip her? Would someone turn her over and beat her arse to more fully open her?

Tesra lowered herself to the ice-cold marble. It would be her body alone shielding that of her lovers, keeping them from the floor. If lovers was the right word for men who would come inside her with no regard for her feelings, her thoughts or even her name. This is what slaves did, humbling themselves, reducing themselves to naked pleasure objects at the disposal of clothed men, and even women who may or may not offer them kindness or any form of human regard.

Tesra thought of the slaves she knew. Drusia and Vorra and now Ameliadora, and how they would live this way all the rest of their days. And these girls in the palace, and the thousands, maybe millions who were owned by men in every corner of the world. For Tesra it was a choice, a dark one, but still a choice. She could take it back. She could rise to her feet. But not for the rest of them.

The first of the soldiers was the captain. Without bothering to look her in the eye he knelt between her legs, opened his heavy breeches and pulled forth his spear. He claimed her with military precision as though ravishing wenches on the governor's floor were part of his duties. For all she knew it was. His cock felt good; it had been too long for Tesra. Most of the time now she burned, just as Serena burned, or used to burn before she was enslaved and given to the governor's soldiers. Was she suffering and moaning and coming right now in the barracks, her naked body preyed upon by whips and cocks and rough, uncaring hands?

Tesra felt a bite of envy, knowing things would remain ever more restrained here in the court. The captain grit his teeth, concentrating. Tesra tried to breathe. The man's burnished chest armor was heavy and hard on her skin. It made her feel that much more a slut, to be so sandwiched between metal and marble. The fact that he didn't bother to undress only made it worse - or better. She pictured his cock as a snake, uncoiling inside of her, despoiling her, tainting her in the presence of all these witnesses, all these tightly repressed, carefully bound men and women who, if released from their inhibitions, would be doing exactly as she was.

How strange were these people of the outside world. On the Isle of Dreams there was no sex because it was unknown, hidden. Here it was well known and yet, as near as she could tell, masters and slaves only engaged in the practice - on pirate ships and barracks and marble floors. With a grunt the officer relieved himself efficiently, then rose, ceding his place to another.

This man was a sergeant, a burly man with wild red eyes. His teeth flashed like a wolf's as he took up his place. Steadying himself by means of his hands pressed down on her exposed breasts, he jammed his way to the hilt. His cock was long and hard and at the first feel of it she began to orgasm. The sergeant sniggered wickedly, enjoying his power over her. Drool ran from his lips onto her chest, the act of degradation only serving to turn him on that much more. Aggressively he shunted himself in and out and she rode with him, unable to resist, unable to avoid responding, even as poorly as he was treating her.

'Good girl.' He patted her head when he was done, as if she were little better than a dog.

The next man, a corporal, wasted no time positioning his ass on her breasts to plant his crotch on her face. 'Do me slow, bitch,' he warned, 'or I'll slice you wide open.' Tesra obeyed, imitating what she had seen the other slaves do, delicately pleasing the man's dick to build his anticipation. 'Yeah, that's it,' he encouraged, flapping his enormous penis over her tongue. 'Come on, slut.'

When he was tired of her teasing he grabbed her head and positioned her to take him deep. She thought she might gag, but as he pushed himself deeper she found herself absorbing all of him. The corporal used her mouth like a vagina, but when

110

it came time to climax he withdrew, ejaculating on her face and breasts. The spray was warm and sticky. She thought of all the lords and ladies watching, thinking how she really was nothing but a little slave, worthy to be trotted off to the barracks with Serena.

There were three more after this; each, she noted, of declining rank.

'Any others?' the governor wanted to know after the last of these was done with her. Tesra lay there, the semen dripping back out of her overfull cunt, caking the fine hairs of her vaginal fleece, and she did not know if she should be relieved or insulted there were not more takers. 'Sorry, my dear, the slaves are ever so much more popular.' He summoned her back to her feet.

'But you will spare Marcellus now?'

'I shall not seek to shorten his life, if that's what you mean. I should point out, though, that your self-styled king was right all along; it is not actually in my power to end his life. It seems the two of you are destined to sail to the capital, by order of his imperial highness. Congratulations. I myself have been seeking an audience with the emperor for three years now, unsuccessfully. Take them away,' he commanded.

'Separate cells?' enquired the captain.

The governor thought for a minute. 'No, together, I think. Let them have a little fun on their last night together. And to make it a little more interesting, shackle the pirate in some compromising position. We shall see by morning what has arisen.'

There was laughter throughout the assembly. As the governor stood, signaling the end of the session, applause followed, indicating that his brand of justice was, if not legally sound, at least entertaining.

Tesra bowed with the others as he passed, ahead of his courtiers. Already her mind was hard at work, thinking of ways to take advantage of a shackled man. A delicious chill passed down her spine. They may not know what tomorrow would bring, but till then the world was their oyster.

Marcellus was stretched painfully, his wrists and ankles pinched cruelly in the Talassian metal, his back already bitten by the rough stone floor of the Talassian dungeon. The cruelty of the accommodation, of course, were to be expected, as was the governor's little joke, allowing him a last night with the nymph but at the same time depriving him of the freedom of movement to enjoy her.

It had been so long since he'd been able to make use of her or any other female, but the choice was not his. Once the goddess Persistrata had touched him, back on the ship, he'd been required to remain pure and focused on his objective. It had never occurred to him that his one selfish little prayer could so unhinge the power of the world.

In asking to steal from the dragar that which the man most valued, he had unwittingly made himself a tool in a struggle for divine supremacy. Dragar Teradon it seemed, had pretensions of godhood, based on the legacy of the founding of the original City of Talas by the god Talar. He was now seeking to consolidate that power with every means at his disposal, including the use of witches and seers to attack the other royal personages.

The ring made of ruby was to have been one such avenue. By its use the emperor had intended to find the Isle of Dreams for himself. Whereas Marcellus had settled upon one lovely nymph, the dragar planned to enslave the whole of the sisterhood, engaging their powers against both Persistrata and Nephisis both. The only place the ring was safe was in the underworld. The bird was a courier of that place, and the volcano on which they'd stood was the one place on earth where the underworld creatures could emerge at the gods' behest.

The dragar's soldiers had intercepted them too late. He had accomplished his mission and now, no matter what they did to him, the emperor would never find the island.

Unless, of course, he managed to find out through Tesra, which meant that her life was very much in danger. This was the one thing that concerned him, and as he lay in chains, ready to die, he could think only of her future.

Even more pressing, though, was the girl's present. At the moment she was in the corner of the cell, curled up, sobbing like a child. He'd hurt her feelings again. She wanted to make love and he'd rebuffed her. Even if he wished he could not begin to explain to her now why it was so crucial for her to keep away from him.

Marcellus thought of his own words, which might one day soon come back to haunt him. We are toys, he'd said, in the hands of the gods. But which gods controlled and for how long?

'Tesra, it will do you no good to make a scene like that all night. I am resolved.'

'You do not care for me at all,' said the woman, employing no form of reason he could understand. 'You never have. I am ugly to you and stupid.'

'This is not about caring, Tesra. I must keep my mind sharp, to communicate with the goddess.'

'But I need you. Like Serena needed her husband... her master.'

'I am neither to you, girl, nor would I be any good at either of them.'

'You would to me. Sir, let me give you pleasure. Your body may be shackled but I can free your spirit. Let me do that, my lord, let me pleasure you.'

Tesra was crawling towards him, a look of mayhem in her eye. What a tawny little thing she was, with her golden hair luxuriant to the shoulders of her shapely body. So innocent behind those blue eyes, like a babe, and yet how wanton had been her responses to his possession of her flesh. 'Do not touch me,' he warned sternly, 'or you will be...'

'Will be what, sir?' said the minx softly, trailing her hair over his lips.

'Punished,' said he, though for the life of him he had no idea how.

Her kiss was like fire, like an itch at once created and scratched. He could hold out no longer, not after this much time. Forgive me, Persistrata, I must turn from you this one time.

'I do not wish to displease you, my lord,' she whispered humbly.

'Indeed, you do not,' he replied sternly. 'Which is why you will submit to my voice, as though to iron.'

'Yes.' She lowered her lips to his once more. 'That way it will really be you who is free and I who am bound.'

'Sit up,' he ordered, 'slave girl.'

'Yes, master.' She shivered, for tonight that is what she was.

'Put your hair back; show me your breasts. Good. The nipples, they are not hard enough. Pinch them.'

She obeyed, tentatively pressing them between thumb and forefinger.

'Harder.' Much harder, in fact, is what he needed. Correction and discipline for the wench, that is what he wanted. Tesra winced at the pain. 'Touch your tummy. Is it warm? Fine, now slide your hand lower. Yes, lower still, good.' She was moaning already. Clearly she was his property despite her supposed freedom. 'Between your legs, tell me how wet you are.'

'Like a fountain, master.'

'You enjoyed having all those cocks in you today, didn't you? Your naked body used like that of any slut?'

'I did it for you,' she breathed.

'Left nipple,' he commanded abruptly, 'twist it until you scream.'

Tesra abused herself according to his orders. The fact of her conformity to his will made her hot and him hard as a rock. She arched her back, unleashing the desired cry of pain, a plaintive female wail that carried to the high rock ceiling of their dimly lit abyss.

'Enough.'

She collapsed back on her heels, catching her breath.

'Lick the sweat from my body, slave girl, every inch of it.'

'Oh, yes,' she replied throatily, her lips slack and pouting, 'my lord.'

'Do it well and you will be allowed to take me between your legs.' Tesra sucked his nipples, indicating how badly she wanted that very thing. It was good to have the attentions of a female's tongue, small and eager to please, the girl intent on satisfying him, working her hardest to earn the right to a fuck. She'd have to go on top, needless to say, on account of his current predicament. No matter, a strong man controlled his lovemaking regardless of the position of his female. Riding his cock the girl would be every bit his prisoner as if she were the one chained. And in the end she would come on command and clean his dick with her mouth.

'Do I please you, master?' She dabbed at the inside of his thigh.

'Yes, and you had best stop chattering and attend to your work.'

'Why,' she giggled, 'what will master do if I don't?'

'Master will feed his little Yellow Pelt to the sharks, as I should have done the day I found you.' It was good to have this game as an escape. He was as unlikely to command a ship again as this cell was to crack open of its accord yielding a stairway to the moon.

'Master was cunning to catch me that day in the pool. Was I the loveliest of my kind that you saw?'

'No, wench, just the slowest.'

She kissed the head of his prick. He groaned, nearly ready to expend himself already. Fists balled, he strained at the irons. Tesra seemed excited by this - so much male power constrained so completely.

'Will master allow his slave to mount him?' she wondered aloud.

'If his slave will stop wagging her tongue, perhaps.'

'Please, master?' she begged prettily.

'Permission granted.' He feigned indifference.

She took him in a single smooth motion, amazing him with all she'd learned. Apparently the slave girls had been busy with her education back in the hold. 'Slow down, wench, or the sport will end before it begins.'

'Am I more woman,' she grinned down at him, pausing for air, 'than master can handle?'

'You will pay for that,' he promised, with a good-natured growl.

At once her demeanor grew serious. 'Promise?'

They both knew the implications of this. For him to ever have power over her again they would both need to be free - free of this dungeon and of the horrors of Talassia. 'Promise,' said Marcellus, well aware that he had never in his life broken his word.

Persistrata, he prayed. You have brought me thus far. Please tell me you have a plan the rest of the way.

Tesra began to cry. 'I am sorry, my lord, it is all too much.'

He invited her to lie upon him, her cheek on his chest. As long as there was breath in his body, as long as his heart beat in his chest, he would protect this female. 'Trust in me, Tesra,' he said. 'Trust in the goddess.'

'I do,' she sniffled.

'Then ride me, wench. I command you to take your pleasure. Now.'

Wiping away her tears she resumed her place upon his throbbing cock. With long slow strokes she fed him in and out of her opening, the tension building.

'Now,' he hissed. 'Let go now.'

She threw back her head, grasped her own breasts and rocked herself to the most splendidly female climax he had ever seen.

Waiting till the last possible second he released his own, riding with her over the crest of the waterfall, and even as he fell he wondered if he could ever have enough of this woman or if life without her could have any meaning.

Chapter 10

Talas City rose in gleaming gold from out of the sea, like an artificial mountain, or rather a collection of them, spires of many sizes and shapes topped with slender rods and flags and banners. The sun herself could scarce cast enough light to reflect the splendor of the whole of it, from the colored stones and gems in the harbor walls, the marble-coated battlements to the endless array of ships lining the harbor, representing every nation and people in the world.

It was said that the capital city of the Talassian Empire was well over ten thousand years old, and that the First People themselves had laid the cornerstone of what was now the old wall. Noble Talas, seat of the greatest empire the world had ever known, home of its strongest people and of its emperor, the dragar, held to be sacred among all who bowed to the green and yellow of the imperial flag.

Tesra had an excellent view of all this from the deck of the Talassian naval flag ship as it glided slowly into the mouth of the harbor. Patrol craft surrounded on every side, as if somehow the girl might escape and require vigorous pursuit. As it was she was quite entirely helpless, her hands manacled behind her back, her ankles shackled heavily. A guard stood at either side of her, attentive to her every breath. Neither would dare make sexual use of the captive at this juncture, though both seemed more than eager for a last go at her.

Many times she'd been had on the sea journey here. She doubted this was supposed to occur, but she'd been advised it was best to go along and not to complain. Marcellus and the men were on a different ship and in her great aloneness she had for the most part welcomed the slobbering mouths, the thrusting pricks in the dark of the ship's hold, long into the wave-tossed nights.

The upper echelon officers took no never mind of the crew's games with her and, surprisingly enough, did not seek her favors for themselves. Perhaps they had more to fear from their superiors. Either that or they regarded the woman as too low to be worth sinking their penises into.

The ship docked quite smoothly, and at once a large landing ramp was slid down from the side of the naval vessel onto the dock where a contingent of high-ranking officers were waiting. Two admirals accompanied Tesra off the ship, turning her over to a pair of red-robed men with masks of black. The masks were expressionless and when each of the men took her by one of her upper arms she felt a chill that reminded her distinctly of death, as she had experienced it among the oldest members of the sisterhood.

Flanking the mysterious escorts were two dozen soldiers in gold armor, one dozen on each side. Their body armor shone like dawn and they carried large and heavy swords. She could not see their faces below the visors of their equally gold helmets, but it was a good guess none of the men were cracking a smile.

At first Tesra thought they were going to walk from the crowded, bustling harbor onto the street, but she saw now that there was a carriage and a pair of heavy wagons, the tops framed in wood overlaid with fine silk. She was helped into one of the latter, and her escorts rode with her, sitting opposite her on the benches along the outside walls. She had no idea who might be in the carriage.

Tesra heard the cracking of whips - a sound that brought back memories of her own punishments. With a jolt the wagon started forward. Soldiers were shouting for the way to be cleared in the name of the dragar. A thousand strange smells and sounds assaulted Tesra's senses through the barred doors and windows. She could hear unknown languages. Everything from quick, staccato chops to delicate singsong. And smell the odors of the marketplace, with its strange animals and foods. And all manner of people; interesting people with so many stories to tell. If only she had the time to investigate. If only she wasn't a prisoner, naked, on her way to see a brutal monarch who, it was rumored, was so bloodthirsty that he had one of his own wives killed for interrupting his train of thought by passing beneath his window one morning humming a little tune.

Compared to what she'd heard from the sailors on board the Talassian navy ship, the governor indeed seemed a saint in comparison to Emperor Teradon. And all she could possibly do to oppose him was to continue praying, hoping against all hope the long-absent goddess would deign to reappear, choosing this of all times to intervene in some miraculous and spectacular way.

The wagons and carriage traveled for a good long way through the streets of the sprawling city. There were more people here, she reasoned, than had ever even lived back home on the Isle of Dreams in its entire history. And in even one of these minds, by her detecting, there seemed to be more distortion, more potential for violence than the whole of the sisterhood could ever contrive had it a million years.

Tesra did her best to shut her mind against all such thoughts. This was something she hadn't bargained on - tuning in to the mental activity of such a locus of humanity; such a twisted mass of contradictory, distorted wishes, confessions and rationalizations. It was no wonder the gods put so little stock in the race of men, choosing to rule them from afar.

The wagons stopped twice at what Tesra presumed to be checkpoints. The wheels bumped over cobblestone past the second one, then vibrated over stone and finally a clacking platform of wood. A drawbridge, perhaps?

Behind her she heard the screech of metal, slowly grinding, and an ominous crunching sound loud as thunder. She imagined huge doors shutting her in. Tesra was let out into a courtyard of stone. The walls were thick and gray and above her she could see just a small thatch of blue sky between the monstrous ramparts. Inhaling, she sensed something ominous in the air - something hanging and oppressive.

No words were spoken as the prisoner was transferred to a new set of guards, wearing purple robes and high black boots. It was these men who led her, or rather half dragged her, inside to a long corridor decorated by small marble columns and ornate suits of armor.

Rudely, with no explanation, they shoved her inside one of a long series of rooms. The stout wooden door was slammed shut behind her and Tesra was sure she'd been left to rot here forever. If so, at least it was richly appointed, with red woven carpeting, ornate wall hangings and a large four-poster bed with crimson brocaded coverings. There were even fresh flowers sitting in a crystal vase on a nightstand. If this was Talassian slavery, she decided, she could get used to it.

'I am Fiona,' said the busty, longhaired matron, barefoot in her pink chemise. 'I am here to prepare you.'

Tesra beheld the lushly curved woman, fuller and more luxuriant than any human she'd ever seen. 'You're so...'

'Fat? It's all right to say it. I'm comfortable with myself.'

'Actually I was going to say, you're so full of life.'

'Much better,' the woman nodded, hiding her pleasure behind a comic-serious mask. 'I can live with that.'

'But you are beautiful.' Why is it these off-islanders did not see in themselves how each was made in the image of the gods, just as they were - beautiful and miraculous?

'We have work to do,' Fiona sighed, beholding the bedraggled girl. 'For starters, let's see about these chains.'

116

Tesra noted the gold belt at the woman's waist, perfectly offset by the scandalously thin covering. Keys hung from it, presumably to many locks. 'Can you open every door?'

Fiona fiddled with the wrist cuffs. 'You mean can I help you escape? No. I'm a prisoner here, like you. For life. But if you cooperate, over time it can become quite pleasant.'

'I am here to see the dragar,' said Tesra, as if to prove her case exceptional and therefore inapplicable to the woman's rules.

'Yes,' agreed Fiona, kneeling to undo the ankle shackles, 'and that is very unusual for a newcomer. I gather you know him from somewhere?'

'I have never laid eyes on him,' she replied, though she wondered if in her dreams, perhaps, she already had.

'You are a beauty,' Fiona cupped her chin softly, 'that's for sure.'

Tesra stood perfectly still, knowing better than to resist anyone with so many keys.

'I have rights over you.' Fiona read her question. 'I can do what I like... so long as it leaves no scars.'

Tesra contemplated the many possibilities. 'Please,' she managed thinly, feeling suddenly the fatigue of her long journey and all that had transpired before it, 'do not hurt me.'

'It's all right,' Fiona cooed, reaching up to play with her straggling blonde curls. 'Women are not like men; if I hurt you it's only so I can comfort you afterwards all the better and have the joy of wiping away your tears.'

'I... I do not understand.'

Fiona caressed, ever so lightly, between the girl's thighs. 'Don't worry,' she said huskily, 'I will teach you.'

'I am in love,' Tesra revealed, 'with another prisoner who was brought here with me.'

Where had that come from? She'd never even thought of it much less considered saying it out loud?

'We all left people behind, sweetie. We have each other now.'

Fiona led her to the adjoining bathroom where a tub of warm, sudsy water had already been drawn. It felt like heaven as she plunged in one tentative foot. She didn't need to be told twice to immerse herself, putting her back to the porcelain wall so as to cover her body up to the neck. Closing her eyes she thought of the Pool of Reflection. The wonders of home, the touch of the mother seers, the great peace she'd known being held in their arms when she was little, in hysterics from some injury or other.

'Just release yourself,' encouraged Fiona, kneeling beside the tub. 'Allow the pain, the tension to flow from you.'

Tesra's nipples quite naturally capped just below the bubbling surface. In the same way, of their own accord, her legs spread wide. Her juices were already flowing, happily mingling with the waters.

'You may touch yourself,' said Fiona, 'so long as you understand this body is not your own.'

'Not... my own,' she breathed, eyes sliding shut, head leaning back in delicious surrender.

'That's right. You are the property of the dragar, and indirectly of me.'

Tesra caressed her swollen lips. It felt wicked to be doing this in front of another woman. To think, all the times she had bathed with naked girls, lived with them and never once had it occurred to do this for their benefit.

'What is he like?' Tesra wanted to know.

'Who? The dragar?' Fiona slid her fingers down over Tesra's breasts, sending arcs of fire up and down her spine. 'He is... more than human.' The woman chose her words carefully.

'Does he, I mean has he...?'

'Fucked me?' Fiona supplied, tickled by the girl's shyness. 'Goodness, what a reserved little thing you are. What is your name?'

Tesra thought for a moment. 'Most recently,' she whispered, her throat tightly constricted, swollen with conspiracy, 'I was called Yellow Pelt.'

'I wonder why,' Fiona teased, finding her nether forest.

Tesra lifted her hips, inviting. 'Tell me,' she wheedled, like she'd known Fiona all her life, 'what is it like, to be with an emperor?'

'Like being branded,' said Fiona. 'On your soul.'

The sexually aroused blonde tried hard to imagine this. 'The man I love is called Marcellus.'

'Was he your first?'

'Yes,' she nodded eagerly. 'Before him I did not know men even existed.'

'Hmm, he showed you what a man is for, eh?' she asked knowingly.

'No, Fiona, I mean before him I did not know literally that men existed.' Fiona's laugh was a delicious trill, a melodious trickle down her throat like the wine of the pirate king. 'I need to climax,' said Tesra, amazed at how far she'd come sexually in so short a span of time.

'Well, you can't,' she took Tesra's wrists, 'until I say so.'

The velvet ropes hung from the ceiling. Fiona secured them at the precise height so that Tesra's arms were drawn taut over her head, her buttocks still planted on the bottom of the bathtub.

'The dragar likes breasts,' explained Fiona, brushing Tesra's engorged nipples in a manner most teasing and frustrating. 'He suckled, you know, from the breasts of dryads, semi-divine wood nymphs.'

'Will he suckle mine?'

Fiona applied her long fingernails, tracing circles over the large, filmy mounds, now defenseless. 'He will drink from them, Yellow Pelt. He will take his fill. Biting, chewing. He will hurt you, my little dear, and he will enjoy immensely making you cry.'

'Is there no escape?' moaned Tesra, throwing back her head.

'You can beg,' Fiona nibbled at the tiny buds, one after another, 'and you can plead, but it will only make him angrier.'

'I do not think I can bear it...'

Fiona took Tesra's cunt with two fingers. 'You have no choice, do you, my yellow-haired slut?'

'N-no.'

'No, mistress.'

'N-no, mistress.'

'Do you want to come, slave girl?'

'Very much, mistress.'

'Then you must serve me. Give me pleasure, slave, and I will consider allowing yours.'

Tesra pulled helplessly at the rope. She could neither cover her breasts nor rise. 'Yes, mistress,' she moaned, knowing the woman would hold her like this indefinitely, on the brink of pleasure and pain.

'Yes, what?'

'I will serve you, mistress.'

'Beg for it then, beg to lick my pussy, beg to be the slave of a slave.'

Tesra said the words for her mistress, replaying them again and again till Fiona was satisfied.

'Do it, slut.' Fiona stepped into the water, facing Tesra and soaking the bottom of her sheer dress in the process. Lifting the hem, straddling the girl's face, she revealed a clean-shaven, completely available pair of sex lips.

Tesra wanted it herself by now, just as bad as the other woman. Greedily, a suspended prisoner, she plunged her tongue into the uncharted territory, and Fiona's pussy blossomed and gushed in response.

'That's it, sweet bitch,' moaned the woman, massaging the captive's head. 'Talk to me.'

Tesra rubbed her thighs together, jealous for the contact she needed so badly herself. If she were the slave of the slave, then who tended to her needs? Perhaps if she pleased her mistress enough the favor would be returned?

'Think of this,' Fiona was saying, her voice a strange cadenced moan, 'when you are with his Majesty. Imagine me... if you can.'

If she could? Why couldn't she think of anything she wished?

When Fiona had taken her fill she continued Tesra's bath, cleaning the very needy girl with her hands. Tesra was not released from her bonds till her breasts, legs and tummy had been soaped and cleaned. Fiona was keenly cruel, knowing precisely how to complete the bathing task without in any way allowing her true sexual relief.

'You must remain this way,' Fiona explained, after untying her and helping her from the tepid waters, 'until he gives you audience and finds you worthy.'

Fiona's words held a special urgency. There was a warning in this, plainly. But how could Tesra control her own body's reactions, especially now with so much to be feared? There was her safety and far more importantly, his. Marcellus'. For his sake if not her own, Tesra resolved she would continue to cooperate, offering herself as her new jailors desired. For the moment that meant Fiona, but soon enough it would be the dragar himself whom she would need to appease... and satisfy.

The pirate king sat upright against the rough-hewn stone wall, appraising the situation. A number of his fellow prisoners, those still able to rise to their feet, were scrambling for the scraps of food being tossed through the bars. They resembled more closely animals than men, their filthy rag-covered bodies bent over, teeth snarling as they tore into each other's flesh for the right to consume the bits of gristle and stale, moldy bread discarded with utter contempt by the lords of the palace above them.

How long had these poor devils been in this dungeon? Years, from the looks of it. As for the ones already dead or dying little could be done, except to offer prayers. In the far corner, as a reminder perhaps, was a skeleton, the bones collapsed round a set of manacles chained to a heavy iron ball, a confinement device which had one day held a brigand like himself, or a thief, or maybe a tax evader, or simply one unfortunate enough to have crossed the wrong man.

The question was survival, and whatever Marcellus intended to do, best to do it quickly, for with each moment of indecision he would only grow weaker. For the moment he enjoyed a brief advantage. He was strong and quick, relatively, having come from the outside. The perpetual darkness and squalor of the dragar's dungeons had not yet broken him.

Nor had he yet felt the reality of the torture that might very readily deter him in the future. There was no question that he must act. The only question was what to do. Escape was impossible; at least not without having a coherent plan, a good command structure. This he would have to build. The place to begin, then, was to establish his position.

Marcellus, king of pirates, would be reborn as Marcellus, king of prisoners.

First he must study just a little longer. Two things he had learned. First, he'd discovered that the guards depended on the men's being at each other's throats. In this main cell, some fifty yards by fifty, there were a hundred men. If they should rush all at once when the door was open, say when the guards came in to change the straw on the floor, or throw in a female slave for discipline, there would be no stopping them.

The second thing he'd learned was that the endless squabbling for turf, for meat, for water, for the right to fuck the slave girls first was an abysmal waste; of energy, time and morale, not to mention of meat and women. In his two days here so far he had seen three girls killed, literally torn apart after just a few minutes in the dungeon. Under his reign they would last the night, and they would fuck and suck each man to his fill. This would be his first gift to his new subjects, though it would hardly be the last.

Tesra examined herself in the mirror, beholding the finished product. According to Fiona she was now dressed in the ceremonial garb of a Talassian pleasure girl. She could not deny that the results of the woman's hard work in dressing her were dazzling. The tunic was of white, a dress of sorts that hung to her knees, with a plunging neckline trimmed in gold, as was the hem. She was barefoot, both ankles being ringed in delicate gold. Several of her toes bore rings, also gold, unadorned and hammered from the mines of far away Rantor.

The nakedness of her feet was in stark contrast to the ornate decorations in her hair, which was swept up in tresses impossibly high and steep. Jewels, woven in and strung on the finest filaments of silver, reflected the highlights of blonde reminding Tesra very much of the city itself as it had appeared upon her first approach. The truly remarkable element of her costume, though, aside from the jewel-encrusted cuffs of fourteen-karat gold binding her wrists together at her belly, was the mask. Covering entirely her face and made of the same yellow metal, it lent her the appearance of a statue, or perhaps a goddess, one of the silent ones such as harmony or justice.

She considered the thing to be far more beautiful than her own face, with its arrogantly carved cheeks, the lines above the eyes and exquisite chin, though there was also a cruelty to it that might well frighten a small child.

Certainly Tesra felt a little like one herself. Kept up half the night being primped and preened, all the while awaiting the command to come at the beck and call of the mighty ruler, before whom even kings trembled and queens abased themselves as slaves.

A child, and yet, at the same time, ever so much more.

According to Fiona, Tesra's potential debut this night as pleasure girl to the emperor was of exquisite significance not only to her own existence, but to that of the empire itself. In Talassian society the pleasure girls played a unique and crucial role. Higher than a servant or whore, the pleasure girl was in some ways like a consort and wife. And yet she was also like a slave in the sense that it was upon her flesh the Talassian lord unleashed his full lordship and right of possession, pouring without mercy the darkest most sacred of the sex visions in his mind. To be such a girl one must be beautiful and intelligent, radiant beyond measure, unequalled in her class. She must also be fortunate to be chosen, captured, raffled or otherwise acquired. There were means within the social structure to make such girls out of noble families, though there were complex taboos surrounding this and it was not spoken of in polite households, though the evidence was generally right underfoot. Pleasure girls were black holes in the society, sacred spaces where none, not even warriors tread.

To be the pleasure girl of a high officer, an admiral or governor, was to wield immeasurable power. To be so for the emperor of Talassia was to be tantamount to its goddess. Teradon the Fourth, relatively new in his reign despite the high number of his daughters claimed no such woman for himself. Fiona would not say if Tesra's being thusly prepared was a jest or a serious overture. There was no reading the mind of the dragar. To even attempt to do so invited untimely death for one's self and one's family.

Hence the secrecy of her preparations, and the long wait - a wait that was about to end; for this look in the mirror was the final one in preparation to make her journey.

'Enough,' said her mistress, almost kindly. 'It is time.'

Marcellus stood, chest heaving, over the body of the terrified, whimpering girl. She was barely eighteen, a blonde like Tesra, though with shorter hair and smaller breasts. On her thigh was a brand, that of the island of Miros. She wore a scrap of a rag upon her hips and nothing more.

'The next man to touch her,' warned the king of pirates, 'dies.'

He had fought off a dozen of them so far. Fortunately it had not occurred to them to work in unison. One by one he had dispatched them, inflicting damaging though not severe wounds. Broken limbs were not something he could afford among his soon-to-be troops. At any rate, it was time to end this lesson before he grew too drained of strength to continue his plan.

The prisoners, bewildered, brought to life in a way they'd not expected, regarded Marcellus as well as one another. Several began to grunt and growl, this being the degenerated form of speech most common in the dungeon.

'You are men,' Marcellus challenged. 'Speak as such.'

One man, large and hairy, did, or attempted to at any rate. 'You... claim woman?'

'This is not about the woman.' He shook his head, though he intended to be using her richly in a few short moments. 'It is about our manhood.'

'What... what do you mean?'

Marcellus thumped his fist upon his bare, unwashed breast, which the little slave would shortly lick clean with her tongue. 'I am a man. I am Marcellus and I claim before you the rights of manhood.'

'What rights?' asked another, an old timer with nary a tooth in his head.

'The right to command a slave to my pleasure, with dignity, the right to enjoy her to my contentment.'

'We, too, want the slave.'

Marcellus nodded. Good, they were beginning to reason. 'We all do, that is why I propose we share, in an orderly manner.'

'Share?'

'We use her,' Marcellus explained, 'one after another, till we are all satisfied.'

'Please, no,' wheedled the cowering girl. 'I serve only you; you are the strongest.'

Marcellus lifted the girl by her hair. 'Behold,' he presented her, 'this is the slave put here to be punished. Does she not belong to us tonight?'

'Aye,' shouted more than one man.

'And who is strongest among us?' Marcellus continued, coming to perhaps the more difficult question.

'You,' said the old timer, pointing amidst the silence. 'You are strongest.'

'Who?' He bent back the neck of the half naked girl slave.

'You are!' she cried.

'You are, *master*.' Marcellus looked around the dungeon. 'Does any here challenge me?'

They looked to the big man, who considered doing so, only to retreat once more.

'By right of combat, then, I am strongest,' declared Marcellus. 'But this is not enough.'

'What more is there?' wondered the old timer.

'Beasts rule by strength alone. Men rule by wit and generosity. You,' he said to the old timer, 'what is your name?'

'I was called Goragno.' He straightened himself, saying a word he had likely not spoken in many years. 'Son of Malato.'

'And you are called so again,' declared Marcellus. 'Goragno,' he addressed him now, 'son of Malato, will you acknowledge me?'

'Yes,' he replied, grasping quickly the import. 'Marcellus, strongest in the dungeon, I acknowledge you.'

'Good. In that case I give to you first rights over the slave. When you have finished with her she shall go to the next man in line. Let us draw lots now for our places.'

'No!' screamed the girl. 'I serve you, not him. Please... master, I will lick and suck you as if you were a lord of Talassia, a free man, I will give you much pleasure.'

Marcellus cuffed her to the floor. 'Do not insult me again, slave girl. We in the dungeon are free by our own declaring. We are named by one another, and we would sooner die than imitate the ways of the spineless bastards who imprison us.'

'Forgive me,' said the girl hoarsely, 'master.'

'Crawl on your belly to Goragno, son of Malato, who is your master now. Beg his forgiveness.'

'Yes, master.' Knowing herself in the presence of men, the lithe female slave, her body muchly desired by all in the dungeon, made her way across the cold damp floor, the stone of the dungeon, her belly never leaving the surface.

'Forgive me,' she asked of Goragno, her head at his feet.

Goragno, son of Malato drew a deep breath. 'It has been a long time,' said he to Marcellus, 'since I have the pleasure of commanding a woman properly.'

'Is this not better, my new friend, than tearing the wenches limb from limb, depriving yourselves of all pleasure?'

'It is,' the man agreed, wiggling his dirt-blackened toes. 'Slave girl,' said he, 'lick and kiss my feet.'

'Yes,' the girl shuddered, 'master.'

Her tongue was blackened and her person much humbled. There was no way to remove all the dirt, but when Goragno had had enough of this he commanded her to kiss her way up his legs, till she came to the disgusting loincloth that hung from his bony frame. Marcellus imagined it being a fine robe, just as Goragno must once have worn when he was young and strong.

'I do not know,' grunted the old man, suddenly self-conscious, 'if after so long I will be able to...'

'That is not your concern, my new compatriot. It is the slave's. Isn't that so, girl?' She looked at Marcellus, fear and uncertainty in her eyes. 'You will bring your master Goragno to erection, then you will take him down your throat and allow him to ejaculate into your mouth. Afterwards you will swallow. If you cannot accomplish this goal we shall return to the old way of dealing with female slaves.'

The girl's face grew pale. She did not want to die, did not want to be torn apart, her arms and legs ripped from their sockets. So very diligently did she attend to the wizened cock of the old timer. Employing great skills acquired in service to her Talassian masters, the female began by licking the tip of him very gently. His cock was as filthy as his feet. Still, as she ran her tongue along the underside and sucked each of his balls in turn, she treated him with the same deference due an admiral or even the dragar himself.

How fitting for girls to be slaves, thought Marcellus. How natural for this young beauty to subjugate herself sexually to this less than handsome old man, the age of her grandfather. How right it seemed for her, naked and on her knees to be serving, her whole life devoted to his pleasure.

Goragno grunted in joy as he beheld the swelling organ. The girl was good. She must have been quite a highly trained slave. 'By the gods!' he exclaimed. 'I am like a young man again.'

The girl took the swollen cock deep, again showing her great expertise and familiarity with the pleasuring of male organs. Marcellus was pleased to see she was not rushing the old man, but was giving him the respect and time due his age. As he neared his climax he put his hands on her head for support, which of course she allowed since her body, at the moment at least, was his property to do with as he wished.

Obediently she drank him down and then gave him a final lick clean. It was a nice touch, the sort of thing one learns in the harem of the dragar, no doubt. Seizing his opportunity, Marcellus made his enquiry. 'Slave girl.'

'Yes, master?' She turned to him, her body alert and alive the way a girl's always was when at the business of pleasing and obeying men.

'What did you do to land yourself down here?'

The slave blushed, looking more child than woman. 'I stole a cookie, master.'

'Why would you do such a thing?"

'I was hungry, master. I had not eaten for two days.'

'Talassian masters are hard.'

She narrowed her eyes catlike, licking her lips. 'So are dungeon masters,' she said huskily, offering Marcellus her firm, apple-like breasts. 'Will you use your girl now, master?'

Marcellus shook his head. 'We have drawn lots. My number is fourteen. Who has drawn the first lot?'

'I,' said the big man with the barrel chest who had nearly challenged Marcellus earlier, 'have the first lot.' He held himself proudly. His eyes were brighter. Thanks to Marcellus, he knew himself once more a man. 'I would enjoy the experience more had I a whip,' he observed wistfully.

The slave girl lowered her eyes and shivered. From the looks of her she'd been beaten many times, but no matter how many times a girl tastes the lash, it is said, she never loses her fear.

Marcellus raised his palm and smiled. 'Did not the gods give us instruments to discipline our slaves already built in?'

'Indeed,' he laughed, the sound a startling novelty in such a somber place, 'they did.'

Ordering the tiny creature to all fours - she looked scarcely to be half his weight - the big man proceeded to deliver loud, cracking smacks to her arse. The blows were both efficient and terrifying. With each blow, no matter how hard she tried to brace herself, she was pushed forward, down onto her smallish but proud breasts. Her bottom was throbbing red and she was sobbing and moaning as though he really had employed a whip.

'What do you need, slave?' He towered over her, the smell of her thick in the fetid air.

'I need to be fucked, master,' she acknowledged her wetness, her slave's heat. 'Please, will not master fuck me?'

'If I fuck you it shall be in your arse.'

She went slack, hardly able to stay upright. 'I yield myself to you, master,' said she throatily. 'All of me.'

He pushed her face to the floor, angling her hips higher in the air. 'Lubricate yourself,' commanded the big man. 'And spread your cheeks for me.'

Reaching back she found her sopping pussy, and she transferred to her tight, puckered anus the sweet liquid that would allow the man to more easily invade her.

'Hands on top of your head.'

The slave laced her glistening fingers, the excess seeping onto her hair and forehead. Cheek to the dungeon floor, breasts pressed hard, knees drawn to her tensed stomach, blatantly open for penetration, she waited.

The big man was big in every sense of the word. Were the girl not a trained pleasure slave Marcellus would never allow the huge spear to enter her slender form. As it was she would be open for him, having likely given herself this way in the past almost as much as in the other two more common orifices.

Grasping her hips like those of a toy doll, the sex-starved man thrust himself deep, burying the monster cock halfway on the first thrust.

'You will take him to the hilt,' ordered Marcellus, to further humiliate and torture her, 'or I shall have every man relieve himself on your prone body.'

'Please no, master.' She squirmed, loosening herself as best she could so as not to risk being soiled by the slaves as punishment.

It was pleasant to see the girl's discomfort, her dilemma, naturally wanting to please but finding herself pushed beyond her limits. Tesra had squirmed like this too, and she made the same little noises as he was using her. He missed the little slut more than he realized, but pushing the thought from his mind that he might never see her again, Marcellus pressed on.

'To whom do you belong?' he enquired.

'To you,' she moaned.

'To all of us,' he corrected, as the big man settled forward yet another inch.

'Yes, master.' She clawed helplessly at the stone beneath her fingers.

'You will serve every one of us, and treat us each as the dragar himself.'

'I shall, master.'

'Are you hot, slave girl?'

'My cunt burns,' she confessed, eyes tightly shut.

'You would like to be satisfied?'

'Y-yes, master.'

Marcellus looked about the chamber. 'Who holds the next lot?'

A smallish man, his nose showing signs of having been broken more than once, called out. 'Here, sir, it is I.'

'The mouth,' said Marcellus to him, 'is yours if you wish.'

The male slave did not need to be asked twice. Ambling forward with a limp, he produced a thick rod from under his tattered loincloth. 'Kiss it,' said the man, taking his place in front of the buggered slave girl who, pummeled as she was from behind, obeyed. 'Mmm, that's it, girlie, now lick it like it's a real treat.'

She ran her tongue over him, preparing to worship her second cock for the night, though by no means her last. The man had little endurance and in moments he was shoving himself hard to the back of her throat, shivering. The slave, speared fore and aft, seemed contented now; her place in life, her training fulfilled. She was, if not born for this, then at least molded to it. The Talassians knew well their work of subjugation, Marcellus admitted this much. This little creature lived only for her masters, as their slut and whore, and he and his fellows were exploiting the fact well.

'Behold,' said he, as both men began one after another to release themselves inside the girl, 'the beaten, prone body of Talassia herself. The naked form of her noble women, waiting to be plucked from the vine. By the blood in my veins,' he raised a single fist, 'I promise you we shall not die in this stinking place. Who is with me?'

'I am,' called one man, and then a moment later another, till every man with a voice was affirming his allegiance. They were risking alerting the guards, but it was a chance they must take.

'It is settled then. In the meantime, who holds the next lots?'

Two more stepped forward, a spring in their steps, and licking their lips they took the places occupied by the others.

Looking directly at the slave girl, her mouth reoccupied, and now also her cunt, Marcellus said, 'Remember your numbers, lads, for your second turns later on.'

The little slave beheld him with defeated eyes, liquid eyes, desirous eyes. She wanted him, Marcellus, king of prisoners, as a girl naturally wants the strongest in any group. And he would have her, but not till all the others, for he was a leader not merely a bully as had been Rodrigo.

Yes, he began to stroke himself in anticipation, he would enjoy with great satisfaction his turn with the girl, though he would be hard pressed not to think of another, one who by this time was quite possibly dead.

'Care for her, Persistrata,' said he to the goddess who had indirectly brought him here. 'If she be alive deliver her into my hands, that I may fight for her. And,' he added as an afterthought, beholding his cock in his hand, 'forgive me yielding to my weaknesses as a man... again.'

The chamber was pure white, as had been the corridor leading to it. White, almost as pure as a cloud, or as the cliffs of her native island at dawn. Tesra, clothed in the ceremonial garb of the woman of pleasure, found it ironic that one with such a reputation for darkness as the Emperor Teradon should surround himself with this color of purity.

It was odd, too, the lack of windows or wall decorations anywhere in the circular, vaulted space. There was, upon the white marble floor no carpet, and in the corners not even so much as a stick of furniture or a speck of dust. For a split second she wondered if the dragar were not some sort of germophobe, or even insane.

'Not insane,' replied a voice, melodiously masculine, 'but rather divine.'

The shackled, masked girl, her feet bare on the cold marble, tensed instantly. He was reading her thoughts.

'That is correct,' the voice indicated approvingly, as if she were a small child. 'But that is what you are to me.'

What? A small child?

'Yes... a little girl, a nestling, a kitten...'

She heard the footsteps behind her, precise clicks upon the marble, as from high-heeled shoes. A woman's shoes? And where was the man coming from? The double doors had closed behind her upon entry and had not reopened.

A touch to her shoulder, feather light, made her scream. Though when she opened her mouth she had no voice. Just like in a nightmare, she thought. Turn. She must turn to see for herself. But then she would be staring him in the face... or was it an 'it'?

'Now you're hurting my feelings.'

A figure, gold-masked like herself, a metal-hewn smile appeared in front of her face. Long tendrils, like insect whiskers, filaments, protruded ray-like from the top and sides of the facial covering. The eyes were slits; behind them something was moving, living, cold. Barely her height and slender, he - and it was a he after all - was dressed in white, a long gown like her own, some sort of gold shoes on his feet and many, many rings. Dazzling rings; gems with changing patterns; the glare concealing something.

A dagger... he holds a dagger. Smiling, he puts one hand light and soft on her shoulder, while the other hand, hard as iron, is lifting the knife. He is going to kill me, she thinks. But in this room, she wonders, are things really what they seem?

'They are whatever you think them to be,' replied the emperor, who was more than an emperor.

Tesra fell to the marble floor, stabbed, the blood running white from her body.

Chapter 11

The slave girl did not wish to leave the dungeon the next morning. The guards had never seen anything like it and as the naked blonde clung to the feet of Marcellus, he who had used her last and most richly of all, they regarded him with wariness, a new respect, mingled perhaps with fear. The prisoners all saw this, which was very good, because it put them one step closer to escape.

'What is this, slut?' the sergeant wanted to know. 'Since when does a little cunt like you desire more punishment?'

'I belong to them, master,' said she, breathing heavily, breasts heaving, in the clutch of the guards, all thought of her own safety banished in the face of her bodily needs. 'They have conquered me as no others... he has conquered me.'

'Him?' the sergeant pointed, amused. 'Well, at least you have some discernment, for a slave.'

'What do you mean, master?'

'That is no ordinary dungeon scum,' pointed the beefy, bearded jailer with his club, well worn from striking the backs of helpless louts. 'That is none other than Marcellus, the brigand captain. He's been the biggest thorn in the side of the navy for years. Not that the navy is worth much, if you ask me, compared to the army.'

'Marcellus,' breathed the slave girl, pronouncing upon her lips the name of the one who had conquered her as no other. 'My master.'

'Take her away,' the sergeant snorted, 'and have this one flogged for insolence,' he added as an afterthought.

The girl was crying out and fighting back, risking punishment all over again as they dragged her from the cell to take her back to her Talassian lords. Meanwhile, Marcellus was stretched across the rack and richly whipped, in plain view of the others.

'This is your pirate king,' the sergeant snarled, unleashing the bullwhip with full fury again and again. 'Why don't you bow down to him now?'

The men were silent... deathly silent. Even through his pain Marcellus could read in the air the tension, the anticipation. Soon, very soon they would be ready to fight for him, and if need be, to die.

Tesra awoke beside the Pool of Reflection, lying naked upon her back, her flesh gently warmed by the morning sun. A breeze wafted over the shimmering water, delivering natural coolness as somewhere above, a te-te bird trilled its happy call as it circled artfully in the spiral sky.

She sat up on her elbows. She was home. Had it all been a dream?

'Yes, and no.'

A shadow loomed over her, blocking the sun. It was a man, slender and naked with fine auburn hair, angled cheekbones and a boyish physique. She noticed at once his rosy-red nipples and long, dangling cock, the head of which was pierced with a gold ring.

'Who are you?' She spoke out loud, though he'd been reading her mind a moment before.

'The keeper of your dreams.' He indicated the enchanted vista, the white-capped mountains and blue-green lushness. 'The keeper of your heart's fancy.'

Tesra cocked her head. The voice was familiar. Was it the man in the mask of gold? She leaped to her feet, compelled to check for wounds on her chest from the knife. She found nothing.

'Who are you?' she demanded, matching his height. 'Or more properly, what are you?'

'Why don't you take a guess?'

'I take you for a demon, a warlock,' she speculated. 'Though presumably you are him. The emperor.'

'At your service,' bowed the dragar.

'What do you want from me?'

He pinched her chin. 'Everything, my dear.'

The touch was like ice, and yet it warmed her, too. Almost irresistible was the urge to thrust herself against him, to take that dangling penis inside her, to be defiled by it, even though the act be sacrilege on her island.

Tesra pulled back, her action causing his enigmatic, almost angelic features to cloud instantly. She was reminded at once of the danger she was in.

'You shouldn't have done that,' he said, sounding more boy than man now. 'You are my toy, and I will touch my toys when and how I like.'

'I am no toy and you are no child,' she countered recklessly, her words lacking all conviction.

'Indeed.' He reached for her engorged nipple. 'What are you, then?'

She was powerless to resist. 'No, please, do not do that... not here.'

'Why not? Don't you like it?' He was mocking her.

Tesra was panting. He was making her need him, as a female needs a male. He need only say the word, issue the command and she would be his, but she sensed he needed more than her mere body. He needed her mind. Her heart. And perhaps her very soul.

The dragar smiled, though there was no mirth in his countenance. Clapping his hands he drew thunderclaps in the sky and in a flash, he was gone.

Tesra was alone. More alone than she had ever been, for while this place looked like home she was quite sure now that it was not. Wherever she was it was an illusion, something dredged from the depths of her memories.

'Tesra,' whispered the voice in her ear, 'how are babies born?'

It was a child's voice mocking. She looked down and there was a very small girl with wide blue eyes, nearly invisible skin and white-blonde hair to her knees.

'How are babies born,' the child repeated, '*Tesra?*'

Tesra retreated, frightened. This was not her island, not her home, not even the inside of her own mind.

'Oh,' spoke the unseen dragar, 'but it is.'

There was a crack of thunder and Tesra found herself running through the jungle. Someone, something, was behind her closing fast. She must not allow herself to be caught. The girl's voice laughed in her head, the question ringing about the babies, and she did not want to know the answer.

The thing was closing. Hot and snarling. A beast with claws, snapping limbs, tearing the greenery behind her, swathing a path of destruction. She was nearly out of breath. Her chest heaved and she was aroused, inexplicably, the fear of being hunted, the helpless feeling of pursuit working at odds with her need to flee at all costs. A part of her, very strong, did not wish to fight, but knew, soon, very soon, it must yield nonetheless.

She heard the creature snarl and roar and then, instinctively she knew it was airborne, springing at her. Tesra went down beneath it, belly first onto the jungle floor. It was on her, hot and fur-matted, teeth and claws sharp and deadly. She dared not move a muscle.

Oh, goddess, why were her thighs tingling and trickling so? Why were her sweat-covered breasts so swollen and why were her hips pressing down into the dirt, undulating?

The thing was sniffing and licking at her, up and down her back. She cringed at the prickling tongue, slavering past her ear, down to her buttocks, whip-like. Then all at once the monster flipped her to her back. It was dark now and very fast and before she could get a good look it was sniffing elsewhere, at the source of what had attracted it in the first place.

Her sopping wet cunt.

Terror flashed through her mind as she realized what it wanted. It is going to rape me, she thought, the words icing her overheated skin. I am to be raped by a beast.

'No,' said the voice of the man-child, the impossibly old, impossibly young dragar. 'It cannot be an act of rape if you spread willingly.'

'But it will hurt me,' she replied to the thoughts invading her mind. 'It will force itself and show no mercy.'

'And this is precisely what you crave, is it not?'

'No,' she denied. 'There is no reason in this. What could the thing want from me, or I from it?'

'What indeed?'

The beast mounted her, but it was no longer a beast.

'Marcellus?'

He smiled lovingly as he thrust his cock to the hilt in her warm silkiness. 'I shall give you seed,' said he. 'And you shall bear me sons.'

'That cannot be, Marcellus. Only the goddess creates anew the flesh of the male and female. She herself forges the bodies of infants, delivering them from the sacred volcano.'

'That is a fairytale told to silly little nymphs.' He shook his head, his motions in and out beginning to drive her to distraction. 'It is the cock, the sperm which fertilizes the womb. Your own belly is where the babies are forged, Tesra.'

'No,' she squirmed. 'You lie and you are not Marcellus.'

'I am close enough for your purposes. I have his memory, his experience. I can tell you how we met and how you are my slave, she whom I will impregnate. And I can tell you other things, like how his grandfather went to your island many years ago, as have many sailors, to make babies in secret. The babies you think are plucked from the volcano.'

'Get off me!' She bucked beneath him on the jungle floor, biting and kicking as though she herself were the beast.

'Lie still,' said he to her, delivering a hard smack across her face, 'girl.'

Tesra ceased her useless struggle. 'Please,' she begged, 'at least show me the respect to appear as your true self, dragar. Why pretend? We are still in your palace. I am not fooled.'

The image of Marcellus smiled thinly, the cock, the touch all too real. 'This is all you need to know, female. On your back, receiving the seed of your male. Your master, Marcellus. Move beneath me, Tesra, increase my pleasure now or I shall take my belt to your pretty arse. Just as I did the day we met.'

Tesra shook her head back and forth. This could not be happening.

'Acknowledge me, slave.' He savaged her nipple between his teeth.

'Yes,' she wailed, 'master.'

Of all the possible attacks from the dragar, this was the only one she'd not anticipated. His use of the very form of Marcellus, which so dominated her heart and body. A form she could not help but respond to, though she knew it was an illusion. But still there was at the heart of it all a lie. She would not, could not bear children this way. Tesra moved her hips obediently, unable to stop herself.

'Your belly will swell, Tesra. A child shall squirm within it and kick, the very child grown from the issue of my cock. Through this child we will rule the world, from a new capital upon the Isle of Dreams.'

'No, only the goddess gives us children,' she defied, though her body continued to respond, pleasuring him. 'You speak madness.'

'I own you, Tesra,' said the image of Marcellus, 'and your thoughts as well. You cannot contradict me.'

She saw the red in the eyes, the sudden temper, and it occurred to her the dragar had a weakness.

'The blazes I can't.' She spat full in his face.

'Bitch,' hissed the emperor, returning to his own form, his eyes like the underworld, his breath burning hot on her face, his hands at her throat. 'I will never release you. Not till you give me what I want. That fool Marcellus cheated me of the ring by which I would have found your island for myself. But you will tell me. You will reveal everything to me. You will open to me, or you will die!'

Tesra looked in his eyes, seeing his intention at last, and it was more terrible than she'd imagined. It was not only the world he sought to rule, but the domain of the gods as well. Her screams rose to the illusory skies, threatening to break them apart. She could not let him do this thing; it was not only her fate, but that of all creation at stake.

'Too late,' the dragar laughed, ejaculating deep inside her. 'Too late.'

Marcellus signaled his men into position at the top of the dungeon stairs. Overcoming the jailors as they'd opened the cell doors to deliver fresh water had been an easy enough affair, but now they would be dealing with the dragar's soldiers, the crack troops of his palace guard. Truthfully he'd needed more time for reconnaissance, but Tesra's cries had come to him, even in the bowels of the abyss below the palace.

As had those of Persistrata. 'Go to her,' had said the image of the goddess, delivering into his hands by her own miraculous power his own recovered sword, that which had been taken from him on the island.

To their credit, and perhaps his own as well, the men did not question his plan of attack. He took only volunteers, saying that the mission would be dangerous and likely suicidal. Of all those able to walk, not one refused to follow.

'Better to die as men than live as dogs,' had said the old man, his countenance greatly improved by a night with the blonde slave girl.

Marcellus' plan, such as it was, involved fighting their way level by level to the uppermost chambers of the palace, where the dragar was holding Tesra prisoner.

Marcellus estimated the odds at a hundred to one or better, in the enemy's favor. Then again, they did not have Nephisis and Persistrata on their side.

'Now!' commanded the pirate king, pushing on the heavy wooden doors, the men pouring up the stairs at his back.

'Earthquake!' cried a soldier, running down the corridor in which they found themselves. Indeed, the palace had begun to shake quite unexpectedly.

The work of the sea god, Marcellus determined. He who commands not only the waters of the deep, but also the great lands below them. 'This is our chance, men, make for the upper floors!'

They met little resistance along the way. The whole of the building was shaking and the guards were on the run. Amidst the falling columns and smashed treasures they made their way to the dragar's private rooms. One after another they searched them, finding nothing.

'She is gone,' shouted the big man, just barely protecting Marcellus from a falling statue.

'No,' cried Marcellus, though he feared the man might be right, 'she is still here. We must look again. The dragar is a wizard. She may be more carefully hidden than we can imagine!'

Tesra's body was in convulsions beneath the emperor. Everything around her was vibrating ferociously and she did not think it was of the dragar's doing. The dream he had placed her in was crumbling and now she was witnessing shards of nightmare, images of her island under attack by the dragar's soldiers, the temple in flames, the sisters run down by soldiers, thrown onto their backs and raped. She saw Marcellus as well, hung by a rope, swinging dead from a gallows, the vision having come true that he would die at the dragar's hand.

Oh, her poor love, and her poor sisters too. Before her inner eyes she could see the faces of women crying out, their bodies invaded, their resistance crushed, whips cracking on their backs, cocks pounding at every orifice till at last they explode filling their wombs with the dreaded seed. There is more thunder and more shaking, screaming everywhere and now the women are running too. As they flee past her she sees the lumps in their bellies, their hands on the horrible swellings. The look in their eyes bespeaks the horror. They have been impregnated.

'Come with me,' the dragar called to her, his voice mesmerizing as the hiss of a snake. 'Sit beside me and rule the world.'

'No,' she defied. She wanted Marcellus. She could feel his heart beating. Could it be he was close at hand? Lifting upon inner wings she sought to fly and reach him. But the dragar made a final attempt to keep her. Sleek and black and fast he took off after her in the guise of a bird of prey. Tesra flaps for her life. She wants to go back home. But she knows if she takes him there he will bring ruin to her sisters. And death. She has no choice but to go down, even into the flames if that is what it takes to stop him. The bird of prey seized her neck but it could not hold on. With a mighty screech it let go and veered off.

It is gone, she thought. Or was it?

Tesra called out Marcellus' name and pulled at the fastenings on her wrists.

Opening her eyes she saw she was back in the white room where it all began, naked and bound to a chair.

'Do not leave me,' she heard the dragar cry, seeking to pull her back into the dream, sounding more slave than master.

'Tesra, are you in there? Can you hear me?'

The earthquake stopped.

It was he, Marcellus, on the other side of the wall. The real one, and though Tesra could not speak to answer she wept with joy all the same.

Marcellus was sure she was behind this stretch of wall, as surely as he knew his own heartbeat. 'It must be a hidden door,' he called out. 'I feel her presence. Fetch a battering ram.'

The big man brought a downed column from the wreckage, and in short order they had smashed enough of the stucco for a man to fit through.

'I go in alone,' said Marcellus. The big man looked at him. 'You will stay.' He put his hand on the man's shoulder. 'That is an order.'

The room inside was dark, despite the hour of the day. He drew his sword, stepping over the rubble. From behind the old man handed him a torch. Holding it forth in front of his face he beheld her. Tesra was sitting on a chair, naked, her wrists and ankles tied to it. She was wearing a mask of some sort.

'Give me a moment,' he pulled off the mask, 'and I shall free you.'

The face of Rodrigo grinned at him. 'Yes, free me, please.'

Marcellus took a step back. There was wizardry afoot. Offering prayers to Persistrata and Nephisis both, he placed his sword at the creature's neck. 'Release her,' he said to the face of Rodrigo as though Tesra were inside it, and in a way she was, which is why he must coax her out.

'To the pits of fire with you,' spat back Rodrigo, whose real body was laid in a coffin at the top of a mountain half an ocean away.

Marcellus lifted the sword overhead, preparing to strike. 'Then I will slice you open and retrieve her myself.'

The room exploded upon contact of metal and flesh. Several men cried out from the hallway. Marcellus was blown backwards, landing on a soft carpet of green. A moment later he stood. They were no longer in the white room but a green forest.

Tesra was cowering at his feet, clinging for dear life. 'Oh, master, thank you!' she cried.

'The girl is mine,' said a tall and most ugly giant, who had broken his way through the trees. 'I have filled her with my seed and she will bear my children.' The giant, obviously, was the dragar. And this jungle was some sort of sorcery.

'You have many children already,' Marcellus noted, his sword at the ready.

'None like she will issue. None capable of seeing all that will happen in the world before it transpires. None capable of building me a new empire, more powerful even than the realm of the gods.'

So that was the emperor's game. Cosmic domination. An old story among men of his kind. The question, though, was how to stop him?

'Am I to take it, dragar,' he asked calmly, 'that you have already impregnated this slave of mine?'

'I have,' he offered eagerly. 'Indeed I have.'

Marcellus closed his eyes. The goddess was communing with him, telling him much that he needed to know. 'No, dragar, begging your pardon, you have not. Touch her womb and see for yourself.'

The dragar snorted. 'You don't know what you're talking about. Come here, girl, I shall prove it. With one touch I will know.'

'Go to him,' said he to Tesra in a tone he hoped would remind her of her promise to trust him above all others. 'Now.'

She obeyed. How he admired her strength, to be able to walk with such courage back into the clutches of a creature such as this. And all without having the slightest notion how Marcellus would yet save her or himself.

The pirate king waited till the exact moment of contact between them before acting. Encircling her waist with just one of his huge hands the giant lifted her from the ground, in readiness to be probed by the index finger of his other hand, and as soon as the tip of the finger touched her belly and the giant's eyes slid shut in concentration, Marcellus slung the sword, like a knife, landing it hilt deep in the giant's forehead.

The giant went stiff, his eyes wide with amazement, as much over the results of his analysis as the fatal wound he now bore. 'Impossible,' he gasped. 'She is not yet pregnant.'

It had been the hands of the goddess that had guided his throw. As the giant began to stagger Marcellus ran forward, catching the girl as he released her. The ground was shaking again. Lightning was tearing into the trees. Falling to the jungle floor Marcellus covered Tesra's body with his own, waiting for the storm to pass. The winds were fierce, and at a certain point he and Tesra were separated.

In a few moments everything was silent again and they were back in the white room. Marcellus heard screaming. He found her on the other side of the room, pinned beneath the dragar, who was making one final attempt at impregnation. The pirate king pulled the man off and threw him to his back. Before he could leap up Marcellus fell down upon him, grasping his throat with both hands.

'Please,' the dragar begged, his voice reverting to that of a small boy, 'let me go. I won't hurt anyone.'

Marcellus was not fooled by the ruse, and sure enough the body of the dragar turned into that of a lizard creature. 'Do not seek to provoke me,' Marcellus warned. 'Or I will squeeze the life from you.'

The emperor turned human again, this time into an old man, the oldest Marcellus had ever seen. 'Oh no,' he cackled, a fearsome, death rattle of a croak, 'it is I who will squeeze. Forever. Behold, my power... eternal...'

The emperor's body began to convulse. Foam poured from his mouth. He was like a man possessed. Smoke poured forth from him, but Marcellus did not let go. The dragar shrieked and began to dissolve, his flesh wasting before the pirate king's eyes, and at last there was nothing left beneath Marcellus but dust.

'Marcellus, what is happening to me? Help me!' It was Tesra. By all the gods and goddesses she looked ready to explode, her belly fully swollen with child.

What black magic had the dragar worked?

He ran to her side, cradling her. 'It will be all right, hold still.'

The child came of its own accord, at her feet, covered in warm afterbirth, drenched in fluid, gestated miraculously in a matter of minutes. Marcellus bent to retrieve it, severing the umbilical with his knife. It was alive, its mouth and hands and fingers moving wildly in sheer joy of life. So beautiful and yet...

'It is his,' said Marcellus, more statement than question.

'No,' smiled the very tired, very pleased Tesra, 'it is ours.'

He cocked his head. 'How is it possible?'

'You were with me first, were you not, before I ever laid eyes on the dragar?' He nodded in the affirmative. 'Then it is you who first had me and you who fertilized me. Therefore, I and the baby are yours.'

'You were already pregnant and you did not tell me?'

'You were otherwise preoccupied, master.' She took their child into her arms. 'Besides, I did not know at the time what was happening. Persistrata has only now explained it all to me. The dragar sought to possess my womb, but was able only to accelerate the process already begun by you.'

'That is a poor excuse,' said he with mock sternness, 'for keeping the father of your child in ignorance. We shall tend to your punishment later on.'

'Yes,' Tesra lowered her eyes, her cheeks glowing delightfully, 'my lord.'

'All attempts to butter me up,' he further informed her, enjoying the game immensely, 'shall fall on deaf ears.'

Tesra gave him a gleaming smile, laying her head back against his shoulder. Indeed, he would torture her richly and with delight, as soon as they found a nursemaid.

'Sir,' called one of his rag-tag pirates, having entered through the makeshift door, 'word has come to us of a rebellion, from the palace guard. They demand a new dragar.'

Marcellus had expected as much. 'We shall lay low till it blows over.'

Goragno, son of Malato frowned, hesitating.

'Speak,' growled the pirate king, no malice intended, 'the wench grows cold.'

'Word of your exploits has spread, from the times before and of today, as well. There is talk that the emperor's guardsmen wish to crown you dragar.'

Marcellus laughed heartily. 'Just my luck,' he muttered. 'Tell them I shall meet with them presently, when I have finished some rather more pressing business.'

A short while later, the baby safe in the arms of one of the royal nursemaids, Marcellus sequestered himself with the nymph, who for a woman having just given birth, was remarkably recovered.

'At last,' he announced, 'the battle I have been waiting for.' Without preamble he tossed her down onto the silk-covered bed, her shapely body lost in the sea of thick fabric.

'You are rough with me,' she teased, 'my dragar.'

Marcellus frowned, flipping her onto her belly. 'You shall pay for that,' he promised.

'I hope so,' she sighed, wriggling her body, her bottom well exposed.

He gave no answer, save the thundering crack of his palm against her deliciously vulnerable cheeks.

Also by Reese Gabriel and available to order as paperbacks at AMAZON

Caralissa's Conquest
Possessing Allura

www.ingramcontent.com/pod-product-compliance
Lightning Source LLC
Chambersburg PA
CBHW060937120626
46557CB00003B/1037